Tressa: Twin of Passion

Norma Lopez-Stewart

Table of Contents

Prologue

Before the Dark Days

Once upon a time, the world was connected in every way. Life was good for everyone, and all the hardships from the past were forgotten. Everything a person needed was at the tip of their fingers. The reason behind this prosperity was that the world was attached to technology. Even the most remote places on earth were connected to some kind of electronic device.

The high-speed intercontinental rails connected people to the other side of the world, making it easy for travelers to ride in luxury. People had all kinds of luxuries available – conference rooms, restaurants, spas, bars, shops of all kinds, barbershops, hair and makeup salons, spas, gyms, you name it. Everything was for a person's pleasure, even a companion. However, all for a price.

If you were wealthy, you could enjoy all the bounties of life. People who had money could afford a space pod for private use. This means of transport could be parked on the roof of their homes or in their own landing space. Since airplanes were no longer used after the fuel wars- all airports were forced to shut down, and it became illegal to have your own private plane. The five-year fuel wars had devastated some countries. Since then, solar transportation has replaced just about all electric devices.

Skyways helped alleviate the traffic problems, moving most of the traffic to the roads high above the normal land traffic. These skyway bridges were faster and used solar magnetic power.

This was the age of high technology. Cell phones were part of a person's existence, installed in the back of the ear or hand, under the skin. They monitored your health, money transactions, and other activities, depending on how you wanted to program your life.

Artificial Intelligence had taken over all minimal chores, even childcare. Life was grand, and people everywhere were living their best lives. Simply put, technology ruled.

However, it had made people weak and vulnerable, unable to survive what was coming. It took the world by surprise. There was no time to hide from the darkness that assaulted the world. Not even those who had shelters in the mountains or underground were saved. The evil or men and women once again trumped into destroying humanity. The armed viruses swept through the world like swarms of locusts devouring the world's populations, throwing the world into chaos.

As the world crumbled under devastation, fanatic religious groups took it upon themselves to add to the chaos the world was already trying to deal with. They blew up anything, burned down buildings, and destroyed most of the technology along the way. Their mission was to rid the world of all technology, that God was punishing the world.

However, there was a great reset. Those that survived had the task of rebuilding. What took three months to destroy was evident everywhere and would take perhaps three centuries to rebuild. Forty years had passed, and the countries were still trying to dig themselves out of the hole. Great strides were made to stabilize the land. It was a time of going back to a simpler way of life.

In the midst of all this chaos, people continued to move forward. They worked hard, married, had children, and looked toward better times. However, leaders were sworn never wanting to repeat the past.

Agencies were developed to keep countries accountable, leaving the past buried and not allowing to develop weapons of mass destruction that could uncover what should be kept buried.

Chapter 1: The Mission

Tressa Quintanilla looked over her shoulder, making sure she wasn't being followed. As quickly as possible, she walked down the dirt road that was part of the main business marketplace. It was early morning, and the marketplace was already buzzing with activity. The merchants were busy getting ready for another exhausting day. The sun was already beaming down on her. She felt damp as trickles of sweat ran down her neck. Struggling to walk in the burka that hid her appearance but was too clumsy to walk in, Tressa wondered how the women in this country kept their sanity, having to wear this type of heavy garment without passing out from the heat. It was hard to see as she tried to blend in with the rest of the women, hoping no one noticed how awkward she was walking in the oversize garment.

Tressa hated coming to this part of the world. Women were still oppressed, and the tribal leaders were always changing their minds about women's rights. Though most women now wore regular clothing, there were still those married men who insisted their wives wear the full covering. This gave Tressa the perfect cover for the operation.

Two Days Before

Tressa was a chameleon. She had to disguise herself from top to bottom. When she was detained coming off the ramp of the ship, she had to look like she was on vacation or a celebrity. She put on a blond wig, heavy makeup to lighten her skin, and blue contacts, wearing jeans, a purple top, shiny pumps, and expensive sunglasses. Her makeup was flawless.

They searched her baggage, and after arguing feverishly with them, they let her go. One of the guards followed her inside the terminal, wanting to know if she had a husband or boyfriend. It made her sick in the stomach when he blocked her path.

"Young lady," the guard stopped her, smiling. "Are you traveling alone? I would love to be your special guide if you permit me," he said with eyes full of lust. He stared at her body from head to toe, unable to take his eyes off her.

Tressa was good at thinking on her feet, "Well, is this a special service you provide?" she asked, smiling, not wanting to anger him.

He laughed, "No, only to exceptional beauties. I am very cheap, but for you… I will do this for free," he winked.

"Ah, as tempting as the offer is, I'm really sorry, but I am meeting my… my boyfriend, thank you."

"That's a shame. A young beauty like you can turn even the King's head. You should not dwell on small fish when you can get the shark." He crept closer to her and made a face. The strong odor coming from his body made Teressa unable to stand.

"Ah, I appreciate the compliment, but I'm not here looking for a husband, and I don't need a guide. So please don't waste your time on me. I'm sure there are plenty of other beautiful women in your country that would love to catch a shark."

He grabbed her by the arm. "You're an American, they are different than our women, and I can tell you are educated."

She pulled away. "Oh, I see," her anger was coming to the surface. "Now, I don't know what you think about American women, but this one... doesn't like strangers touching her."

Within a few minutes, her contact appeared, cussing and waving the stranger to get away. After a heated discussion, he left.

"Tressa, thank God you made it safely. I'm sorry I didn't make it to see you off the ship, but these bastards started to fight among each other and held up the line. Did you have any trouble?"

"Just at customs; they wanted to search my things, and then that asshole followed me. I was ready to drop-kick his ass into the crowd when he grabbed my arm."

"Well, I have everything arranged for you; everything was sent to your hotel room. Are you ready for this? I was surprised and shocked they sent you on this dangerous mission," Drew asked curiously.

"It's not the first dangerous mission we've been on. Plus, I'm the only one who has the training, and I can scale a wall. Don't worry, Drew. I will be alright as long as I have everything in place. I will have everything timed to the second."

"I'll be watching you from a distance and will disappear when the fireworks go off."

"Will I see you before I leave?"

"I think not. The ship returns in two days, and you need to be on it. I got you a totally different-looking disguise. You're going to love it." He said, throwing a wicked smile.

"Sure, just like the last one you picked out for me, I looked like a dominatrix."

"Sweetheart, you were rocking that leather. I didn't go that far, but you're going to look awesome. The map is in one of the pockets; you know what to do after you memorize it."

"Alright, give my regards to your family; love you." They kissed and hugged each other before she took a cab to her hotel. The cab driver kept on looking back at her as if he recognized her. She avoided his stare as much as possible.

"Miss, have you been to our country before? You look familiar," he said, grinning. His stained teeth made her feel nauseous. When she spoke to him in his language, he backed off.

Everything was in place; her room was on the first floor towards the back, facing the back alley. Tressa sat down on the wicker chair and paged through the instructions. In the bathroom tub, she lit the papers on fire and washed the ashes down the drain.

She rolled up her burka and put on her black sneakers. Then she hung the 'do not disturb' sign on her door and went out the window. She could hear the street noise as she lowered herself to the ground.

They had a dirt road with pieces of concrete damage from after the Dark Days. Most of the main streets were destroyed by fires. The damage was so massive they were never repaired, but people did what they needed to do to survive and used what was left.

The hotel she was staying in was one of the few hotels that were not totally destroyed by the fires. It was damaged, but it served the purpose, and the staff always made sure their guest had the best service possible. Quickly she mimicked the women's walk patterns. She made sure to stay away from any military group that would stop her. Taking the narrow streets of the marketplace, she went weaving in and out until she reached the other side. Her target was half a mile from her hotel. Tressa surveyed the area and realized that security was stationed by the dug site next to an office building. She found her target and returned to the hotel before someone could notice she was gone. Tressa had dinner purposely on the open patio so she could be seen in her disguise and prepared herself mentally for the task at hand.

The hotel was packed with visitors from other cities for one of their holidays. With so much distraction, it gave her a great opportunity to sneak in and out before anyone noticed.

Early the next day, she went shopping in order to get through customs, to show she was a tourist. That evening, dressed in black spandex pants, shirt, and sneakers, she strapped the explosives to her body and all the equipment she needed, carefully making her way toward the office building, which was once the defense building. This building held many secret plans for creating superweapons.

During the riots, it was one of the first buildings that were bombed, burying all the secrets with them. Tressa disappeared behind a huge wall and waited until it was dark. Quickly she took off her burka, folded it, and hid it in a safe place. Women were not allowed in the street alone after dark. Tressa found her target. Underneath the building, government workers were digging in certain areas of the building, excavating anything that looked official. For months they had been searching through the rubble for information to bring back the past weapons blueprints that needed to stay bu ed. After a few hours, she had dug twelve holes, filling them with explosives.

She could hear the guards playing cards and drinking in the front part of the building on the other side where they were excavating. They never got up to walk around and see if anyone was around. After planting the explosives and setting them to go off in the morning, she sat down to wait until daylight. Climbing on top of some boxes where she could see what was going on until she had an opportunity to get away safely. At sunrise, the guards had fallen asleep; she tipped-toed over them, slipping into her burka.

Tressa was rushed by some women arguing about the price of fruit. The place came alive as merchants chased people to buy their wear. She strode, dodging some merchants as they tried to get her attention. They shoved food in her face raving their food was of great quality. She pushed them aside, striving to get as far as possible from the explosion ns. In a few minutes, the local police would be all over the place, and she wanted to be indoors when the blasts occurred.

Tressa needed to make it to the hotel, which was only a few blocks away. She tried to walk even faster without looking suspicious. The heat was blaring down on her making her sweat. If everything went as planned, room service would deliver her breakfast in a few minutes. Then in a few hours, her cab would be picking her up, dropping her off at the port where she would be on the next ship back to New America.

The back window was still ajar just as she lifted it, pulling herself up into the room. Off came the burka as she wrapped herself in a robe. A few moments after climbing in the window, the porter was at the door with her breakfast. Tressa thanked him in his native language and tipped him generously. The young man had a grin on his face; he knew she was an American woman and tried to say something cute in English. "Thank you, Miss, thank you very much."

Tressa took the rest of the clothes off and placed the garment into a plastic bag to dispose of it later. She changed into more active attire and brushed her red wig. The short bob cut made her look like a celebrity. The body makeup lightened her beautiful tan skin, and the green contacts completed her transformation.

Nervously she looked at her watch and began to pace back and forth. One of the maids came to her room to bring her clean towels. Just then, the ear-splitting explosion shook the hotel. Tressa screamed and hung on to the pole of the bed. The maid was also terrified. Scared, the two women looked at each other.

"What... what was... that?" Tressa asked in the woman's language, trying to look shocked and concerned. The poor maid shrugged her shoulders and ran out of the room down the hall to the office.

The second explosion made some windows crack; dust and debris flew everywhere. Tressa joined the others out front. The military police were everywhere as people fled, running from the explosion. The firemen's sirens screamed as they tried to make their way through the crowded streets.

Tressa covered her eyes, the dust from the explosion made it hard to see.

The target site had been empty, and the guards were in the middle of shift change when the bombs went off. The site-building was once the Headquarters for the high-tech weapons division. The information that was destroyed was old documents that would allow them to make weapons of mass destruction. Some of the top world leaders had outlawed this type of weapon, not wanting to repeat the mistakes of the past.

One of the inside informants notified the agency. Secret manuscripts were found in a vault in a secure government building. It was dug out from under its destruction after so many years. This information was something the world needed to keep buried, never to be built, letting the past stay in the past, dying along with the old. This idea was argued at Headquarters for days before Tressa was asked to set the twelve bombs and keep documents from getting into the wrong hands.

Like clockwork, the cab arrived to pick her up to take her to catch the ship that would bring her back home. Again, like before, security stopped her, questioning the nature of her trip. After fifteen minutes of heated arguments in their language, she threatened them or not following their procedures about foreigners.

"What is the problem?" she said, "My papers are in order, and here is my travel ticket."

The head of security was surprised she knew their language, "Well, I see you know our language very well. Most vacationers bring an interpreter with them."

Her stare made them nervous. They usually harass foreigners to pay them money in order to avoid missing their baggage.

"I also know a few other languages. Would you like me to repeat the same thing I just told you? My papers are in order. Why I'm being detained again? Is it because I am a woman you think I am weak and you can continue to harass me, or that I am an American? I think I will call the American Embassy, gentlemen," she said harshly, trying to remain as calm as possible.

The head of security looked at his men and nodded, "I am sorry for the delay, but as you know, there was a bombing in the city you came from, and so we need to be extra careful."

"I understand, gentlemen, but I am on a tight schedule, and you have annoyed me to no end."

They were surprised that she spoke to them with such authority, never showing any fear, "I'll have someone take you to the boarding ramp."

Tressa was relieved when they were finally on their way. She would stay in disguise all the way home. It was one of those work trips where she stayed to herself. Men propositioned her, sending her drinks and asking if she would accompany them for drinks.

But Tressa's mind was elsewhere, back her home. When she had first started with the agency, Samuel always preoccupied her thoughts all the time, but now with rumors of him running around with other women, she had to figure out if there was even a future for them.

Bureau of National Security - Eastern Branch

Harley barged into Mr. Jesse Lee's office just as he was about to putt. Lee fumbled and missed, and the golf ball was lost under the radiator.

"Damn it, Harley, it better be good news,"

Lee reached under the dusty radiator to retrieve his ball, "I had a perfect shot."

"You told me to notify you when Tressa entered the country."

Mr. Lee blew the dust off his golf ball. "When was the last time someone cleaned under there?"

"I don't know; never if I have to guess."

He pushed his glasses back up his face, "So where's my girl now?"

"She'll be here any minute. She called me from the station. We have sent a car for her."

Harley always hated when she was sent on dangerous secret missions. Lee was always on edge.

Lee adjusted his tie and sat at his desk. He had been so worried about sending her to that part of the country where women had no voice. After the Dark Days, women's roles reverted back to old traditional ways.

Women of great beauty were always sort after and used to satisfy wealthy men's lust. She would bring a higher price because of who she was. However, Lee knew she was the only one capable of getting the job done.

Tressa was the only agent who knew the city; she spent some time undercover and learned the language.

"Thank you, Harry; Lord knows I've been praying for her safe return," Lee said. He could relax now that she was safe and back in Washington.

Her uncle Jesse was not happy when he found out that she was sent on such a sensitive and dangerous mission. Tressa was a natural with her background and her sense of safety. Lee trusted her judgment and her abilities. Now all he wanted was to see her pretty face.

Mr. Lee couldn't stop tapping his foot; he was so nervous. He called for Harley on his intercom, "Damnit, Harley, where the hell is she? You know I can't rest until I see her face to face."

"Calm down, sir; she just stopped downstairs to grab some coffee."

"Alright… have her come in as soon as she gets here."

Tressa walked into the office as Harley was hanging up. "Thank God you're here; the beast is in hell mode," he said, relieved.

They greeted each other with a big hug and kisses.

"You look great… let me see."

Tressa modeled her black mini leather skirt with a white lacey low-cut sleeveless shirt and boots with a four-inch heel.

"Glad you're back… it's been hell around here. Apparently, your uncle Jesse found out, and he hit the roof."

"I called him already to let him know I was back and called my parents too. I'm surprised he is so angry. Uncle Jesse knows the nature of my work. Well, he can relax now I'm back."

"Thank you, Harry."

"Jesse carved him out a new asshole… so you better go in before he starts crying."

"Gotch, why don't I give him my shoulder to cry on? He should learn to relax."

Mr. Lee breathed a sigh of relief when she entered his office. She sat down on a comfortable chair right across from him. "Baby, you look marvelous. I'm so glad you're back… I had no doubt you could accomplish this mission. But I also understand how dangerous it is for extraordinary women in that country. It is still a very volatile society."

"It seems like women's rights went out the window after the Dark Days. It's a bitch not to kick some of the men in the balls for their foulness, but it went well. Drew was right; I saw the vault. It melted through the base and destroyed everything from the inside out. The explosives took out the rest of the place, sending it deeper into the rubble. By the time they get it back out, everything in it will be ashes.

"That was our biggest worry that some fanatics try to build one of these unstable bombs, and without the shield, we had in the past, we would not be able to defend ourselves. I'm truly happy everything went as planned. And at least they didn't get to see the real you; how was it besides uncomfortable."

"It was very… intriguing, to say the less, but it's over; this was my last assignment. I can't take any more badgering from my parents. They made it clear they want me married someday and want grandchildren," she laughed.

"I can understand that… so we received all your paperwork for release, and all you have to do is go through a briefing session. However, you did say you would be available to give training sessions for new recruits."

"Sure, just send me a schedule, and I'll take it from there. I will miss the adventures, but that's life."

"So, what are your plans? Have you thought about getting married to that douchebag you're engaged to? Now that you aren't going to be away so much, you can plan your wedding."

She laughed, Lee was like a father to her, and he didn't think Samuel was good enough for her. "I don't know about this wedding thing… I do want to get married… it's just that I'm not sure about the groom."

"Really," he said with wide eyes, "I think you should take it slow. You've been through hell with that boy. You have no idea how many times I've wanted to punch him in the face. He came this close to getting a beating from me," he tried to putt again and missed.

"I had a lot to think about on my long trip back home… we've been engaged for almost four years, and I swear I don't know if I truly know my own fiancé."

"Hey, why rush into this? Take a few more months till you're sure about taking that step; it won't make a difference."

"I guess you're right; I'll be staying with my parents for a few weeks… I miss my brothers. Plus, Samuel and I need bonding time to make sure this is what we want." Tressa got up to leave.

"Come here and give me a hug, we're going to miss you around here, but you have to do what is best for you. I'll be in touch with you soon."

"Alright… I'll miss you guys too, but I will come and visit… making sure you ain't screwing things up."

They both laughed out loud.

***

Tressa paused, looking down the hall. The open floor had many cubicles. She would miss all the action and noise. There were boxes on her desk filled with her personal items. A picture of her and Samuel sitting on a rock during a fishing trip. She remembered the day they took that picture. She had worn red shorts and a navy blue top. The day had started out beautifully until Samuel started a fight with one of her male friends.

She touched the picture fondly. They did have some good times. She wrapped the picture of her with her sister Yadira. They held up a winning trophy along with another picture of her parents and her brothers.

She remembered how excited she was when they recruited her for this job. She was going to make a difference in the world like her uncle Jesse. But the pressure from her parents and their state of mind weighed heavy on her heart.

Tressa thought about her future. She would miss the thrill of the hunt and investigations. The last argument she had with Samuel made her think about their relationship and how she had to make an effort to make it work. She had been crazy about Samuel ever since they came to live in Lutzville thirteen years ago. Her parents would not allow her to date until she graduated from high school. When she was only sixteen, her father would take her to fighting matches with her sister. At eighteen, she went into the academy for training and got her master's degree in science.

She and Samuel were unofficial high school sweethearts. For as long as she could remember, Samuel loved her. He was always sending her love notes, and they met secretly behind her parents' backs. But Samuel also loved other women, he had an eye for the ladies, and they also went after him.

He was one of those charming pretty boys with bedroom eyes; he was a sweet-talking guy with a killer smile and lots of money to spend. Samuel Delapaz came from one of the well-to-do and connected families in the area. His parents spoiled him and always covered up his mistakes no matter how bad they were. He was their golden boy and was very popular in school. It didn't matter what age, young and old women flocked to him. He flirted his way through school and out of any trouble.

The Delapaz family loved Tressa and was always pushing for a wedding date. They were prepared to pay for everything. However, Tressa was never intimate with him. There were times she almost gave in, but Samuel always did something to make her change her mind.

Samuel insisted they get married right after graduation, but after a huge fight, she enlisted in the academy and joined the agency. Tressa's parents were not happy with the rumors that Samuel had fathered a child with one of the Mason girls. He swore it wasn't true.

Holly Mason was a lovely girl, thin, with blond hair and pretty blue eyes; she came from a very poor family. Samuel denied having any relationship with the poor girl and even brought her to Tressa to collaborate on his story. Poor Holly was terrified of Tressa; she was soft-spoken and very shy when Tressa asked her questions. Samuel dominated the whole conversation and, like always, convinced Tressa that people had it out for him, so that's how the rumors started. Still, something deep inside Tressa questioned their relationship and made her uncomfortable.

Holly had a son but had refused to name the father, and since her mother worked for the family, she was always around. Tressa had caught Samuel in other suspicious situations. However, he always managed to find an explanation and make her feel as if it was her imagination.

Their relationship also created a rift between Tressa and her parents. Demi, her overprotective father, didn't like the constant rumors, and he let her know just how he felt. "Tressa, I'm a man. I know how men think. He's lying to you," he said, trying to protect her reputation and feelings.

She remembered the shouting matches with her parents. Tressa always found the need to defend Samuel and wanted to give him the benefit of the doubt.

Since their relationship was long-distance, she wasn't sure about her feelings anymore. They constantly talked on the phone, and he would come to visit every now and then. However, she refused to become sexually intimate with him because of his past relationships. They constantly argued about her celibacy. It wasn't that she wanted to wait until marriage; it was based on the fact that she didn't trust him and held on to a part of her she knew he wasn't allowed to touch until she was ready.

Tressa thought for a long time about their relationship on her trip back home. She didn't even know if she loved him anymore. This was a critical time for both of them. She would give it a few months and see how she felt about him and their future together.

The long bus ride home allowed her to reflect on what she wanted to do now that she wasn't at the agency anymore and would be on call. Samuel's last conversation with her made her think about why he wanted to get married so quickly. He nagged her to start making wedding plans. Tressa wanted to be married and have a family. But something was stopping her from taking that step forward. It was fun when they were together, and he made her feel special.

Nevertheless, even when they were together, his eye would wander and the flirting never stopped. Samuel would tease her and laugh, saying she was overreacting. Tressa was overly sensitive about how casually he dismissed her feelings when she bought up the subject.

His family was very protective of their oldest son. They loved Tressa and would always treat her like a daughter. However, sometimes she felt they were hiding things from her, especially when Holly and her baby were present. Tressa made a list of the good things she loved about him and what she hated. When the hated list became longer, she ripped up the paper and threw it in the trash. Tressa tried to make sense of everything and wondered why she even bothered to hold on. She had men throwing themselves at her feet constantly, begging her for a date. But her thoughts always went back to Samuel and how things would play out between them.

The streets were deserted when the cab dropped her off at her parents' home. It felt good to be home, she thought. There was a sense of peace, the air was crisp, and it was almost daylight when Demi answered the front door. Tressa smiled at her father, watching his expression of relief.

"Thank God you're home," He picked her up and swung her around as if she was five years old. "I'm so glad to see you, honey."

"I miss you too, Dad. I'm so glad to be home. Is Mom awake?" Demi put his arm around her shoulder, walking back to the kitchen. Even though she hadn't lived with them in a few years, she still considered it her home. It was always warm and inviting.

"She was in the bathroom when I heard you knocking. Where are your keys,"

"I'd have to dig in my bags. I'm so tired, Dad," she hugged him again.

"I understand, baby girl. What I want to hear now is that you're done with the agency. No more I-spy shit, it's too dangerous, and I cannot bear it if I lose you," he kissed her cheek. She hugged her father feeling like a little girl once again.

"I know you worry, Daddy. I'll be teaching recruits, maybe traveling to different places training."

"I'm sure your mother will sleep easier," Demi said before leaving the kitchen to check on the boys.

Audrey rushed into the kitchen. "I thought I heard your voice… oh, my God! Let me hold you," Audrey squeezed her tight, welcoming her daughter home. "I'm so glad you are home, sweetie. I can finally relax now."

"I've missed you too, Mami," her mother had a way of making her feel like a little girl all over again.

"You look wonderful. How about some breakfast so we can catch up?" Audrey suggested wanting to spoil her.

"Thank you, Mami. I am hungry."

"Tell me what your plans are now?"

Tressa poured herself some coffee and sat at the kitchen counter.

"Well, I'm going to bunk with Yadira for a while until I find out where Samuel and I stand. We have so much to talk about if there's going to be a marriage someday."

Audrey tried not to react to Samuel's name being mentioned. "You know we plan on moving to the ranch next year after Demi Jr. finishes his school year. Most of the renovations will be done by then. I think it's just a burden on your father to have to go back and forth all the time."

"No, I agree. The last time I spoke to Yadira, she was planning on moving. We talked about getting a house and sharing for a while. That's if things don't work out with Samuel, then I'm leaving. I'm just tired, Mami. It's just not welcoming around here anymore."

"What about Samuel? Will he be alright moving away from his parent's safety net? You know how he relies on them," Audrey mentioned.

"Well, I've been thinking about our relationship a lot. If we do decide to get married, I'm not living anywhere near his parent's influence. Don't get me wrong, they are the sweetest people, but I think they are the reason Samuel never grew up. It will take me a few months before I figure out where I want to go. If I feel things aren't progressing, then it's time to cut my ties with him and move on."

"Wow, that's a very grown-up decision coming from you," Audrey replied.

"I have to grow up sometime… being away from home so much has helped me grow up and start to evaluate my own happiness."

Demi returned to the kitchen, drawn by the aroma of fresh coffee, "So where's the coffee," Demi said, sitting next to Tressa. "How long are you staying this time?"

"Well, after breakfast, I'm going to Samuel's house," Demi made a face when she mentioned Samuel. "Dad, why the attitude?" Tressa whined, making a pouty face.

Audrey put her hand on his. "Think before you speak. You have a way of antagonizing your daughters."

"No, Mami," she turned to her father, "Dad, come on, speak your mind… you never held back before, so why stop now."

Demi took a deep breath and looked at his wife and then his daughter. "Tressa… there are many rumors about this guy. I saw him and the Mason girl at Barney's shopping for clothes for the little boy. Who just so happens to look just like him; why would he go out of his way to do that? He didn't see me; I followed them around for a few minutes. They were very friendly. There is something going on between them. I was getting really angry, so I went out the back way. But I tell you, I wanted to beat the crap out of him."

Tressa looked down at her coffee, feeling the anger rising inside. "Daddy, why don't you tell me how you really feel? Why are you rehashing this thing with Holly again?"

"Open your eyes, honey. See what everyone in this town sees but you." Audrey was silent. It took a lot for Demi not to attack the boy in the store. She had to stop him from going to his house and confronting him.

"Dad, I know you love me. Sometimes I feel as if no one meets your expectations… however, to appease both of you, I will go over there this morning unannounced and get some answers."

"Honey, it's 6 in the morning. He's probably sleeping in on the weekend. What would they think?" Audrey said, almost laughing, trying hard to defuse the situation. She didn't want Demi to chase her away again by being overbearing.

"Well, he better be sleeping alone; that's all I have to say. This way, I'll catch him off guard. However, Dad, if I find him alone in his bed, all warm and cozy under his covers, can we drop the subject that he's cheating on me?"

"Alright, I can live with that for now. How about you, Audrey?"

Audrey didn't want her to go alone. "Can I come with you? I'd like to see you get around the guard dogs at the front door."

"I have my ways, Mami. I learned from the best. Remember, I was a spy, and what they do best… avoid confrontation."

"Good luck, sweetheart. I hope for your sake, you're right, now kiss your mother and eat your breakfast. I can't have you knocking on someone's door this early in the morning on an empty stomach."

"I love you too, Mami."

The cold morning air felt wonderful against her face. The sun was finally overhead. It was a perfect morning for a nice brisk walk. The streets were still deserted as she took the familiar path down to Rushbrook Pine, where all the massive estate stood proud. These neighborhoods were beautifully kept with huge oak trees and cherry blossoms. Mrs. Walker waved at her as she walked her dog Stormy a beautiful white Siberian husky with one blue and one brown eye.

Samuel's home sat between the two wealthiest families in the town. The homes on this street were some of the loveliest estates in town. Sometimes you could catch as many as a dozen artists finding inspiration from the amazing historical homes. Samuel's father had a rod iron fence placed around his property to keep undesirables away. Mr. Delapaz took great pride in his perfect landscaping and awesome kept stables. The mansion had tall white columns in the entryway flanked by two stone lions.

Tressa punched in the eight-digit security code. The dogs started to bark, but as soon as they saw it was her, tails began to wag, welcoming her with kisses. She looked around to see not much had changed. When Rita opened the door in her robe, she had a look of shock on her face when she saw it was her. "Miss Tressa, you should have called ahead of time."

"Why I know Sam is here," she turned to go up to Samuel's room, annoyed when Rita tried to stop her.

"Miss Tressa, please let me get him for you," she said nervously.

"Rita, what's wrong with you… I know where his room is," she was getting suspicious. Tressa moved her out of the way and continued towards the second-floor suite where Samuel slept. She tried to open the door, but it was locked. Samuel never locked his door. She wiggled the doorknob and began to bang on the door. Samuel opened the door abruptly, wondering who had the nerve to bang on his door that early in the morning. Tressa stood with her arms crossed in front of him, watching the color drain from his face. He closed the door behind him.

"Sweetheart, you're here. Why didn't you call? I would have been dressed when you arrived," there was a nervous tone in his voice. Tressa heard movement behind the closed door.

She smiled at him sarcastically. "Had I called ahead of time, you wouldn't have had the pleasure of introducing me to the person you're sleeping with."

Samuel lost his voice for a moment. "Um… there's no one in there… it's one of the dogs," he laughed nervously.

"I have a feeling you're going to come up with fleas," Tressa didn't give him a chance to talk his way out of this one. She pushed him into the door opening it wide. When she entered the bedroom, it was empty, but the bathroom door was closed.

"See, I told you no one's here," he smiled. "I can't believe you don't trust me, baby," he tried to sound wounded. Tressa walked towards the bathroom door and heard a child crying from inside. She knocked hard on the door. By this time, the rest of the house had awakened.

"Please come out," she shouted.

"Baby, there's no one there. Why don't we go downstairs so we can talk."

"Go to hell!" She yelled at him. "Whoever is in there, you have until three before I kick down the door... one," there was a click as the bathroom door unlocked from the inside.

"Baby, please, I can explain," he tried to pull her away.

"Don't touch me, Sam, because I am surely going to kick your ass," she said, pointing at him. Samuel's mother was shocked when she stood at the door and saw Tressa standing by the bathroom door, just about to open it. The bathroom door opened very slowly. Tressa crossed her arms, waiting for the person to come out.

"Daddy, it's me, Sammy. You found us," Samuel's three-year-old son comes running out of the bathroom and into his arms. Holly stood by the shower wearing just a pajama top. She tried to hide her tiny belly.

"Everyone get out of my room," he yelled at his family and Holly, who had just enough time to wrap herself in a towel and grab little Sammy. Tressa was frozen on the spot… she felt a knot forming in her throat. The last thing she wanted was to cry in front of him. However, the pain was too real. Her eyes began to swell with tears. When she turned to look at Samuel, the pain had turned into anger, and the word revenge entered her mind.

"So, when were you going to tell me you had a child and another on the way? During our vows or maybe during our honeymoon… we were together last month on the beach, talking about a possible life together… you are dog shit to me!" She yelled in his face.

"I can explain," Samuel said, coming towards her, "I know this looks pretty bad."

Tressa found her voice under all the anger. "You can explain, ah, what could you possibly say to make this look better? Stay away from me, you pig! She started to walk towards the door, but Samuel blocked her path. He tried to hold her, but she pushed him away.

"Had we been intimate, this would have never happened," he said, trying to rationalize his relationship with Holly.

She pushed him away from her, "So this is my fault... I didn't give you sex, so it's my fault you couldn't keep your pants on! I'm glad I didn't have sex with you. It wasn't because I didn't want to, I truly did, but I guess I never trusted you. And I was right; I will never regret not sleeping with you!"

"Oh, is that right? You never gave me any indication you wanted to have sex with me... you pushed me away every time. I tried to be patient, and so every time I came home from seeing you, Holly was there waiting for me to satisfy my sexual needs."

She slapped him hard in the face, "Well, the way I see it, she can continue to satisfy your sexual needs. I'm disgusted with you. You lied and betrayed me in the worst way possible. Be happy with your life. You deserve everything you get," she yelled at him, crying with anger, she tried to leave, but he picked her up and tackled her to the bed, pinning her down.

"You belong to me, ice princess. I'll turn you into a hot sex slave by the time I'm finished with you." Samuel struggled to pull off her pants, but Tressa pulled his hair back and punched him in the face. She wiggled away from him, heading towards the door where his parents were waiting, afraid of what would happen to their son and Tressa.

"Tressa, my dear, please let's sit down and talk this out like adults," Mrs. Delapaz pleaded, following her to the stairway. Samuel caught her and held her from behind.

"Tressa, please talk to me." He pulled her back into the room and forced her to sit on the bed, and knelt between her legs.

"Tressa baby, now that all this is in the open, we can start over," he tried to touch her, but she slapped his hands away.

"Had you been honest with me from the beginning, maybe we could have salvaged our relationship, but this… everyone knew you were cheating on me!" She couldn't stop the tears, "they knew about Holly and baby Jr. Your parents condoned this… this life of yours, how sick is that," she yelled.

"Had I told you about Holly before, you would have left me?"

"I would have been hurt and angry, but I would have forgiven you," the anger was building up inside of her. Samuel tried to hold her, but she pushed him away.

"Tressa, please forgive me, stay with me, let me make love to you and show you how much I love you… we can have our own baby and build a life together." Tressa's anger took on a new course. She pushed him so hard he fell back.

"You're pathetic. Once a cheater, always a cheater," Tressa stormed out of the bedroom and ran into Holly, who was holding her son, crying.

"Tressa, please forgive me. I never meant to hurt you," she saw the pain in her eyes and knew she was also hurt by his lies.

"Holly, you're too good for him. You can have him. Have a good life together."

Tressa slammed the door behind her; she was so numb she couldn't even feel the cool air against her face. She was living a lie. All this time, she dreamt of marriage, a home, and children with Samuel. She tried to stop the tears of pain and anger, but the betrayal was too great. Almost by instinct, she turned and ran to her grandmother's house, only a few blocks away and three blocks over on Divine Street. Her grandmother Alex was on vacation with her new husband and kept a spare in a hidden place.

Tressa fumbled for her keys as tears clouded her eyes. When she opened the door, she could feel the warmth from her grandmother's home rushing to greet her. The familiar sweet smell of pine was in the air. She found the oversized chair, the one she and her sister used to fight over when her grandmother sat in it. Tressa collapsed in it, pulling the quilted blanket over her, and sobbed until there were no more tears to shed.

So many nights, they would have long conversations about everything under the sun with her. Alex always understood and would laugh at some of the stupid things she said. Tressa could only speak to her about Samuel, who didn't try to judge her, and though sometimes she wanted to say something and shake her. Instead, Alex would get quiet and hold her.

"The truths will come out, dear. Lies have a way of surfacing. Just take your time. You're young," then she would smother her with hugs and kisses.

Tressa fell into a deep sleep. When she awakened hours later, it was getting dark, she had slept for hours, and her head was pounding. "Oh, God make the pain go away," she cried. It was time to go home. Her family would be concerned.

Tressa washed her face trying to put cold towels on her sullen red eyes. *Why did she not see what he was,* she thought. She had so many fights with her family because of him; even her sister tried to tell her, and she defended him.

On the way home, anger was building up inside her. She made up her mind that from now on, she would do with her life what she wanted. In her heart, she would get as far as possible from this town and the awful memories it held for her. She imagined people looking at her and laughing… what a fool to believe someone like Samuel could be loyal to anyone. Let alone a woman, her mind raced with so many thoughts.

The streets seemed colder and darker than usual as she passed Samuel's house. She stopped and wondered what had happened after she walked out. Suppose she could be a fly on the wall as they discussed what happened. Slowly she made her way down to her parent's home, all the outside lights were on, and when the door opened, Demi rushed to meet her.

"Tressa, oh, my God. Where have you been? We've been going crazy looking for you." Tressa fell into her father's arms. A new flood of tears threatened to fall, but she fought them back.

"Daddy, it was terrible… I went to my grandmother's… I'm alright."

"Let's get inside, it's cold out here, and your mother is going crazy with worry." Audrey embraced Tressa as she entered the house. "Mami," Tressa cried like she did when she was very young and hurt.

"What did that bastard do to you?" Audrey asked, holding her tight. "Samuel was here earlier making a scene. I had to keep your father from going outside and beating the shit out of him."

Tressa made her way into the warm kitchen. "I'm so hungry. I haven't eaten anything since breakfast, and my head is pounding."

"Sit down, sweetheart. Tell us what happened?" Audrey asked, "Samuel kept on yelling to forgive him. I called the police to have him removed," Audrey held her tight. Tressa mustered up the strength to tell them what happened, but her father was out of control and punched the wall. Yadira rushed into the kitchen, wondering what all the commotion was about.

"Thank God you're home," Yadira hugged her sister. "I looked all over for you. I'm sorry I heard what happened. We got into a shouting match right outside. Boy, can we really choose them? Two broke down no good losers," Yadira said, holding her sister's hand.

"Twins to the end, you still thinking of getting out of town? I have to get out of here," Tressa said urgently. "I can't stand being around here anymore."

"So, we're still on, then? I have the school, but I've been thinking of selling it for a long time now. I feel suffocated here, and now that Mami and Dad are moving, the only one left is the grandmother."

"Definitely, now I know what you were talking about... I may go ahead and find a place for us," Tressa said sadly, "There are a few areas I want to check out. I'm going to do some freelancing with the agency, training is good money, and I can come and go as I please."

"I think our time here is done, sis. Let me know what you come up with. It will take me a while to get things wrapped up."

Demi couldn't stand to watch his girls hurting so much, wishing he knew what to say to make them feel better. "Look... girls, I understand about pain. When I lost your mother, I wanted to die a hundred deaths. I used to find ways to end my life when the pain was unbearable at times." Audrey put her hand on his shoulder as he looked at her with so much love in his eyes. "Don't give up on love, girls. I guarantee you that the right man will come into your lives."

Yadira smiled at her father, "Daddy, you're romantic, but I know one thing. I'm not going to find someone in this town. It's been two years for me, and this fool is still on my ass."

"I know, sweetie, but you'll see good strong men instead of these punk ass mama's boys around here," Demi said, getting angry again.

"Your father is right. The young men you two were involved with are pampered and don't know what a good day of hard work is… their idea of a hard day's work is holding their hand out to ask their parents for money."

Tressa laid her head against her father's chest. "I know it will take me a little while to put this all behind. I understand now what you were trying to tell me, Daddy, but I'm going to be alright," Tressa said in a small voice.

"You're my blood. We are strong. I have no doubt it's going to take some time. Set goals for the future. It's not the end of the world," Demi said, holding both his girls.

Tressa spent the next two weeks relaxing and enjoying herself with her younger brothers; there was so much to do to get ready for their move. Tressa busied herself with helping her parents pack and clearing years of clutter. Samuel tried to call her so they could talk, but she refused him, and her parents intervened all the time. He would send flowers, and they were sent back. Tressa was shocked to see his parents at the door one evening. Audrey peeped out the window.

"Sweetheart, let your mother handle this. You go upstairs with your brothers."

Audrey opened the door, "Good evening, Audrey, may we speak to Tressa," Ms. Delapaz pleaded.

"Karen, Sam… I'm sorry to say that Tressa is not receiving guests. But if you have something to say, you can say it to me. Please come in."

Karen felt uncomfortable sitting in their family room. Most of the walls were bare, and some of the furniture was missing. "Are you leaving?" She asked, surprised.

"Yes, in a few months, once the boys finish school. We just built a beautiful ranch. So, what is this all about?" Audrey asked, pretending she didn't know the nature of their visit. She sat with her arms crossed. Wondering what they could possibly say to repair a broken heart.

Samuel senior cleaned his glasses. He was nervous, "Let me talk, honey, my wife, is terribly upset at this… development."

"I don't know what you're not understanding. My daughter found your son in bed with another very pregnant woman. Is there anything more to say?" Audrey felt the heat of anger rising within her.

"Audrey, it was unfortunate that this happened. But I assure you that Sam loves Tressa. He's all bent out of shape. He never meant for her to find out this way. He swore to me he would talk to her the minute she came home. But she beat him to it, and it was a tragedy that she didn't give him a chance to explain his side."

Audrey looked at him as if he had grown another head, "Are you serious, Sam? How stupid does that sound? What could he possibly say that would have my daughter consider taking him back? You must be just as crazy as your son. The bottom line is that your son couldn't keep his dick in his pants and knocked up this girl not once but twice. How much love did he have for my daughter when he was screwing Holly?" She yelled.

Karen sprang from her seat, "Audrey, really! Must you be so vulgar?"

"Sit down, Karen. I haven't even started," Audrey paced with anger. "So, Sam, what could you possibly tell my daughter that would ease the pain she has endured and shame? Tell me about the shame she feels knowing you two knew he'd been with this girl for over three years now. How old is your grandson?"

Karen avoided her stare, looking at her husband for an answer. "Audrey, I understand this is still very raw for everyone. I just wanted you to know that Sammy didn't set out to have a relationship with Holly. They were just good friends. When Sammy and Tressa had that huge blowup, and she left to join the agency, Sammy was extremely upset. He was inconsolable. Holly was there to listen to his problems. One thing led to another, and she got pregnant."

"I guess she did a great job consoling your son. You lied to her and us. If my daughter goes back to your son, I will disown her. So, there is no possible way she will take that liar and cheater back."

"Really, Audrey, how could you say that? Maybe we should stay out of it and allow them to work things out."

Audrey took a deep breath, guarding her tongue with those hateful words she wanted to say. "I'm going to have to ask you to leave before my husband gets home. He won't be as nice as I am."

"Won't you please, as one mother to another," Karen pleaded as Audrey walked them to the door. "Ask her to at least hear him out."

"Goodbye, my daughter is going to do what she wants, and if she decides not to speak to Samuel, then I support her decision." She slammed the door behind them. Tressa was on the stairs listening to all that had transpired.

"Mami, would you really disown me?" She asked, surprised.

"Don't be ridiculous, dear. They just won't take no for an answer. There is nothing you can do to make me disown you or any of my children," she held Tressa tight.

"I want you to know that there is nothing he can say that will make me go back to him. I do have feelings for him, and the betrayal is horrific. Yesterday as I was walking home, I felt a huge weight off my shoulders. I could breathe even though my heart was heavy."

"It will pass; no one wants to be made a fool. He will get what he deserves in due time."

Tressa spent some much-needed time with her family. Her brothers were growing like weeds and followed her everywhere. She helped Demi Jr. with his fighting techniques, proud of how he handled the practice sword Yadira gave him for his lessons.

It was a clear and beautiful morning, spring was coming, and the boys were itching to get outdoors and play. Demi Jr. couldn't wait to break in his new baseball glove.

"Come on, guys, get your jackets on. It's still chilly outside," Tressa said, helping the boys with their jackets. Tressa tossed Demi Jr. the ball for a while. Baby Julian pretended to hit the balls with his bat. Demi and Audrey watched from the kitchen's glass door as they drank their second cup of coffee.

"It's so good to have her home, even if only for a little while," Audrey said, smiling.

"Yeah, I know she's grown up, but she's still our little girl… and Yadira. I swear she's given me all my gray hairs," they laughed.

"But Tressa is the more emotional of the two. Remember when Yadira broke up with Danny, I felt sorry for the boy. She beat him up, stepped over him, and put him in the hospital," Audrey said, remembering how proud of her they were.

"That's my girl, brutal to the max. That bastard deserved what he got," Demi added.

Tressa and the boys continued to play, but in the distance, she noticed a single man traveling their way. As he got closer, she realized it was Samuel. Demi Jr. became defensive when Samuel jumped their fence.

"Get away from my sister, punk," he yelled at him swinging his bat.

"Demi, take little Julian inside."

"What about you, Tress?" He asked, concerned for his sister.

"I'll be fine, buddy, trust me," she said, assuring him everything would be alright.

Audrey noticed the look on Demi's face, agitated, "Baby, stay out of it. She's a big girl and needs to learn how to handle this situation." Audrey warned Demi, who was ready to open the door, "Let her handle her business… she knows what to do."

Samuel fell to his knees before her. "Tressa, please talk to me," he begged. "I've been waiting patiently to see you outside to talk to you and beg you to give me another chance."

"What is there left to say, Sam? There's nothing left of us. Whatever I thought we had is gone. How could I ever trust you after this? I deserve better than a cheating and a lying husband.”

“Don’t say that. It will always be us; you belong to me in body and spirit. We are meant to be together. You know that.” he pleaded, trying to make her see he’s changed.

Tressa shook her head. “Samuel, it’s over… it’s never been right between us, be a man and marry that poor girl who is about to give you another child. I can tell she truly loves you.”

“Sweetheart, I don’t love her. Please understand that she is a nice girl, but I don’t love her like I always loved you. Tressa, I was lonely, you were gone most of the time, and sometimes you were indifferent towards me. Holly was there to listen to my heartache, and we became close. The baby was my fault. We were angry at each other; I got drunk, and I didn’t use a condom. She was going to have an abortion, and I stopped her. I told her I would take care of her and the baby. She knows I love you.”

She couldn’t stand to look at him. “You are a worthless piece of shit. You were lovers for a few years. She wasn’t just a one-night stand. What kind of man are you?”

“Call me whatever you want, but that’s all she was.”

Tressa looked at him with disgust. "You're lying. The only reason you won't marry her is that she is poor, and her mother is your cleaning woman. You will never change, Sam. Every time we get into a fight, it would be your excuse to sleep around. I would wonder every time you stepped out of the house where you were going and who you were screwing. I don't love you anymore, Sam. Whatever I felt for you is dead, and I want to start my life with a good honest man. Please don't come here anymore." She turned to leave, but he held on to her hand.

"Look, I know you're still hurt, and I'm going to give you a little space. You're speaking out of your pain and anger… I'll be back in a few weeks, and we can talk when you're not so emotional. I love you so much, Tressa, and I know you love me too. I know our love cannot die like this but will be stronger because… we have been through so much."

"You're delusional," she walked away from him towards the door.

"I love you, Tressa. Our love won't die like this," he shouted, turning to leave the same way he came. Tressa shook her head in disbelief. He was still under the assumption that they could get back together someday.

"Are you alright," Demi asked.

"Swell, Dad. He's pulling at straws. I realize something… seeing him again. He can't hurt me anymore, and I think that even though this is painful, I'm glad it happened this way. I killed the illusion I had about us, and I can move on."

"I'm glad to hear that. You deserve better, sweetheart. There is someone very special for you, I believe it."

"Your right, Dad. I do deserve better. Time will heal my achy heart," he kissed her forehead.

"Pain sometimes goes with growing up, but we manage to live on."

Chapter 2: The Journey

Demi was startled when the doorbell rang at three in the morning. Jason arrived exhausted with a frantic message from the Agency calling her back to headquarters. Jason took his hat off before he entered their home.

"I'm sorry to disturb everyone this late, but I have a message for Miss Tressa."

She broke the seal to read the urgent message from Mr. Lee, which only states it's a code red incidence of great importance. Tressa looked at Jason, shivering, looking pale, and tired from the long trip.

"Why didn't he just call? He has my number?"

"He was afraid someone would intercept the call. You know the phone lines are not a hundred percent secure or reliable."

"Well, I guess it can wait until after you have rested?"

"Yes, we're going to have to. The train line is not opened at this time. I was lucky to get here. I walked about two miles," Jason said, weary.

"If we go on horseback, we can make better time. Going by train takes twice as long. You must be hungry and tired. Come in the kitchen and eat something while I make your bed on the couch," Tressa suggested.

Audrey was a concern. She didn't like late-night messengers banging on her door. She bought out extra blankets and pillows to help Tressa make a bed for him.

"Honey, what's going on? This has to be serious if they're sending you a messenger in the middle of the night."

Tressa tried to relieve her anxiety, "I wasn't briefed after finishing my last job. Lee will get in trouble if he doesn't file this report. And I think he may have a training assignment for me, so I just may take off from there. It would be ideal; I can use it sometimes, away from Samuel. He's not going to let up until I do something to hurt him."

"Send us word. You worry me, and you know your dad; he's always a wreck."

"Don't worry. I'll let you know. I think I may be sent to New Los Angeles. They are heading up a special tasks force."

"Stay in touch, and don't worry about Samuel. He'll bounce back."

Early the next morning, Tressa said her goodbyes to her family. It was about nine o'clock before the boys let go of her neck. She waved goodbye to her family and to her painful past with Samuel.

Jason had a hard time keeping up with her pace. They rode straight through, only stopping to eat and water the horses. It was almost five o'clock when she arrived, signing into the security desk and up the elevator to the seventh floor. Everyone had left for the day, but she could hear Lee arguing with someone.

Logan sprung from his chair when she walked in, "Thank God you're here!" Logan cried with an anxious look on his face, "Lee is going crazy and taking me down with him. Hurry, he's in his office digging a hole in the carpet, pacing back and forth." Lee was on the intercom with Dr. Kumar. Logan had her take a seat, still puzzled, wondering what the urgency was. She regretted having to lie to her parent so they wouldn't worry.

"What's going on, Logan? When did you get back in town?" he motions for her to be silent. Lee rubbed his balding head.

"What's wrong, Lee?" Tressa asked again, not liking the sound of his voice

Lee turned his attention toward her with a worried look on his face. "Tressa, we have a situation, and unfortunately, you're right in the middle of it…" Lee took a deep breath. "I am sorry to get you here like this, but we have a problem. We just received word from Drew that after the bombing, police went door to door conducting an investigation. It seems that the hotel we booked for you also came with a peeping tom."

"So, what does that have to do with me?"

"You were in the pictures."

"You're kidding. Was someone taking pictures of me? But I was very careful. I backtracked to make sure no one was following me," Tressa started to get concerned.

"No, my dear, I wish that were the half of it… it seems like you weren't the only woman he has on film. However, you were the only woman that caught the eye of Prince Ahessa.

She laughed, "He is one of the last persons I ever want to meet up with." Tressa replied, starting to get scared about the whole situation, "he's a spoiled brat."

"Yes, my dear, he's young, spoiled, and very rich. After the explosion, they went house to house, looking for any connections to the bomber. One of the managers from the hotel had their teenage son at work with them. Well, he said he'd never seemed such a beautiful American woman and planted his camera in your bathroom while you went out to see what happened. The boy tried to hide his camera, but one of the guards took it and started to look at the pictures, and low and behold, there you were in all your glory. Now you are the poster girl for this spoiled prince."

"So, what's the problem? He has my picture… so what."

"Tressa, he has your naked picture with your shiny black hair flowing down your pretty ass." Logan interjected, "The prince knows you are an American, and so he is using that to connect you to the bombing. However, there is one good thing."

"Oh, there's a good side… please inform me because I fail to see the humor in it all."

Lee pulled his chair closer to her. "Look, honey, the good thing is that he has no proof that you were involved in the bombing, but that's not going to stop him from coming after you."

Logan tried to make her understand, "The prince has a huge boner for you and a price on your head, enough money to make anyone help find you for him. Apparently, his desires for you are very strong, and he will do anything to have you."

"You can't be serious? So, what are you saying that this fool can come and knock on my door and just swish me away? Please tell me how safe I am supposed to feel."

Logan was feeling her frustration. "Tressa, we can stop him legally, but it's going to take a few weeks. He has a legal passport, and we have to petition the courts to take it away, but he's rich. The snot can buy anyone to help him," Logan explained. Logan was the head of their security department.

"Just listen, sweetie, Logan and I are working on a petition, but in the meantime, we need to keep you in a safe place for a few days. We are trying to find you a safe house… unfortunately, because it's an international problem, they have to handle these matters with delicacy. But Logan has a plan."

Tressa sat back, crossing her arms, "I am all ears; I still can't believe he can track me down."

"Sweetheart, think of what you just said. There aren't many like you running around. I'm sorry for putting you in this predicament. We're trying to work something out as soon as possible. Logan is working on something."

"Well, you see, I have a close friend who is the owner of The Pink Lady's & Things."

Tressa was confused, "That's a whore house…is that your idea. Take me off the edge here because nothing is making sense."

"Just listen; the plan is great. This is the last place they'll be looking for you. The prince is very proud and thinks everyone is beneath him. He wouldn't be caught dead with a whore."

"Lee, did you two think this through…because there's something you left out. These women are all mutes… you know I can't stay quiet for an hour, let alone a few days. Hell, you can send me on the most dangerous mission, and I'll be fine, but keeping quiet for days it's the hardest thing for me to do."

Logan tried to calm her down. "Listen to me. We have everything covered. I wouldn't do anything to harm you."

She looked at Lee and saw the strain on his face. "So, this is your plan… pretend to be a whore. What other options do I have."

"It will just be for a few days."

"Lee, I know your worry about me. I'll do it. I have all the time in the world. I hope you know I'm on the payroll because you're paying me for this shit. If I'm going to be a concubine, I may as well get paid." she said, trying to ease his mind.

"Anything you want. Logan will take you downstairs to see Professor Kumar while I work on the transportation."

"I hope this doesn't take long. So, what does a prostitute on leave do to occupy her time?"

"It won't be as bad as you think. Two days is all I need to get you moved somewhere safe," Mr. Lee tried to assure her.

Professor Kumar's office was just how you would imagine him, with thick wireframe glasses, a dingy white lab coat, and books everywhere. Professor Kumar was a hardcore 20th-century study. He had just about every single product the century produced and analyzed every component and ingredient. So much was lost during the holocaust of the Dark Days. Buildings burnt down, taking wonderful information with them forever.

Dr. Kumar smiled when she walked into his over-cluttered office. Tressa sat at his desk, moving some books. "Ah, the most beautiful spy in the world. How are you, my sweet?"

Tressa laughed. He was her favorite person in the Agency. "What do you have for me in your goodie bag?" She teased.

"Well, my dear… let's see." He felt her neck to make sure she was a good candidate for the procedure. "You're a perfect specimen, my lovely."

"Professor, all we need is something that will silence her for a few days." Logan added, "Do you have something safe?"

"Mr. Logan, I have just the thing they use to relax the vocal cords when doctors need to perform a delicate surgery."

"Does it hurt? That's all I want to know?" She asked, pulling away.

"Not at all… I will, however, numb the area just in case. I promise you won't feel a thing. I tried it on myself. It was the best week my wife had." Everyone laughed. His jokes were as dry as he was geeky. "For your lovely black hair, I have this temporary hair coloring it comes out when you shampoo your hair. I hope red is ok with you, and for those sexy brown eyes, I have these green contacts that will do the job. They won't irritate your eyes if you leave them in a few days."

"Woo, sexy redhead. I think I'll visit the Pink ladies," Logan teased.

"It's not funny, Logan. Maybe I should put your ass in a dress so you can keep me company."

"Sweetheart, I don't do dresses, plus my sister will kill me. I have better legs than her."

It took Tressa an hour to get the contacts in her eyes, but when everything was done, she looked like a totally different person. The green dress they gave her to wear was so tight she could hardly breathe, and the shoes were extra high and pointy.

"You look beautiful, Tressa. Now you let me do all the talking," Logan teased.

Tressa flicked him the bird feeling the effect so quickly.

The Pink Ladies was nothing that she expected. It was plush and beautifully decorated in pink and black. Jeffery Lambert didn't spare any expense when it came to making his clients feel special. Jeffery met them at the door dressed flamboyantly with extravagant jewelry. "Logan, you devil. It's great to see you. Let me look at you." He teased, "my, you're looking mighty delicious these days. I was thrilled that you would let me help you in your time of need. Please come in. Glenda, sweetie, bring my guest something to drink." His office was just as flamboyant as his dress. Black, white and pink everywhere. He was mesmerized by Tressa. "I must say you are divine. What a lovely creature, oh I bow to you."

"Snap out of it, Jeff. We need Tressa to hide out here for a couple of days. Can you do that for us?"

"For you, anything, my love… you, my dear, are so welcome to stay as long as you want. If I may say, what a perfect tan you have, sweetheart. Tell me what you use? I would love to have some for my girls."

"Maybe some other time, Jeff. This is serious top-secret shit."

"Oh yes, please forgive me, love. Glenda!" he called, "Glenda darling can you take Miss Tressa and find her something suitable for her to wear so she blends in with the rest of my beauties? Good lord, she can make me rich with her sweet ass."

"Don't even think about it. She's one of us. Jeff, this is a really sensitive mission, so please keep it hush-hush."

"Not a word, my good man. She is free to mingle with the girls. She can make herself at home."

"I appreciate this, Jeff. I will be in touch with you as soon as we can make a move safely."

"She will blend in beautifully with the others. I will keep her in the back when the guest begins to arrive. But that won't be for a few hours."

"Great, I will call you and send Mr. Lee the bill."

"Oh, don't worry, I will send him my babysitting bill. You can count on that."

Tressa fought with Glenda over what to wear. Everything was so skimpy she was embarrassed just looking at the items. Finally, she settled on a lacy full body suit and wore a black and white short jacket to cover her breast and back. The banquet room was the meeting place for all the girls. It had white and pink lacy curtains and oversized cushions in black and pink. Along one of the walls were four vanity tables with chairs. Girls took turns styling their hair and putting on their makeup.

Glenda worked on Tressa, pressing her hair straight and putting on some makeup. She gasped when she looked in the mirror and saw the caked-on eyeshadow and deep red lipstick. Quickly she wiped the blood-red lipstick off and just added a soft mauve color, and toned down the overdone green eye shadow.

The two large tables on the opposite side of the room were laden with fruits, vegetables, seafood, and sweet appetizers. On the side were two fountains of fruit drinks. Tressa loaded her plate and sat down on one of the armchairs facing the ceiling-to-floor windows. After having her fill with food and drinking two glasses of ruby red drink, she started to get sleepy. Before she realized it, she was fast asleep in the armchair. She curled up in a little ball and forgot where she was.

Hotel Su nrise

Felix and Lydia arrived ahead of the rest to make sure the accommodations were to their master's specifications. The concierge followed them around the two-bedroom suite, "Sir, if there is anything I can help you with, just ring," knowing they were big spenders.

"I'm with the Montenegro party… he shall be arriving in about an hour, and I wanted to make sure everything was perfect for his arrival," Felix continued to look in every room and bathroom, making sure they had enough towels and that everything was clean. "I would like you to bring up two bottles of your best wine… he's going to need something to snack on, so some cheese and bread would be nice."

"We have some nuts and fresh fruit, sir…"

"Yes, that would be great my master needs to relax."

"I'll have someone bring that right up, sir. We also have a directory where you can order just about anything. It is right there on the desk. He paused, "forgive me for asking if your master isn't married or with his wife. We can arrange… some female company."

Felix thought about it a second, "You know that's not a bad idea…um… I'll have to see about that. My wife and I will unpack for Mr. Montenegro, and if I need your help, I will ring for you."

"Any time, sir, the directory has those amenities listed."

Felix brought in his master's bags as Lydia busied herself, turning down the bed and arranging everything so that when Cruz arrived, everything was done.

Cruz Montenegro was bigger than life. His presence demanded respect everywhere he went. After two long weeks in meetings at the Inner Cities, he needed to relax.

Felix wanted to make sure everything was perfect. He had just acquired the position and wanted to make a good impression. Cruz Montenegro was the only person who believed in him, rescuing Felix and his family from a miserable life of extreme poverty. For two years, he served as his butler and was content. When he was asked to be his personal assistant, he nearly fainted. Felix was so honored and thankful. His wife was also promoted to travel with them to help out with other duties. He was thankful to be able to bring his wife on their trips so that they could be together. There were other reasons, Lydia was one hell of a cook, and she could put together a feast on a rock.

Felix and Lydia made a powerful twosome, and Cruz capitalized on the pair.

When Cruz and his men arrived, Felix had already laid out fresh clothes, and Lydia was cooking a lit dish for him. Felix opened up the double doors to his suite. "Welcome, sir. I have unpacked for you, and Lydia is preparing something for you to eat."

"Thank you, Felix, everything looks great, and Lydia… umm, now, she is special," he commented.

Felix smiled at his approval. "I know, sir; that is why I married her," they both smiled. "Are you tired, sir? Maybe you can use a massage?"

"I'm not tired…I just can't unwind for some reason. I need to relax."

"Sir, if I can be presumptuous…I know what makes me relax… some good wine and a warm body at your side are what you may need."

Cruz smiled, "I knew there was a good reason why I hired you… I have to eat, take a shower and go over a few things. I don't know if I want to get dressed and go through all that."

"Sir, if you allow, Lydia and I will go for you and pick out a beautiful, sweet woman for you… Lydia has an eye for pretty women… and there's a place not too far from here. You stay and eat; shower, and we will bring her to you."

"If she's not of your liking, we can always take her back," Lydia added, hoping he'd say yes. They really wanted to make a good impression, and he was very good to them.

"Hum… let's see…you know I trust you, and it's only for one night, anyway, so why not."

"Wonderful, you will not be disappointed. You just allow Lydia and I to prepare a nice romantic date as you get ready." Felix was beside himself, wanting to please him.

The Pink Lady

When Jeff opened the parcel, he almost fell to the ground. "Oh my God! I'm ruined! Glenda, oh my God… Glenda, come here quickly!" She reached his office, out of breath, and found Jeff going through his file cabinet.

"Jeff, what's wrong?"

"Glenda dear, I will be ruined. I need you to get my brother and tell Richard to get his ass down here right now! And pack some clothes. I have to save my business." Richard was Jeff's brother, who was partly owned at one time until he started to gamble. Richard sold Jeff his half of the business. Richard was a better businessman than Jeff; he was better with numbers and knew how to negotiate. When Richard arrived, Jeff was still in a panic.

Richard was at the country bar when Glenda pulled him out. "Jeff needs you. It's urgent."

"Ah, what does my brother want now?" Richard said, finishing his beer.

"I don't know. Something about the business being ruined. You know what kind of drama queen your brother is."

When Richard arrived, Jeff was in a tizzy, "What's wrong with you?" Richard yelled, trying to make sense of what Jeff was saying.

"Glenda dear, please finish packing… Richard, I need a favor from you. I have a major crisis on my hands. The port is holding my merchandise. If I don't get there in three days with a bill of sales, I will lose my pants. I need you to stay and look after the girls. Anything we make, you can have half. I'm expecting some big spenders in a few hours."

"So, Fajardo is up to his old tricks again," Richard chuckled.

"That son-of-a-bitch is going to get killed one day… Glenda, honey, are you almost ready!"

"Don't worry, Jeff, I'll take care of everything. You go on and settle things with the port authority." Richard said, happy to be making some extra money. Jeff was famous for having some of the prettiest girls in the area. He treated them well, and they loved him.

"Alright… I think I have everything. I've got to go. Glenda, honey, bring our things. Take care of my customers, Richard. You know they come first."

"Don't worry, I got this," Richard waved them off.

Tressa could hardly keep her eyes open. She managed to pull herself off the armchair and tried to walk whatever she drank off. However, the more she tried, her feet were like lead. Sitting back on the chair, she had a hard time focusing. The sun had gone down, and the room was lit by a bunch of small white lights placed in certain areas of the room. The music was hypnotic, and the girls seemed to sway with the music. One of the girls pulled Tressa to her feet and lined her up in a row. Felix and Lydia went girl to girl, looking for the perfect woman to please their master for the night. "Oh, Felix, this is going to be hard to choose. They are so beautiful."

"Yes, Madame," Richard replied, "We only pick the finest in all the land and overseas. They all get checked every week by our doctor. We take every precaution when it comes to our girls. We cater only to a very special class of men and women."

"Well, my employer is special, and I want to make sure he is well pleased. Money is not an issue."

Richard grinned.

"Felix, what about this one? She's exquisite," she stopped in front of Tressa, who felt like she was in a dreamland.

"Huh…yes, my dear. She is remarkable. Has she been altered?"

"No, sir, we do not alter our girls. What you see is what you get," Richard was surprised by his question.

Tressa couldn't even make out what anyone was saying. She was drugged, and all she could do was be led by whoever held her hand or gave a command.

Richard couldn't find any paperwork on Tressa, but Felix insisted that she was the girl he wanted. "I will pay whatever it takes."

Richard only saw the gold and dollar signs. "Well, how long will you want her for? I can always do her paperwork when she is returned."

"Perfect, it will only be for a night. We are traveling tomorrow morning. Here is our information."

"Huh… you're staying where the rich and famous stay."

"Only the best for our employer," Lydia said, smiling proudly

"If she pleases my employer, there will be an extra something tomorrow."

"I am positive she will be to his liking… we guarantee our product."

Tressa sat like a zombie between Felix and Lydia. When they arrived at the hotel, she tripped and fell in the mud getting her clothes dirty. "Oh, my poor dear," Lydia cried, helping her to her feet.

"You'll have to get her washed up… I will go and prepare the room," Felix said, afraid she was hurt.

"Alright… come dear, we'll get you washed up and pretty again in no time."

Lydia helped her into the shower. The warm water felt weird against her skin. Lydia handed her some shampoo and some scented soap. "Wash your hair, dear. That is the best shampoo and conditioner made."

Tressa did as she was told, washing her hair and rubbing her eyes, letting the red dye and green contacts run down the drain. When she stepped out of the shower, she was a different woman. Lydia's eyes grew as big as saucers. "Oh my God, she whispered." Lydia wrapped Tressa in one of the towels and wrapped her hair in another.

When Felix entered the bathroom, he noticed the strange look on his wife's face. "What is wrong, my dear?"

"I don't know what happened, but…" Lydia removed the towel from her hair, letting her black hair stream down her back. When she opened her eyes, they were no longer green but brown.

"Oh shit, what happened?"

"I don't know… she was in the shower, and when she came out, her hair had turned black, and her eyes were no longer green… the shampoo… I don't know."

"Don't panic… get her ready… I bought you some sexy clothes for her. It will be dark soon. What we can do is when Mr. Cruz falls asleep, I'll get her back… I'll darken the lights some more… here give her this wine. It will help her relax."

"She is actually more beautiful than before. I don't think he would mind. Felix, she has black hair and brown eyes. Do you know how rare that is?" Lydia busied herself, blow-drying her hair and putting on a little makeup. The red outfit was made to entice any man. When Felix returned with another glass of wine, he could only stare at the beautiful woman who sat finishing the last of the red wine. "Felix, you can put your tongue back in your mouth."

"I'm sorry, my love, it's just that you… created a masterpiece. There are no words to describe it. Come, let's get her into bed and let Mr. Cruz know she is ready for him." Felix placed another bottle of wine with two glasses on the nearby table. Lydia arranged the lacy curtains to give the room a sense of intimacy.

Tressa felt like she was in a dream remembering the waterfalls and the warm breeze. She saw everything in a tunnel, and the bed felt good underneath her. She laid back on the huge pillows hoping the dream wouldn't end. *This must be heaven,* she thought. From a distance, she saw a flash of light and the shape of a man as he came closer. In her dream state, she tried to focus. He was a very powerful, built, handsome man. She felt him sit by her and say something, but she didn't understand a word.

He gently touched her hair and captured her lips. Her brain exploded into a million sensations. Her body reacted to his touch and his kisses. She felt a fire rise within her as he kissed her neck and captured her lips once again. Tressa pulled him closer as she couldn't get enough of him. He caressed her body and touched her in places she was never touched before, opening herself to him as he tried hard to hold back. She began to breathe heavily as he touched between the legs and then stopped… something stopped him. Cruz reached for the light and was stunned. Tressa had curled into a little ball. *Felix and Lydia had outdone themselves,* he thought. Not only had they bought him one of the most beautiful women he'd ever seen, but she was a virgin. Cruz smiled and started where he had left off. He tried to be gentle since it was her first time. He felt her stiffen under him as she tried to push him off, but when he kissed her again and again, she began to respond to him. She felt her skin getting hot and closed her eyes, surrendering to his passion with waves of ecstasy overcoming her body and soul. Her body trembled as he pulled her into his powerful embrace. When they were finished, she fell asleep to the rhythm of his heartbeat.

Cruz tried to remove the sheet from under her and replace it. For almost an hour, he sat and drank in the beauty of the shape of her delicate face, neck… breasts, and perfectly shaped legs. He wanted her; he was her first and wanted to keep it that way. Cruz summoned the nervous Felix to his room. Lydia followed him to explain what happened in the bathroom." "Come in," Cruz said, looking for something in the desk drawer.

"Sir, did she not please you?" Felix asked, surprised. Cruz smiled

"You and Lydia… outstanding…she is perfect. How did you manage to get a virgin? It must have cost you a nice sum?" Felix was shocked.

"But she's a concubine, sir… are you sure we are talking about the same girl, long black hair and her eyes."

"Brown eyes…"

"Yes, sir, an almond color, very beautiful. But if that is not to your liking, I can take her back."

"Felix, she is to my liking, and I have the proof of her purity. I want you to buy her for me and offer him what he wants."

"Sir… yes, I will right now… I'm happy you are pleased I will bring you her papers tonight."

"Very well… and Felix, you did well. Hey… you know the house we were working on with the French tile and the pool."

"Yes, sir, the one with the pretty garden and flower beds."

"It's yours and Lydia… you have pleased me greatly. Now go get me that bill of sales. I have to get back to my dark angel," he grinned, satisfied.

Felix could not content himself when they walked outside. He began to cry, "Did you hear that love he is pleased with."

"And we got the house we wanted." Lydia cried.

"I knew it. He is a good employer, my love." Felix said, kissing passionately. *The hard times were finally over,* Felix thought.

When Cruz returned to bed, she was still in the same position he had left her. Tressa was dreaming that this gorgeous man had just made love to her. Cruz touched her, and she reacted as if she had no will of her own. This time when he took her, she wrapped her arms around him, wanting him more, and let herself go completely.

The next morning, she woke up in a panic. She was naked and in a strange bed. Everything that happened the night before was a blur. Lydia came in carrying some clothes and motioned to the waitress where to place her breakfast. Tressa grabbed her by the arms trying to make her understand.

"Don't worry, my sweet girl… everything is taken care of. I bought you some clothes we have some clean towels for you and breakfast. There are toothbrushes in the bathroom. You let me know what else I can do for you. Mr. Cruz had to go out for a minute, but he will be back soon. Try to eat something before we leave." Tressa ran into the bathroom and slammed the door. When she looked in the mirror, she realized that her hair was no longer red, and her contacts were gone. Quickly she showered, brushed her teeth and hair, and tried to sneak out the door. When Tressa opened the bedroom door, she bumped into Cruz. He surprised her, and before she could react, he kissed her, making her body react to his kiss. Her mind was racing a mile a minute, thinking it wasn't a dream, but this gorgeous man was real.

"I see the clothes fit you. God, you're beautiful. I couldn't think of anything else but you." He pulled her in an embrace. "Don't worry. I'll take care of you." He kissed her tenderly and pushed her gently away, "Ok, we have time for lovemaking later… eat something, my sweet, it's a long ride." he kissed her on the forehead. "Oh, by the way, what do we call you?" She motioned for some paper. "Tressa, like poetry," he kissed her again, leaving her wondering what the hell happened last night.

Tressa watched as he walked away. He was built with broad shoulders and big arms, and when he smiled, she couldn't help but want to be with him. She surprised herself, going with the flow, wondering what to make out of this situation she found herself in.

Tressa showed him that she could handle a horse. So, they took turns riding each other. He took advantage of her, touching places she never let her boyfriend of five years. All she could do was pull away in a playful manner. When they reached the very next town, they ate, and he booked some rooms for the night.

Tressa didn't know what to do or expect. She didn't remember anything that happened, all she knew was that she wasn't a virgin anymore, and this hunk of a man acted as if he owned her. She couldn't talk to call the Agency, and she didn't have money to send a message. Tressa didn't know where she was or where she was going.

Lydia was always around her to help. She laid out some very nice clothes. Filling her bath with steaming hot water and a liquid that turned the oversized bathtub into a giant bubble bath. It was wonderful; Lydia smiled and lit some candles around the tub, pouring out two glasses of wine. Tressa laid back to enjoy the warm water when Cruz walked in wearing nothing but a towel and climbed into the tub with her. Tressa tried not to stare. She had truly never seen a naked man up close in the flesh before. She turned away, feeling her face turn hot with embarrassment.

"Ahh, the water feels good, doesn't it," he came closer. "I've wanted to do this all day," Cruz said, not wasting time.

His kisses were sending tinkling sensations up and down her body. Tressa questioned herself, wondering when this dream would be over. She closed her eyes as his lips fondled her neck and breast. Tressa would never, in her right mind, do something this bold. Her life went from boring to a new sense of excitement, allowing her the freedom to enjoy this stranger's tender caress. His kisses became more demanding, and his hands began to roam her body. It was more than she could handle as he set her body on fire. When he touched her between the legs, she nearly jumped out of her skin. He chuckled, "I'm sorry," he whispered, taking it slower, helping her relax until she responded to his touch and kisses that were breaking her down.

The next two days were full of teasing and lovemaking. Tressa was in a different state of mind. To her, it was a vacation, one that she wished never ended. Tressa watched him as he slept, admiring his beautiful body. For years when she was with Samuel, she wondered how it would feel to make love to him. But something always stopped her. Now here she was with a complete stranger having the time of her life. All the times she yelled at her sister about having sex with Danny, now feeling like a hypocrite. It felt good to be the rebellious twin. In many ways, she envied her sister and her wild side. Now she had a tale to tell Yadira. She smiled.

The night before they were to arrive at his estate, she overheard Cruz talking to Felix and Lydia. "Sir, you look so happy with the lady, but what is going to happen when you bring her to the house?" Lydia asked, aware that the women of the house would not take her presence kindly.

"I am very pleased, and to answer your questions, I don't give a damn what anyone says. It's my house, and if they have a problem with Tressa, they can leave."

"Yes, sir, you are right," Felix said, feeling proud that his employer was standing up to the women of his household.

"Felix, I want you and Lydia to go ahead and make preparations for Tressa. I want to spend one more day with her alone before I introduce her to the madness. And I have a gift for her which won't be ready until late tomorrow. Lydia, I want you to tell our household staff that I am bringing another lady home… a special lady," his voice became low. "I want her to feel special."

"Yes, sir, she is special… I like her very much. Would you like me to explain this to Miranda?"

"No, that won't be necessary… I want to tell her myself." He smiled when he spoke about his daughter.

Tressa could hardly sleep after a round of steamy hot sex. Cruz held her in his arms, surrendering to sleep. She tried to comprehend just what had happened these three days. Things were moving so fast. It was making her head spin out of control, wondering how she was going to explain this new path her life had taken to her parents.

This was out of her character in so many ways. Now it haunted her. She had so many drag-out arguments with her sister about virtue and keeping her virginity until she was sure the relationship with her boyfriend was worth having her. How could she ever justify her own actions? They would never believe she had mad sex with a perfect stranger. A handsome sexy one, but still, he was a stranger, and she didn't want to stop. She laid next to him, pressing her breast against his back, feeling his strong thighs against hers, kissing his back tenderly. He felt like a million dollars in her arms. Tressa began to compare him to Samuel and wondered if she had given in to his demands for sex if it would feel the same.

When making out with Samuel, she was always on guard and could never enjoy herself. In the back of her mind, all she could think of was how many other women he was enjoying. She could learn to love this man, who made her go crazy with pleasure, who handled her like a finely tuned instrument. She made up her mind to enjoy the time they had together.

The next morning after breakfast, Cruz took Tressa shopping. He picked out some clothes he liked and let her pick out whatever she wanted. Among her many purchases, she picked out a pair of sunglasses and a hat to hide her hair. "Baby, you don't have to hide who you are. We'll talk about this later." She held onto his hand, wishing this time would never end as they walked holding hands and exchanging kisses. Tressa had no idea how long this would last but embraced every moment. Together they walked towards the stables where a man waited. He walked towards them, greeting Cruz as if he knew him.

"Mr. Montenegro, he is ready for you. I'll bring him right out." After a few minutes, the man brought out a beautiful chocolate stallion, a stunning creature.

"He's beautiful, just perfect. What do you think, baby?" She smiled, feeling his coat between her fingers.

"The lady knows her animals, nothing but the best for the Montenegro clan."

"Sweetheart, does he meet with your approval?" She looked at him, surprised. "Alright, we'll take him. I knew you'd like him."

The assistant brought out three saddles to choose from. "Which one would you like?" Cruz asked. She pointed to herself, running her hand over the soft leather saddles.

Tressa picked the reddish one with a T branded into it. She couldn't believe he had just bought her this magnificent animal. She kissed him before the help mounted her new horse.

"You look like a lovely natural lady," the salesman commented, checking to see if everything was secure.

"She is in more ways than you think. Can you have someone deliver it early tomorrow to my hotel? We are leaving first thing. I can't wait to show off my new lady."

That night he said so many tender things, holding her so tight, feeling safe. Floods of emotions overcame her. That's when she realized it was more than lust. She started to cry, burying her face in his chest. "Don't cry, my love. I know it's only been a week, but you are my saving grace. I can feel it… soon I will speak to the doctor to see if he can reverse your vocal cords. I can't wait to hear what you sound like." Tressa couldn't stop crying. She ran towards the window to let the cool air soothe her cheeks. "Baby, what's wrong?" She shook her head. "Hey, I don't expect you to love me… but I'm hoping that with time you would come to feel love for me." She wanted so badly to tell him how she felt, taking his hand, kissing it, and placing it by her heart. He held her in his strong arms, letting the sweetness of his voice soothe her anxiety, rocking and kissing her temples, whispering sweet words as she continued to cry.

He had captured her soul. Now she knew how her parents felt and how much it was going to hurt when she had to go away.

Tressa enjoyed stopping at the small eating spots sampling the country cuisine and meeting all the friendly folk. Cruz tried to encourage her to remove her glasses and hat. But she refused. Once they crossed into his territory, she started to see a lot more villages along the way, noticing that people would come out of their stores or stop what they were doing in order to wave at Cruz. He made a point to nod and say hello to everyone. At the end of a long road, her mouth dropped at a massive estate behind a rod iron fence. It dwarfed Samuel's parents' house. There were other smaller homes along the way and another huge home nesting on a cliff. What a spectacular view, she said to herself, bringing back memories of her uncle Joaquin's estate.

There was urgency when Cruz arrived. Cruz helped Tressa down from her horse and walked her into the house. She could have never imagined the elegance and beauty when she entered the great hall. Lydia met Tressa at the door. "You're home, come dear, you look tired," taking control of her immediately.

"Take care of her for me…I have a few things to do." He kissed her before he sent her off with Lydia. Tressa hardly heard a thing Lydia said as she chattered on all the way to her room. They stopped before the double doors. Lydia opened the doors to splendor; the room was as big as her apartment, decorated for a man's taste, grays, blues, and black in straight clean lines. Pictures of a beautiful girl on the fireplace mantel, black and white photos of the family. The gray accent wall had tasteful pictures of families in red frames. The super king-size bed could easily sleep four or five. Tressa was in awe, not expecting something as grand. Lydia ran a bath and brought out some warm towels placing a white terry cloth robe with a set of matching slippers next to the bed. The bathroom was a reflection of the rest of the room, navy blue and white with a rich grey tile patterned. She felt every bone in her body relax in the steamy water shutting out the world and its problems.

Tressa felt like a new person as she emerged from her bath. Lydia laid her down on the massage table to help her relax. She moaned as Lydia worked her magic. All the stress poured out of her like water. Lydia had dinner waiting by the wall-to-wall window that looked out into a long terrace. She ate hardily, savoring the wonderful food and enjoying the solitude for the first time since meeting Cruz. The huge bed called to her, curling into bed and falling fast asleep.

Chapter 3: The Madness

Cruz met his men to get an update on what they accomplished while he was gone. Going over their reports, Miranda comes charging into his office. He scooped her up in his arms. "Daddy, I'm so glad you're home. Did you miss me?" She asked happily, kissing his cheek.

"How could I not miss my little princess? I bought you a present, so I hope you were a good girl," She looked at him with those big innocent eyes that always melted his heart.

"I did everything you said, and I drew a picture for your office," she smiled proudly.

"Good girl, why don't we go to your room so you can show me my new picture," he took her tiny hand in his as she led him. He felt guilty about not spending as much time with her as he wanted. The picture had a huge rainbow, their house, and a stick figure of them holding hands. Miranda had a daisy in her hand, offering it to another figure in an orange dress. "Very nice, but who's that in orange? Is that your aunt Sandra?"

"No, Daddy," she exclaimed, giving him a surprised look, "This is your new friend, the one you bought home with you."

"Who told you about her?" He was not amused, knowing he was trying to find the proper way to introduce Tressa to his daughter.

"Nina told me this morning that you bought a lady friend for a lot of money and that she had to do everything you said."

He held her tight, annoyed that Nina would say such things to her. "Listen to me, princess. Don't listen to your crazy Aunt Nina. Tressa is my new girlfriend, she's different but very nice, and I hope you like her."

"I will, Daddy. If you like her, I'll like her too." She smiled, and he melted.

The buzz spread through the household staff, and everyone wondered about the dark, mysterious woman. They whispered, puzzled why Cruz would bring a woman home. After his divorce, he vowed never to allow a woman in his home unless he was serious.

Troy took Cruz to inspect the excavation where the new hospital was going to be built. From a distance, he saw his brother waving to him. His brother Tajo was in the field, making sure the men were doing what they were supposed to do.

"About time you get your ass home, you lazy pig," Tajo shouted from across the field. "You go on vacation, and I'm stuck with these lazy ass bastards," they embraced.

"I missed you too, brother… I see you kept everyone in line."

"This project is our number one priority, but I did miss you nagging me about everything. And now the women can drive you to suicide," Tajo said, pushing Cruz in a playful manner.

"I don't let them get to me. You got to put them in their place. You know, crack that whip."

"Yeah, whatever…" Tajo was the crazy carefree younger brother. They were the same height, just not as built as Cruz, but they favored each other. Tajo embraced Tanio's Indian side of his family; he wore his redness dark hair long in a braid sometimes.

"Oh yeah. Cruz, what's this? I hear you brought some concubine to your house. Did you lose your mind? Hum, forget you have a young daughter?"

"Don't be stupid. I would never do anything to compromise my baby girl."

"Cruz, you got this woman from one of those whore houses. Which is what they are, whores."

Cruz tried to remain calm, "Relax, brother, I know how it looks, but… I was her first."

"The first what? Trick of the day, come on. That's crazy. What kind of trick are these places pulling now? Virgin, really bro." he rolled his eyes, "man, there hasn't been a virgin in these parts under fourteen… she is over fourteen, I hope."

Cruz chuckled, "You don't have to believe me… but I know what I know."

"Come on, bro…you're going to tell me you bought a woman in one of these brothels, and she was a virgin? You must have paid a pretty penny."

"I've been with a lot of women. I can tell if I've been with a virgin. Anyway, I have proof."

"Really… wow… that's amazing. They're always coming up with new procedures. I hope they didn't take you for a fool."

"I know the truth, and to be honest, it doesn't matter to me if she wasn't. You'll get your chance to meet her tonight at dinner… she's like no woman you've ever met."

Tajo chuckled, "You're such a whore. But whatever makes you happy, it's your life."

"She does make me happy… happier than I've been in a long time. Wait until you meet her. You'll change your mind."

"Man, I don't know what to say. I hate to see the reaction of these bitches when they get a hold of this shit."

"Oh, they weren't very happy this morning, and frankly, I don't give a rat's ass if they like it or not. This is my house. I don't live my life for them. They can move on."

"I heard that. I'll see you tonight. I'm looking forward to being entertained."

Tajo was not convinced about this woman, but Cruz was right. It was his house, his daughter, and his women's trouble. He had enough problems with the women he came across that tried to move in after one date.

Cruz was the Overlord of this province, and not one person he knew crossed him except for one woman. The most hated woman in these parts by everyone. So much was she disliked that not even her family whispered her name in the house, and Cruz wanted it that way.

Tajo tried to stay out of his brother's personal business. He wanted to see him happy, and if the whore did the job, *so be it,* he thought. He was a grown man and made his own decisions.

Nina tried hard to get more information about Tressa. She would interrogate everyone that came in contact with this new woman Cruz bought home. "Mrs. Lydia, who is this…, this thing Cruz paid for? Does she have like long red fingernails, blood-red lips, and tattoos all over?"

Lydia did not like the outspoken Nina, who was always in trouble. "I don't think it is any of your business."

"Come on, spill the juice. What is so special about her? Does she have huge tatas?"

Lydia rolled her eyes, "I think you need to ask Mr. Cruz, and if I were you, I would watch how you speak about his new love interest."

"She's a whore. It's the truth, and what is he going to say to me about the truth, so ha."

Nina couldn't believe her eyes when Cruz introduced her to the staff and Miranda that afternoon, as if she were the new mistress of the house. Nina was confused, expecting someone different. She charged into her mother's room, "Unbelievable, mother, what are you going to do? Have you seen this… this whore? She had your granddaughter by the hand," Nina spoke in her dramatic fashion.

"Nina dear, how many times do I have to tell you to knock before you barge into someone's room," Ellen tried to maintain calm. "You would think I didn't teach you manners."

"Why, it's not like you have a man or anything." Ellen sucked in a deep breath before she addressed Nina again.

"Try to be more considered, my dear. I taught you better. As far as this woman, I'm going to address this right now with the lord and master of the house."

"She's hideous... good luck. You know he's a blockhead," Nina spouted, shoving grapes in her mouth.

"Really dear, use a napkin; you weren't born in a barn. So how do I look?"

Nina shrugged her shoulders. "You look fine... I never understood why you get all dressed up every day."

Ellen wore a satin royal blue dress with graceful black sandals and a pearl necklace. "A woman has to look a certain part, my dear. Now when I go address this manner with Mr. Cruz, he will know that I am not the kind of woman who takes these matters lightly," Ellen straightened out her dress in the mirror and smiled. "Come, Nina, learn something of diplomacy."

"Oh, I wouldn't miss this for the world," Nina followed her mother as they both made their way to Cruz's office.

Nina giggled, "This is going to be great... you let him have it, Mom."

Cruz was contemplating paperwork on his desk when Ellen knocked on his door. "This better be important..." Cruz said, annoyed he was not to be interrupted unless it was an emergency.

"I'm sorry to interrupt you, but I need a word with you," She didn't wait to be asked to come in. Nina followed close behind.

"Mr. Cruz, I demand to have an audience with you right now." Nina stood behind her mother. Troy, one of his foremen's watched the expression on Cruz's face while Ellen stood waiting for him to answer her.

"Boss, do you want me to leave," Troy asked, knowing there was going to be an argument.

Without blinking, Cruz stared Ellen down, making her very uncomfortable. "No, Troy, stay where you are." The look on his face made her think it wasn't a good idea. However, she had to make her concerns known. "Madame, I have always respected you because you are my child's grandmother. But don't ever think you have permission to barge into my office and make any demands. Are we on the same page here?"

"I… I apologize for intruding this way, but I am highly upset. I heard rumors that you have invited a woman of questionable reputation to dwell under your daughter's roof. I feel I have much to say about it." Ellen was becoming more uncomfortable watching the anger growing in Cruz.

"Oh, I see…" Cruz stood up and asked Troy to please close the door. Troy knew what was coming. "First of all, Madame, and you too, Nina, the reputation of this woman is none of your damn business. She is what I want, and my relationship with her is my own business. I trust Tressa with Miranda more than I trust you two bitches with her and the bitch of her mother. Ellen, I suggest you look at your own daughter's reputation before you start looking at someone else's. The girl has been caught in so many compromising situations my staff is afraid to open closets."

Ellen's face was bright red. "I was only concerned for my granddaughter's welfare. She is a very impressionable child."

"I know what my daughter needs. I let you people stay here because I thought that having some of her family here would make a difference in her. But you have surely disappointed me. The only one that pays any attention to my precious daughter is Sandy. So please don't pretend you have her best interest at heart."

"Well, I had no idea you felt that way. You should have made your feelings known sooner, and contrary to your belief, I love my granddaughter dearly and only wish the best for her."

"How could you say that!" Nina interjected, "We always look after her. She's just so needy," Nina was still hiding behind her mother's skirt.

"Needy… you mean wanting a little love from her aunt, who pushes her away every time she comes near. Or her grandmother, who is so busy with her tea parties and special interest events she never has time to even plan some time with her!" He threw his pencil against the desk in anger. "How dare you two even challenge me or question my motives with my child? You two haven't done a damn thing to help with the situation she has suffered. And in conclusion, if I find out that anyone in this house makes Tressa feel even a little bit uncomfortable. They will be out in the street…got that! And that means you too, Nina. So, I suggest you spread the news, I want this woman, and she's not going anywhere." Ellen was so stunned she couldn't even speak. She stood glued in place. "Now, Troy, can you open the door for these fine ladies before I have them thrown out." Troy held down his laughter.

"Well, then when things go wrong, I'll be the first to say I told you so," Ellen said before she turned to leave.

"Get out!" Cruz shouted as his temper flared. Troy tried to calm him down. They should have known better. They come to Cruz with demands. Everyone knew he only tolerated them because of Miranda.

Ellen raced back to the safety of her room, holding her chest. She wiped the sweat from her brow and tried to compose herself. Ellen was still young enough to marry and find happiness, but after her horrific married to her children's father, she swore off men. She powdered her nose and combed back the silky salt & pepper hair that fell into soft curls.

Ellen watched herself go from a beautiful lovely young girl into a tired middle age bitter woman. She was forced to marry a man twenty-two years her senior who had a craving for really young girls and extreme cruelty. Ellen spent most of her youth trying to keep her girls out of the hands of their cruel father and family. She hated her mother for forcing her to marry this man for her own security and comfort. Now she was at the mercy of her own daughter.

When Mary left, she found herself in the streets again, trying to find work and find a place to live. But Cruz had not asked them to leave until now. *What would he do if he married someone else,* Ellen thought, looking around the beautiful furnishing and wonderful liberties she indulged in being Miranda's grandmother. She sat in front of the large window and promised herself that she would not get involved and keep her opinions to herself.

Nina busted into her mother's room again. This time Ellen raised her voice. "Child, can you please start acting like a human being for once," she yelled. Nina was stunned. Her mother never screamed at her.

"Mommy, why are you upset? You know Cruz wouldn't throw us out."

"My child, you live in this dream world... if he marries, his new wife is going to want us out. We have no place to go! Do you understand me?" She tried to stress to Nina, who had a blank look on her face.

"Mommy, he's not like that. Not everyone's like father," Ellen couldn't help but hug Nina. She remembered her father's cruelty, feeling bad for yelling at her youngest daughter, always wondering if things would have been different if she had a son.

"I'm sorry; maybe your right, my angel. He is a good man. I guess he deserves to remarry. Your sister blew her chances for any kind of happiness with him."

"She was a fool to give all this up, but that's Mary for you."

Lydia woke Tressa so she could get ready for dinner. She had fallen asleep after a lengthy ride, and Miranda had worn her out. For a moment, she had forgotten where she was and remembered how wonderful it was to be with Cruz.

"You seem to really need the rest. Mr. Cruz is expecting you for dinner." Tressa stretched out on the oversized bed feeling as if she had slept all night.

Lydia smiled as she looked in the closet for something nice for her to wear, "How about this cute pink dress, hum? It is a wonderful color for you. How I wish I had the body for this dress." Lydia draped it across her slightly plump body and nodded. "Not anytime soon. Anyway, with your beautiful dark hair and sexy body, it will make Mr. Cruz's eyes pop right out of his head." It was one of the dresses Cruz picked for her, fitting her just lose enough to move seductively as she walked. She slipped on a black pair of strappy sandals with a nice heel that gave her beautiful legs and sexy curves.

Lydia brushed her hair until it shined and fell neatly in soft tiny curls cascading down to her waist. After a touch of lip gloss and a little eyebrow pencil to accentuate the eyes, she was ready to meet the rest of the family. "You look absolutely stunning, Miss Tressa. Every woman will envy you at the table. Come, Felix is here to escort you to the formal dining room."

When Lydia opened the door, his eyes popped out. "Wow!" Felix said, "Lydia, my love, you've done it again, my dear. I know Mr. Cruz will be pleased."

"Sweetheart, she could be wearing a potato sack, and he'd be pleased," they laughed.

Tressa was intrigued by the mansion. It reminded her of when they lived at her uncle Joaquin's estate. It was elegant full of beautiful antiques and expensive furnishing expertly decorated. It even had an elevator and nine terraces. Flowers, great artwork, and light fixtures adorned the great halls and masterfully decorated hallways.

Two gentlemen opened the double doors to the dining area. It was breathtaking, with tall, vaulted ceilings, massive crystal chandeliers, and a huge mahogany banquet table. As she entered, the room went silent, she held on to Felix's arm, and he put his hand on hers just to reassure her that everything would be alright. When she saw Cruz's big smile, she smiled back and winked at him. She had not realized that everyone had stood up as she walked in. Her eyes were on him only as he stood at the foot of the table dressed casually but striking, he held out his hand to her, and he kissed it.

"Everyone, this is Tressa, my new love."

Tajo's jaw dropped. Now he understood why she was special. He couldn't take his eyes off of her all evening. He had a stirring in his loins that made him uncomfortable. This was his brother's woman, and he lusted for her at first sight.

After dinner, Cruz introduced her to everyone individually, and he explained about her voice. Everyone was very nice and polite but a little curious about the dark beauty, but she could feel the animosity coming from the females. Tajo greeted her with coldness as he said a speedy hello nice to meet you and left as quickly as he could.

Tajo had not expected to react as he did. They never had the same taste in a woman except for now. *How could he hide his feelings for her if he couldn't stand to be around her,* he thought. His brother noticed his reaction towards her but thought it was because he disapproved of where she came from. So, he overlooked his coldness, hoping he'd warm up to her once he got to know her.

Cruz couldn't wait to show off his estate leading her through the gardens and stealing kisses along the way. Every touch made her feel special, wishing she could speak with him about how she felt. Miranda joined them in the garden; she was such a beautiful child with long hair, rosy cheeks, and dimples when she smiled.

"I like her, Daddy. Can we keep her?" She said, holding Tressa's hand.

"If she wants to stay, this is her home," she looked at him as if to say yes, I will stay with you forever. The three made a wonderful family.

Tajo stood in the darkness on the terrace that faced the garden watching the three-walk hand and hand through the gardens in the moonlight. He felt envy he never had before, making him feel lost, allowing the darkness to take over his spirit.

He would have forsaken everything for her. Her beautiful face, brown eyes, and sexy well-formed lips that didn't have to speak because her eyes spoke loud and clear about how much she cared for his brother. He wanted so much to touch her black hair and kiss the sensual curve of her neck and breast. Tajo was afraid to be near her… she would see the lust in his eyes, and he could never betray his brother that way.

Sandra found him in the darkness, watching them sadly, "I know how you feel, Tajo," she said, expressing her own sorrow.

Tajo knew it was Sandra. She had loved his brother from the beginning. "Sandra… what are you doing here?"

"The same thing you are doing…watching the happy couple, wishing he looked at me the way he looks at her."

"I told you a long time ago not to set your eyes on Cruz… your sister's betrayal is still raw, and he would never trust you."

"It's not like he ever loved her. She got pregnant on purpose to trap him."

"Yeah, and he knew that… but things are different for men. Had she said, Hey, I want a divorce to marry someone else, he would have given her his blessing?"

"Why couldn't he look at me as a woman, Tajo? I really tried… now he found another plaything. Who knows how long this will last?"

"Oh… she is not his plaything," he answered quickly.

Her defense comes to the surface, "What do you mean? Look at her; how long can she keep his attention?" Tajo closed his eyes to her statement, "He bought her from a brothel, for heaven's sake."

"Speaking as a man… forever. She is the kind of woman that could get under any man's skin. He loves her, and it didn't take long, and unfortunately for you, she returns his affections."

"You like her…you like her too, Tajo. You just met her." He turned his face away, choosing his words carefully.

"What's not to like about her? She's beautiful, sexy, dark, and mysterious. Believe me. She can seduce the pants off any man."

"You men are all alike. A woman throws a pair of tits in your face, and you go gaga for her. You're all sick. What is so special about her!" She screamed at him.

"The truth Sandra… the truth is that when I look at her… she arouses me. Everything about her… her hair… those brown eyes, the shape of her legs and hips. Oh shit… I'm going to hell. I get a hard-on for my brother's woman." Sandy covered his mouth with her hand. Tajo would never open up to her as he just did. He was always so cool and aloof around her.

"I'm sorry, Tajo, please, I didn't mean…"

"Please, don't repeat what I just said… out of the three of you women, you're the only one I trust and respect."

"Tajo, I promised I would not repeat this conversation. I'm glad you do trust me enough to speak to me about what was in your heart. But I advise you not to let my mother and sister find out how you feel. They will use it to their advantage."

"Come here," he gave her a hug. "Someday, maybe we will find someone who we can admit makes us feel excited, lustful, and crazy in love," he said.

"Maybe your right. We deserve to be happy too."

They watched until they could no longer hear Miranda singing her happy song.

After a week, Tressa was starting to regain her voice. She could make little sounds, and she needed desperately to get word to the agency and her family. To let them know she was safe and not to worry. They had an outside line, but she needed a code to connect. Cruz had a radio she could use until she could get away and use the phone in the village.

As soon as Cruz fell asleep, she slipped out of the room and downstairs, where the radio control was. Everyone was asleep as she tiptoed, making her way downstairs. Closing the door behind her, she managed to get in touch with one of the Chief Officers asking him to relay the message to Mr. Lee.

When she returned to the room, he was just as she had left him. *God, his gorgeous,* she thought to herself. No wonder the women are giving her strange looks. She had to think of a way to tell him that she could speak and how she was going to explain to him the rest of the story. Right now, she wanted to relish her time with him. He looked like a young, innocent boy laying there half-naked. *So, if this is how love feels,* she thought, *it was wonderful being in love.*

Tressa anguished over the fact that soon he would know the truth, and it will change everything. He would not look at her the same and may even ask her to leave. She will draw into memory everything she can. His kisses made her tingle all over, the touch of his hands and embrace making her feel safe and secure. She would abandon everything if he'd asked her.

She tried to compare it to what she had with Samuel, and it didn't come even close. Somehow, she had to find a way to tell him about herself in a way he would understand. She snuggled close to him, pressing her breast against his back. She put her arm around him and smiled as he took her hand and put it close to his heart.

Cruz watched Tressa closely. There was something about her that didn't add up. He was afraid to bring up the subject, afraid she would leave him if he flooded her with questions. He could tell she had much on her mind and wondered if she had family that was missing her. Where did she come from? These were all the questions that ran through his mind constantly. He remembered there were problems finding her paperwork. This haunted him.

Cruz was tired of looking at all the surveys and blueprints. He couldn't shake off the uneasy feeling that Tressa was a bigger mystery than he thought. Troy dumped another set of blueprints on his desk.

"Are you alright? You look spacey?" Troy asked.

"I'm just worried, Troy… about her. She isn't your normal concubine. She can read, write, and rides like a pro. What if I bought a free woman?"

"I had wanted to mention it before. But I didn't want to ruin your mojo. You looked so happy. Ah, by the way, boss, have you been to your training room lately?"

"Yeah, I hit the gym every morning. Why do you ask?"

"Well, you need to come to the outer court… like right now. I want to show you something." They walk down to the outer courtyard and watch from the field house. Tressa was with three of his men working on the ropes and parallel bars.

"Her time is faster than theirs, I timed her a few minutes ago, and she is extremely strong. Look, she is going for the bow and arrows."

Ned was showing her where the bow and arrows were and the distance between each target. Ned handed her a lighter-weight bow. She tried to balance it in one hand and shook her head. She tried some of the other bows and stopped at a red and black bow with the strongest pull.

"There's no way she can pitch that bow, that's Tajo's bow, and I have a hard time using it," Troy said in suspense.

Tressa felt the grip and smiled at Ned. "Miss, you won't be able to…" she pitched it back with ease, "oh, my bag, I guess you can."

"No way," Troy said. They watched with amazement as she pulled back and hit her target. Ned ran to see how close to the bull's eye she got. He gave them the signal that she hit the mark. Tressa smiled, feeling the strength of the bow, it was skillfully made, and she liked the way it was handled. Cruz was starting to worry.

"Man, I'm in deep shit," he ran his fingers through his hair; "how am I going to find out who she really is? I don't know her last name?"

"Look, if there are any charges to be filed against you, she's the one to file them. Tressa seems very happy with you. Does she feel like you are forcing her into bed? Does she push you away or refuse you?"

"On the contrary, she is just as willing as I am. But I remember that first night… anyone can construe that as rape.

She was drugged, and for a moment there, she tried to push me away… and I just couldn't stop."

"I think you're worrying too much. If she feels for you the way I think she does, I don't think you have anything to worry about."

"I hope so. Hey, are we still going hunting tomorrow?" Cruz asked.

"Yeah, are you thinking what I'm thinking?"

"Let's do it."

Tressa was still feeling out the bow when Cruz and Troy met up with her. He kissed her. She returned his kisses and motioned how much she liked the bow.

"That's Tajo's bow," Cruz said, "She frowns, poking out her lower lip. "I'm sure he'll let you use it. I'll have one made for you if you like," she smiled approvingly. "Tomorrow, we are going hunting for a small game. You want to join us?" Tressa nodded her approval, trying to remember how long it had been since she went hunting.

"Good, we're leaving bright and early," she kissed him this time, but Cruz held her longer. She touched his face tenderly, and he became serious, holding her hand in place and kissing it. He was in love with a strange and beautiful woman.

Cruz and Troy returned to his office, where Tajo was looking over the blueprints on Cruz's desk. "You bums are playing hooky when you should be working. Am I the only one who works around here?"

"Yeah, okay," Cruz teased, "I love your excuses, Mr. sorry I'm late to the meeting because I was too busy banging some chick."

"Hey, a man has needs." He chuckled, "it's alright to have a little recreational fun. All work and no play makes me extremely nasty."

"Hey, tomorrow we're going hunting. You care to go?"

"I was planning to. Why are you canceling the hunt?"

"No, I invited Tressa to go, so I hope you don't have any objections." Tajo smiled and turned his face. "Say what's on your mind, brother," Cruz asked, getting annoyed.

"Look, I know she's your woman… it's just that… she's not who you think she is. I did some research."

"You investigated my woman," Cruz asked, surprised and annoyed.

"No, not her, but how those places operate."

"Well, we kind of figured that," Troy interjected.

"She doesn't match the profile. The women are mute, for sure. However, they are also uneducated. They can't read or write. They are schooled in the Act of lovemaking at the age of sixteen. Bro, someone like her would cost a bundle. She's a natural-born woman, very rare."

"Well, I know she's educated. She can write," Cruz said.

"So, you know then," Tajo said, "Who is she, Cruz? Why was she hiding in such a place?"

Cruz sat at his desk and rubbed his hands together, thinking and wondering what to do next. "I don't know what to tell you. All I know is that I don't want to scare her away. If she is hiding from danger, what if she leaves and something happens, I can't live with myself. At least if she's here, I can protect her if she is in danger from someone."

"I agree; she doesn't seem dangerous, just very mysterious. Cruz, how much did you pay for her, I know it's none of my business, but I really want to know," Tajo asked.

"Her contract was ten thousand."

Tajo was shocked. "Oh my God, you're a thief… you know what she is worth on the human trafficking market if she was a real concubine… over a million is the starting bid."

"You're shitting me… well, to me, she's priceless."

"I think you're right to keep her close… she is running or hiding from danger," Tajo added.

"Oh, by the way, she wants to use your bow tomorrow. I kind of told her she could," Cruz said, smiling at Tajo.

Tajo shook his head. "And she can handle my bow?"

"Like a pro," Troy said, "we watched her shoot it a few times, right boss."

Tajo laughed.

"Smart girl, she figured it out. It's not hard to pull that bow; it's the way you pull it. It doesn't matter if she wants to use it. I have another."

The morning was perfect for a hunt. They gathered at the stables, planning to hunt small game nearby. Tressa felt free for the first time in years, she had a wonderful horse that handled well, and she had plenty of room to ride hard. She rode ahead of the pack with Felix riding close beside her.

"It's beautiful here, Miss, don't you think?" Tressa nodded her approval. She led her horse into the forest. Cruz, Tajo, and Troy lagged behind, arguing about who was a better hunter when Cruz heard his name from far away. When he turned around, one of his men was riding toward them. Edward was out of breath when he reached the men.

"Thank God, I found you... I just got word that there is a cougar on the loose, an old hungry one that just attacked the cattle. Someone shot at it and chased him away before he got to take a bite. He ran into the forest.”

Tajo looked at Cruz.

“Tressa and Felix are in the woods,” Tajo said, worried. They started to call for the both of them until they came to a clearing where Felix’s horse was drinking water. When Tressa turned to look in their direction, she started to gallop towards them, stopping in mid-stride, loaded her bow, pointing it in Cruz’s direction. It was like slow motion watching an arrow fly past Cruz’s shoulder, hitting the cougar in mid-air, clawing the horse, which in turn threw Cruz to the ground. Tressa raced towards Cruz, who was beginning to get up from the ground. Everyone thought she had aimed at Cruz until they turned to see the cougar on the ground a few feet away from where Cruz had fallen. Tressa was in tears by the time she reached Cruz, who had blood on his shirt. She ran into his arms. “I’m okay, baby. It’s not my blood,” she couldn’t stop shaking.

“Right through the neck; great shot,” Tajo said, “for a moment, I thought you were shooting at us.”

“That was too close, man,” Troy said, examining the animal. “Are you hurt?”

“Just my pride from falling from my horse,” Cruz held her tearing face in his hands. “Baby, I’m alright, thanks to you," he kissed her, but she was more shaken than he was. "Let's go home." Cruz rode with Tressa, still feeling her body shaking against him as she leaned against him.

"Did you see that shot? She has one hell of an eye," Tajo said, astonished.

"She has one hell of an aim. The sucker was moving… that's a kill shot," Troy said, admiring the animal.

"Yeah, she is no ordinary woman, and she sure is hell no concubine, which is a mystery."

Tressa insisted he gets checked by the doctor and wouldn't take no for an answer. She waited outside the doctor's office with Tajo and Troy. She found a pad and wrote Tajo a note.

I'm sorry for acting like a baby. I thought the animal had gotten to Cruz before I got to it. I was scared he was injured. Love Tressa.

Tajo read the note out loud. He looked straight into her eyes. "Who taught you how to shoot like that?" She looked down and smiled, asking for the pad and pen back. One day I'll tell you, she wrote and walked away from them and sat in the corner, waiting for Cruz to finish with the doctor's examination.

They can hear him laughing through the door. "I think he's going to be alright. My brother is a big baby. He'd be whining if it was bad." She smiled at him, and all he wanted to do was put his arms around her and comfort her, but he didn't trust himself being that close. It bothered him that she was so miserable. Her heart was pounding, trying to forget how close the cougar got and could have done some damage before he was subdued.

Ellen and Nina continued to give Tressa the cold shoulder, but she didn't care. During the daytime, she spent time with Miranda, who wanted so badly to feel loved by one of her aunts and grandmother, who were too busy to spend time with a very active five-year-old.

Miranda followed her everywhere. Tressa decided she would start by giving her riding lessons. Miranda was beginning to blossom into a confident child. Cruz spent most of his time away since they were planning a big expansion project, and Tajo still maintained his distance. Whenever he saw her, he would find any excuse to leave. Tressa felt Tajo's reproach when he was around her.

Tajo was glad he had his own house on the cliff, away from the madness. If he had to be near her a second longer, he'd break down and cry.

He was tired when he reached his home. Dolores, the housekeeper, met him at the door. "Senor Tajo, thank God for your home," she said in her broken English "that crazy girl is here."

"No, no, no…what does she want?"

Her right eyebrow arched disapproving. "You know what she wants…she's a little fast, mama," Dolores said, waving her chubby arms in her comical ways.

"Get rid of her, Dolores. I don't want to deal with her."

"Too late…she's in the pool, and she will not get out…I tried she will not listen."

"Alright, if you can make me something to eat, I'll love you forever."

"Now that, I can do… okay," she murmured under her breath.

Nina was in his pool naked from the day she was born. Tajo felt the anger rising in him when he saw her. "Get the hell out of my pool and out of my house," he yelled, throwing a towel at her, "get dressed and out of here."

"What's wrong, lover? Why are you angry?

"I don't feel like dealing with you today… and don't call me lover! Just get the hell out! I'm tired of your mess." Nina took her time getting out of the pool, parading her young body before him. "Why aren't you down at the house helping your sister and mother get ready for the party? Instead, you're up here making my life miserable."

"They don't need me… anyway, I want to stay here with you," she tried to put her arms around his neck.

He pulled her arms from him and pushed her away. "Well, I don't want you here, so get dressed and make your way home."

"Why don't you love me, Tajo? You're the only man for me."

"Get out… please, you're only a child, and you're not my type. You're a kid." He yelled in her face.

Nina started to tease him. "So, who is your type," she brushed up against him, "You are lusting after that slut your brother bought home." Tajo tried to keep his temper under control, wanting to grab her by the neck and throw her off the cliff.

"I guess it takes one to know one hum," he said, walking into his living room. She followed close behind him.

"Tajo, how dare you. Why I'll have you know, I'm pure as the driven snow."

"I find that hard to believe. You have been whoring around here since before you grew breast."

"Liar! Why would you say that?" She said, pouting like a young.

"Nina, I would like to eat something and take a shower before I drag myself to the party."

"Okay, alright already, stop being so grumpy, but you have to promise you'll dance with me."

"I'm not promising you a damn thing," he started to move her towards the door.

"Come on, one little dance," she tried to put her arms around his neck again.

"I'll think about it. Now, get out of here…" Tajo just wanted to be left alone, needing to prepare himself for the long night ahead of him. Tressa invaded his dreams and his thoughts. Every time he closed his eyes, the image of her smiling at his brother ripped right through him. He needed to stop obsessing about her. Tonight, he had an excuse to get drunk and forget the sexiest woman he knew was under the same roof with him, and he couldn't do a damn thing about it.

Tressa played a few games with Miranda before she got ready for bed. Miranda didn't care that Tressa couldn't speak. She spoke enough for both of them and kissed and hugged her as much as Tressa would allow her. Tressa embraced the child, knowing all she really needed was a lot of love. Miranda laid her head on her lap; in between yawns, she spoke about how wonderful it was to have her there. Tressa caressed her hair until she was sound asleep.

Miranda was a beautiful child with golden hair and the cutest nose that turned up slightly. She loved to sing and was normally a happy child with a wild imagination. Tressa laid her down, covering her up with a light blanket.

All the tables were set, and food was laid out; the beer was flowing, and the music was bumping. She was nervous about Miranda's room being so close to the pool and not knowing how to swim. Cruz was already drinking and playing poker. He was having fun with the men, and she loved it. Tressa didn't realize how hard he worked until he dragged himself home every day.

She sat by herself on the top balcony that faced the pool, drinking wine and enjoying the view. This was such a beautiful place, and Cruz made sure that the estate was spotless for the party. She was proud that he was a man of integrity and decency, and it didn't bother her that he let Miranda's grandmother and aunts live with him for his daughter's welfare.

The person he never spoke about was his ex-wife. It seemed to be a sore subject around the estate. Surprisingly enough, Miranda never mentioned her mother or the desire to see her. As a child, Tressa couldn't even think about not seeing or talking to her mother. Thinking about the family made her sad. She truly missed her family. She felt so lucky to have a loving, caring family that was always so supportive, even if they didn't agree with her decisions. She wondered if they would be supportive of her now, living with a man she hardly knew, and her feelings for him were deeper than she ever thought they would be.

She loved the fact that his men respected him, they worked hard to please him, and he paid them well, providing them with a nice home and a high income. *Her father would like that,* she thought. Cruz had the same values as her father. She pondered on when to tell Cruz that her voice had returned and who she truly was. But it had to be soon. It was killing her, not knowing if he asked her to leave in fear she would be bringing danger to his door. But not tonight. She would let him enjoy the festivities before she killed his joy.

From where she sat, Tressa could hear Nina and her friends chugging down margaritas and trying to outdo each other. It didn't seem to matter to her mother. Ellen was having her own fun, laughing at the top of her lungs, downing shots with some of her lady friends, and Sandra was not far behind.

The music was loud. Everyone was preoccupied. It was her chance to sneak downstairs and leave Logan and Mr. Lee another message… Lee was so happy when she finally sent him a message he started to cry. The communication room was empty, everyone was drinking, and both guards were out in the back playing dice, having a good time. The familiar message came on, "Lee, this is Tressa… Lee, I am well. I'm in love with a wonderful man, Cruz Montenegro. Tell my parents I will call them soon. Love you, Tressa." She said it, she was in love, and there was no doubt in her heart that she loved him.

When she came back to her seat, she noticed someone splashing the pool with all their clothes on. Leaning closer, she realized that it was Miranda gasping for air. "Oh my God, it's Miranda," cried Nina, too drunk to help her. The music stopped, and all they could see was someone jumping into the pool from the balcony. Tressa scooped her out of the pool and gave her mouth to mouth until Miranda began to spit up water.

"Wasn't anyone paying attention? She could have drowned?" Tressa yelled, holding Miranda in her arms. Cruz stopped in his tracks. He was too far from her when he heard Tressa yelling at the women that were too drunk to save Miranda.

Miranda kept on crying, clinging to Tressa, scared to let go. Tressa had Miranda upstairs and in her room before Cruz could recover from what had just happened. When he walked into Miranda's room, Tressa was on her knees, holding Miranda, who was still shaking. "Tell me what happened?"

"Tressa, you can talk?" She said happily, realizing Tressa was talking to her.

"Yes, I can talk now, let's get you out of those wet clothes, and you're going to tell me why you were downstairs after I put you to bed."

"I was looking for you… I was scared," she kept on crying. "I asked Nina where you were, and she told me she didn't know. She gave me lemonade, and I drank it. They were all laughing at me. So, I walked away, but my nightgown got tangled on the table, and I slipped and fell into the deep side of the pool. I'm sorry, I didn't mean to, really I didn't," she started to cry again.

"It's okay now, listen to me… you're alright; I will teach you to swim so that never happens again."

"You promise?"

"I promise, now I will sit by your bed with you until you fall asleep."

Cruz listened from the door as she changed her nightgown. He could hear them in the changing room.

"Tressa, I like your voice," Miranda said.

"I like it too," Cruz said, who was standing at the foot of the bed when they came out of the bathroom.

"Daddy! She jumped into his arms, holding her tight. "I fell into the deep side of the pool. I was so scared. Tressa saved me."

"I was scared too, pumpkin. How are you feeling now?"

"I'm good now, Daddy… see, Tressa has her voice back."

"I see…" she tried to avoid his stare. "Mrs. Lydia is coming to sit with you until you fall asleep… I have to talk to Tressa for a minute."

"Okay, Daddy," he kissed her and tucked her in bed.

"I love you, Maranda…" While He was tucking her in bed, Tressa decided it was time to leave. She didn't know what to say to him. She was glued to the floor when he walked into the room and slammed the door behind him. He took a few steps forward, and she took a few backs until she rested against the wall where he pinned her arms above her head.

"How long… how long have you had your voice back?"

"A couple of days... it started to come back slowly." Her voice was low and raspy

"Why... why didn't you tell me?"

"I was afraid, and it's a long, complicated story,"

He kissed her neck.

"Um... is that right," their lips were almost touching. "Well, good, then you have a lifetime to tell me," He picked her up and threw her on the bed, resting on top of her.

"I'm wet," she tried not to laugh.

"I don't care, now start talking..."

"Can I change first...? Please," she begged.

"Here, let me help you," he said, smiling. He removed them slowly as she tried desperately to explain what had happened and why she was hiding out in the Pink Lady. He kissed her breast. "So, what you're telling me is that you're a spy."

"Well, I like to call myself an ex-international agent."

"So, if you left the agency, why are you hiding?"

"Ah, I told you I'm being hunted by some douchebag. He wants to kidnap me and take me to some far-off country."

"You're making a joke out of it, but you were hiding."

"I have to make a joke out of it. He's a young punk who thinks he can come and take whatever he wants."

"Well, guess what? He'd have to go through me and my army to get to you. I love you, Tressa. That hasn't changed. Stay with me, and I promise I will protect you."

She giggled. "How can I resist such an invitation? The fact is that I do feel safe with you and free at the same time."

"Alright, then it's settled, this is your home, and you are my woman. One day you will come to love me as I love you."

"You love me, hum. You don't even know me except that I was an international agent."

"What is your last name? Let's start there."

"My last name is… Quintanilla, and yes, my great uncle is Jesse Quintanilla."

"Damn, you're like royalty. How can I compete with that?" He asked curiously.

"You don't have to. My family is really down to earth. My parents are moving to their ranch in a few months. There is nothing special about us."

"You're wrong; you are natural-born, as well as your great-grandmother. That is special."

"I want you to see me as a woman who… loves when you kiss me," she kissed him, "loves the way you touch me and… makes love to me, but mostly makes me feel safe."

"So, it's safe to say you have feelings for me," he kissed her neck, drinking in her essence.

"Yes, and when you're kissing my neck, it's hard to think about anything else. But this I will say," she held his face. "If I didn't have feelings for you… you'll be holding your crotch right now."

"Ouch… okay, I get it. And I couldn't be happier. I never ever thought I would meet someone who made me feel like you do. I promise you this you will come to love me as I love you," he kissed her tenderly, sending a sweet sensation through her body. If he only knew she felt the same way.

By morning everyone knew that Tressa could speak. Tajo was so drunk he didn't even know what happened to Miranda until the following day. When he woke up, Nina was lying next to him naked. He roared with anger picking her up and throwing her out the front door naked, with just a sheet to cover up. It wasn't the first time he had run her out of his bed. It took him more than an hour to compose himself, and it didn't help he had a huge hangover. "How does that little bitch get in," he said out loud.

After a cool shower and painkillers, he made his way down to help clean up the mess running into Troy and Eddy breaking down tables around the pool area.

"Mira Jibaro, it's about damn you come down. We have a lot of work to do."

"I'm sorry, I don't know what train hit me last night, who took me home," Tajo asked

"We took you home. You were too drunk to walk," Troy said, laughing.

"Hey, man, did you hear… Miss Tressa could talk… she had lost her voice, and now it started to come back. Woo, does she sound as good as she looks?" Eddy said, not caring who heard him.

"Don't tell me that," Tajo replied, holding his head.

"I hate to tell you, but it's true, bro… you know that deep sultry voice that drives men loco," Troy said, teasing him.

"Hey, you got to be blind not to notice. The woman is sizzling hot… I'm not blind; I appreciate beauty when I see it," Eddy added high fiving Troy.

"You got that right," Troy said, agreeing with Eddy, "When she walks into a room, you can't help but drool… I mean, look."

"Yeah, don't let Cruz hear you talk about his woman like that. He'll kick your asses," Tajo said, threatening them, knowing what they said was true.

"Hey, Puto," Eddy added, "he knows it. If you don't think every man here fantasizes about her, you got to be gay or something. I'm sure you feel it too."

"Puto, that's my middle name. But we should just chill out and at least act like you have some sense," Tajo said, trying hard to change the subject.

All morning Tajo busied himself cleaning up and putting the place back together. When he heard about Miranda, he felt bad he wasn't sober enough to help. He caught up to Cruz and Tressa on one of the upper terraces. It bothered him that she was sitting on his lap. Cruz had both her arms in a bear hug. He heard her giggle, and it ran chills up his spine. "I hope I'm not interrupting something?"

"Oh, no, brother, we're just enjoying the view." He nodded towards Tressa.

"Nice, I heard you got your voice back."

"Yes, it's been coming in slowly."

"Good, glad to hear that now I don't need to learn sign language," Tajo was trying to sound funny.

"Well, I'm going to let you two alone…" she said. Cruz grabbed her hands

"Where are you going?" He asked.

"Ah… to the little girl's room, and I want to look in on Miranda."

"Alright, I'll catch up with you later," she kissed him before she left; all the while, he followed her with his eyes. "So, brother, tell me what's on your mind," Cruz said, pulling himself back to address Tajo, who stood by so uncomfortable.

"What do you mean?"

"You've been really distant lately, not your crazy self."

"I'm alright. I just have a lot on my mind… you know things. So, what's the story? Did she ever tell you why she was at that place? Because these women have their vocals surgically removed…? I don't understand."

Cruz gave his brother a short version of her dilemma. "I didn't know what to say. I call her my little spy. Can you believe it is an international spy? Please don't repeat this to anyone. She is retired. Her parents would freak out every time she went on one of her missions. I hope you keep it to yourself. I trust you; you're my brother."

Tajo was puzzled, "I will take it to the grave, you know that."

"She was hiding out; apparently, she was working for this secret government organization, and someone compromised her cover. I feel like shit. That night we were together, she was drugged, and… not knowing, I feel as if I took advantage of her."

"So, what kind of things did she do?"

"She was sent to very dangerous countries, but I was afraid to ask what she did."

"Damn, I would have never guessed, but she does things no ordinary woman would do. And I'm glad she's alright. We can keep her safe."

"Oh, but it gets better than that. Guess what her last name is… Quintanilla," he smiled.

"Oh shit, are you sure… I mean, Jesse is not the only Quintanilla around."

"I'm positive she's told me he was her grand uncle."

"Shit, what a coincidence. Anyway, It shouldn't matter. She's of age… so what does it do for your relationship?"

"Are you kidding me? I'm not letting her go that easy… we're cool. She was concerned that I wouldn't want her around when I found out who she was. Anyway, back to you, is there something I can help you with? You don't seem comfortable around her now that you know the truth. Is there still a problem?"

"No, not at all," Tajo said, avoiding his stare.

Cruz pulled his chair closer to him. "Look, I've never seemed you like this, moping around like some puss… tell me before I beat it out of you, remember I can still kick your ass?" He tried to get Tajo to loosen up.

"You want to know the truth… even if it bothers you."

"So, tell me to spill your guts. You're my brother. We've always been truthful, at least I think to each other."

"The truth, wow, the truth is I am jealous of my brother… I am so jealous it's making me sick to my stomach."

Cruz moved closer to Tajo, looking him in his eyes, "Is it because of her or because I'm happy… for the first time in my life. I have a reason to get up in the morning. Bro, I'll shout from any mountain. I'm happy with my life… my newfound love. I won't apologize to know one."

"Your taking things the wrong way… I know what you went through with that monstrous marriage you had with Mary. She was the devil's spawn, and you deserve to be happy, believe me… Tressa is not like other women around here. She is the female version of you but much prettier. I wish I had someone who would challenge me and keep me in check and drive me crazy, but I got to tell you I would never disrespect you or Tressa. She is a beautiful woman, I won't lie about that, and I can tell she makes you happy."

"Look, brother, I know you're going to meet someone special. I never thought I would, not after that bitch. We spent the whole night talking, and I found out she is a college graduate specializing in criminal justice… her parents were separated for a while. Her mother had been ill for a long time. They got remarried and had more children. I think she has a younger sister and two brothers… hey, there's a thought she has a younger sister."

"No thanks, I've had enough of younger sisters. Remember the nightmare I'm living with now, Nina, so please don't do me any favors," Cruz laughed at Tajo's predicament.

"That girl is crazy, she is obsessed with you, man, but I don't think we have to go very far. Look at her crazy sister Mary."

"I never understood why you allowed that woman to even come close to your child, I mean, I know she gave birth to her, but that bitch should be in jail for what she did."

"I tried to give her the benefit of the doubt. I didn't think she would do something to endanger her own daughter."

"Cruz, the woman tried to get you murdered. She is bat shit crazy."

"Yeah, she sure fooled everyone with her fake sweetness. But Tressa makes up for it. She is who she is. The woman has me by the nose… man, she got me bad. However, I have to show her I'm no puss. She doesn't like sissy men."

"How do you know she just started talking yesterday?"

"Little brother, you can tell a lot about a woman by the way she makes love to you."

"Oh really," Tajo replied, laughing.

Cruz made a face, "Like a beast, just the way I like it, Lord have mercy! You know what the day is going to come when you are going to meet that certain woman who is going to kick you in the nut sack of love. That woman is going to walk in your life and drive you insane… in fact, I'm cursing you right now, and I'm hoping she can kick your ass."

"You're a crazy bastard. There ain't a woman alive who can kick my ass or tame this beast."

"I am crazy! I'm in love, and I don't care what anyone says. But you, little brother, will feel the pain and agony I'm going through right now. You dig it!"

"I dig it, bro," they laughed.

"I tell you what. I bet you, and whatever you want, that you will fall hard one day."

"Well, this is one bet I'm going to win. Ain't no bitch bad enough to tame me," they shook on it.

"You remember Mami used to throw those curses around. She taught me how. You know that Puerto Rican mojo shit."

They talked and laughed for hours. Tajo felt better about his feelings for Tressa, they hadn't changed, but he would have to deal with those feelings.

Chapter 4: Mary Cooper

Mary felt trapped in the loveless marriage, but William was rich and adored her. She had to wait on him all the time, but that's what she traded for security and money. Mary would become a very rich woman when William passed, an idea that was very close to her heart. Seeing Cruz bought back so many great memories. Even from a distance, she could see the well-built form of his body. Every now and then, she would drive by one of his construction camps just to get a glimpse of him. For years she was bitter with him for the divorce, but now after seeing him last week, it has awoken something in her again.

She sat in her car waiting for him to bark orders to his workers, afraid for a moment he had seen her car outside, making her duck lower in her seat.

He was always well-built and strong. She realized how much she missed that part of him when he commanded his workers. It was wonderful to have his strong hard body next to her every night. She closed her eyes, trying to remember how it felt when he was on top of her wanting to devour him. Instead, she had to settle for an overweight man with a hairy back and shoulders.

"Sweetheart," William said, bought her back to reality, "are you not well, my dove?"

"I'm fine, darling, just thinking about my daughter, how I miss her."

She wanted to block out all his criticism and complaints about the food again. He was such a baby when no one else was around. To the outside world, William was a tycoon and a fierce businessman, but behind closed doors, he reverted into a child.

"Darling, please; try to eat your soup. The doctor wants you to eat better and cook. Spent hours on this."

William grabbed her hand. "Are you leaving me again, my sweet? I miss you when you're gone so long," he kissed her hand.

"I know, my darling, but a mother has to see her child… she misses me. I have to redo all the terrible things that man puts in her pretty little head."

"I don't understand why she just doesn't live here with us… I have some of the best lawyers in these parts," he whined.

"Not necessary, my love… my mother is there to look after her, and my beloved sisters take wonderful care of her; she's in good hands."

"That's another thing. Why do they have to live with your ex when they can live here? We have more room than we need, and I have tons of money, so it wouldn't be a burden."

"I know, my love. You are so generous, but it's because of Miranda that they stay over there. They want to ensure that she is stable… you understand, don't you, dear?" She kissed his forehead. "Plus, I enjoy having you all to myself," she said in a motherly voice.

"Sweetheart, we've been married five years, and they never once came to visit. Maybe I should extend a formal invitation."

"I have many times even begged them to come for a long visit. However, my mother has many social responsibilities, and Sandra still works for Cruz. I'm happy with you, my love."

"I just want to see you happy, my precious you have been a God sent to me. Will you be staying overnight?"

"Yes, dear… I check in the same room all the time, and someone brings my daughter to the hotel room."

"Alright, my love, I guess I can spare you for one day." he kissed her hand again.

"Now I have to get ready. I'll call Henry to help you get a dress for the day."

"Alright, my sweet, I will find something to occupy my time while you're away. I do have some contracts to redo. Let me know if you want me to call my lawyer. It's a shame your beautiful daughter doesn't live with her mother. Sweetheart, look at all the many sacrifices you make for her. You're such a wonderful mother."

She kissed his cheek, "You're the best husband ever. How lucky can a girl get," she said in her little girly voice.

Mary took a long shower and dressed for her trip to town. The same trip she took every other week. She stared at herself in the mirror and smiled, "You still got it, girl," Mary wished her face wasn't so round, and she hated the dimple in her chin. She never let her straight ultra-blond sun-bleached hair any longer than her shoulders. Mary had her breast done last year and her stomach redone. Her body was her weapon, and she needed to keep it in tip-top shape. She was obsessed with a stay in shape. She was 5' 9" tall, thin, and lived under a sun lamp. Mary was very ambitious, looking for the best way to keep her looking as stunning as possible.

When Mary went after Cruz, she knocked everyone else out of the picture. Her sister Sandra was working as an accountant. Mary bullied Sandra into getting her a job coordinating business lunches and training the new staff. From the start, she has set her eyes on Cruz even though she knew that Sandra was in love with him. After the meetings and lunches, Mary would stick around and pretend she loved what she did. On many occasions, she would stick around and engage Cruz in conversation and drinks. Shortly later, they became lovers, and she manipulated the pregnancy and the marriage.

Cruz had made it clear to her that he did not love her. However, when Miranda was born, he decided that maybe it was a good idea for his child to have a mother and father.

From the start, it was obvious that Mary did not want to be a mother. During her pregnancy, she bullied and bossed everyone around, making everyone's life hell. She switched doctors three times when they refused to do what she wanted. She would spend days in bed suffering from morning sickness, which lasted all day. Mary drove the cook crazy with her special request, which the cook didn't mind making for her but not in the middle of the night. After a while, she nagged Cruz into hiring a gourmet cook to prepare her food.

Cruz made himself as absent as possible. Whenever they were together, they fought about money. Every week it was a new shopping spree, and none of the clothes was for the baby. When Cruz put a limit on how much she could spend, she was furious.

Mary was not into being a mother. She would let Miranda cry for hours and would not attend to her needs. Cruz's mother, Amparo, came to stay with them for a while and help care for her baby granddaughter. Amparo would force Mary to pick up her child and try to feed her. "She hates me! You take the snotty brat. I can't stand all that crying," she would scream and put Miranda in someone else's hands.

Amparo was stunned that a mother would refuse to feed her new infant. Cruz was in the middle of a huge building project and didn't have the time to deal with Mary's bad behavior.

"You are useless as a mother!" Amparo yelled, holding Miranda after finding out she let the newborn cry continually for half an hour."

"She hates me! I want a nanny. I can't stand all this crying and wanting to be held. I want out! Do you want her? You keep her or put her outside a church so someone can deal with her." Mary ran off and left Amparo with a hungry infant. After a few arguments, Amparo found a wet nurse and cared for the baby herself. Mary never made any attempts to hold her or care for her again.

The argument became heated and violent between Cruz and Mary. On several occasions, she went after him with a knife and sometimes drew blood. Most of the time, they fought about money. Cruz was not going to let Mary take charge of the accounts, and she wanted full control with no supervision over all the household money and how it was spent.

"I am the mistress of this house, and I should have control of all the household accounts," Mary cried, slamming her fist on the desk where Cruz had all his paperwork. Cruz had a large amount of money invested in the building expansion.

"Let's get this straight! You know nothing about running a household. I give you a personal allowance to manage here. Make it work." But Mary never let Cruz have the last word. She had to throw the last jab even when she was wrong.

"So, you call the few pennies you throw at me every week a nice allowance… that measly amount supposed to keep me in the kind of lifestyle I'm used to and deserves", she lashed out.

"What you deserve is bullshit. What status and lifestyle are you talking about when you and your family lived in a one-bedroom shit hole!"

"Well, I don't anymore, I demand to be treated with respect, and I deserve better than what you give me."

"You deserve less than you're getting. Your lack of interest in this estate and your very own child reflex what you get. You respect no one, and you deserve the same."

"You're such an ass… I hate you just as much as that baby upstairs that screams all-day driving me crazy. And let's talk about your nosey mother who can't seem to stay out of my business."

Cruz looked up just in time to keep her from hitting him with a baseball bat he had by the door. Felix jumped in the middle and wrestled it from her.

"Get this crazy bitch out of here, Felix, and put a guard on the door… I'll never get any work done with her interruptions."

"Yes, sir," he dragged her outside.

"Let go of me, asshole! I am the mistress here. How dare you touch me," she continued to yell.

"You ain't shit here," said a voice behind her.

She turned to see Tajo coming toward her. "I should have known. It was you, another loser."

"If you ever raise your hand to my brother again, I will lay you out."

"Oh please, like I'm afraid of you, beware, little brother-in-law. I will get what I want."

"You're nuts if you think my brother is going to hand over the accounts. I tell you what. How much will it take for you to just leave? I have money put aside, and I would gladly give it to you if you would just disappear from here and never look back."

"You don't have enough money, but I will get a lawyer. Your brother can not treat me like this, withholding money to keep me in the comfort I'm entitled to."

"You are one sick bitch… come at me as you did to Cruz, and you will need a face job. I have no problem punching you in the face and enjoying it. You've caused enough problems here."

"Aww, you're such a gentleman hitting a woman, asshole."

"Cruz wouldn't hit you because he is a gentleman, but I'm not. You want to fight like a man; I will hit you as a man."

"Well, I guess I can add that to my list of complaints against you. Felix, you are my witness that Tajo is threatening me."

"I'm sorry, but I have seen you attack my boss on many occasions. I would never testify against a good man. You are on your own."

"You men are all the same, a bunch of pusses, but I have my ways. Mark my words, little shithead, I will get what I want."

"I'm sure you will," Tajo replied before he left.

Cruz met with many vendors and would have special dinners with his business consultants. This was something Mary loved playing the part of a dutiful wife. She loved associating herself with people who had money, and she pretended to be a grand lady of society.

It was during one of the dinner meetings that she met William Cooper. Mr. William Cooper was an older widower with lots of money to spend. Mary was determined to make friends with the very rich and powerful Mr. Cooper. He admired Mary's youth, beauty, and outlandish ways.

Mary made no bones about the strain in her marriage. After one of their dinner meetings, Mary invited Mr.

Williams to accompany her to the gardens. Mr. Cooper was quite surprised and intrigued.

"Well, my dear… I was a little apprehensive meeting you out here, knowing your husband is still with the others."

"Oh, don't mind him, he made it very clear that…. well, this is very awkward and personal, but I feel you would be one to understand since you are so wise. My husband stated that he has no love for me… he only married me because of my sweet daughter, which I adore, so I put up with his indifference." William was confused. How could any man not love such a beautiful creature?

"He doesn't love you… really tell me it's not true, a beautiful, sweet woman like you. No, I won't believe it."

"Oh, but it's true. We don't even sleep together since the baby was born," she said, producing some tears. "We have our own separate rooms. We do have our own thing. Like right now, I consider you my most interesting and only friend, really… I don't really have many friends. They've always let me down."

"Well, my dear, I am honored to be considered such a privilege, especially from someone as young as you. However, I think the man is making a huge mistake; women need to be loved and pampered. My wife was spoiled rotten; she was young and pretty but not as pretty as you."

"What happened to her if I am not intruding? You're still a handsome man. Why haven't you remarried?"

"She wanted children badly. Even at my age, I embraced the notion myself, but when she was six months pregnant, she was trampled by one of the horses. She loved to ride… she lingered for a while in a coma and died peacefully. They tried to save the baby, but it was too late, and so it was born dead. Sometimes I wonder how it would have been if she and the baby had lived. She was a lot like you, full of life."

"I can tell you loved her very much. I'm sure you'll find someone just as lovely and wonderful as she was."

"I wish I had met you before you were married. I'd do everything to sweep you off your pretty little feet."

"Thank you, Mr. Cooper, but I hope you don't think I invited you out here to worm compliments out of you." She giggled. Cooper couldn't take his eyes off her young full breast. "You see, out of all of the people who visit, you are the most interesting of them all. I find the others very boring at times."

"I'm glad you feel that way because I feel the same way about you, my dear… I find you very interesting." The lust in his eyes did not go unnoticed.

After a few weeks, Mary spent a lot of time with Mr. Cooper. She would cry and show him the bruises on her arms that Cruz made, trying to hold her down when she came after him. Mr. Cooper would feel sorry for her and always asked what he could do to help her situation.

Cruz asked his mother to take control of the baby until he had more time to spend with her. Mary continued to be cold toward Miranda even while she started to walk and talk.

Every night Amparo would stay up late and tell her son what his little girl was doing. Amparo lived between two estates, hers and her sons, every few weeks. She would take Miranda to her estate so she could spend time with her abuelito, who missed her terribly when she was gone. But soon, she would have to give her back to her father. The trips back and forth were wearing her down. Amparo was becoming more and more concerned with Cruz's safety.

"Mami, I'm so tired...I can't stand looking at that woman,"

"She wants money, son."

"Money, if it were that easy. I'd give her money so she could get out of my life... I am tired of all the drama."

"She wants to be the grand lady of this estate... if she'd control your wallet, she'd have total control of everything."

Cruz hugged his mother. Amparo looked at her older son and ran her fingers through his soft curls.

"Cruz, do not let this woman get to you… she will tire very soon. It's been two years. At least you know if she leaves, you have your daughter. She wants nothing to do with her. However, I do wonder where she goes every evening."

"What do you mean?"

"Talk to your friend Troy's son… I think he has much to say to you."

"Oh crap, he's been trying to see me for weeks. I've been so busy I haven't had time to go to the Northern building projects."

"Well, I just saw him going into the men's quarters. You may want to catch him before he goes home. I'll look in on the baby before I go to bed."

"Thanks, Mami, for all your help. I'll try to catch him before he leaves. It may be important." Cruz kissed his mother's cheek, taking the back stairs leading to the temporary building where the workers slept. Troy was washing up when Cruz met up with him. They greeted each other, but Troy had a strange look on his face.

"What's going on, Troy? I did get your message. It's been so crazy."

"Oh, know, I understand we've been crazy busy. You got my notes on how everything is going, didn't you."

"I'm ecstatic with the progress. You guys are doing a great job. So, what's going on?"

"Let's go somewhere private. There is another matter I need to discuss with you. It's a delicate situation." Cruz prepared himself for the worst. Troy was one of his trusted men.

"I've been working with this contractor Edward Grant. He's doing some subcontracting work on the aqueduct. So, I see him leaving the camp every other day, and I start to get suspicious. I decided to put a tail on him, you know, just to ease my mind. I sent my son Albert to find out where this guy goes. So, Albert comes back a few hours later, pale and scared. Albert says he's going to see a woman. I say, alright, you know that's his business, but he just stands there like he has something to say. I started to put pressure on him. By now, he has me suspicious. He makes me promise not to hurt him. I said what the hell. He said that the woman this guy is meeting up with was the boss's wife, Mary."

Cruz was not surprised or angry. He looked at Troy as if he had just given him a million dollars. "Give that boy a raise… he just gave me a divorce and a way to keep Miranda. Tomorrow we will pay them a visit. I have to catch her in the act, or else she will drag on this divorce for years."

The next evening Cruz, Troy, and his lawyer busted down the door of their hotel room. They were both naked under the covers, scared to death. Edward had no idea Mary was Cruz's wife or that she was even married. Cruz handled Edward his clothes and asked him to leave, and Edward did not hesitate.

Mary was so angry she charged Cruz with a knife missing his heart a few inches. The police came and arrested Mary for attacking Cruz and fighting the officers who tried to arrest her. She kicked and screamed obscenities at the arresting officers biting one on the hand.

Cruz had all her things packed and out the door. By that time, Ellen and Nina had moved in, and we were not making any motion to go anywhere. He wanted to make sure that Miranda had family around her since her mother never cared about her.

Mr. Cooper paid Mary's bail and all her court fees. She cried to him and said that Cruz had made up a story about her being with another man to keep Miranda away from her. She wanted to sue him for custody of Miranda, child & spouse support, and was not going to make things easy for

Cruz. In the meantime, she was given supervised visitations with Miranda, who cried whenever she was with her mother.

Miranda was three years old before the divorce was final. Mary realized all she was going to lose, making a last attempt to get Cruz to change his mind. "You know, one of the reasons we decided to marry was so Miranda would be raised in a two-parent home." To hear her speak that way made Cruz think she was suffering from some memory loss. "I know things weren't the greatest between us, but I'm sure we could have worked out our differences." Cruz looked around the room to see if someone had played tricks on him. This woman was speaking to him in a calm and sensitive manner. Amparo and Ellen looked at each other confused.

"Mary, I think we both went too far." He was trying to have the conversation he had wanted since the beginning of their marriage. "We don't get along… it's like we both can't seem to get the best of each other. Mary… you're a beautiful woman, but I don't love you… I never did, and I just want this to be over with you so we both can get on with our lives."

"So, I come with the white flag, and you're not willing to give us another chance." Her quiet demeanor began to change back to the real Mary. "I should have known that there was no reasoning with an asshole like you!"

"Now that's the Mary I know. This is why I don't want it… I'm tired of fighting and the insults."

"This is not going to be easy…you can't just throw me away and expect me to just go away without a fight. I will own you…"

"Mary dear… the child is listening to you. Please, for her sake, keep things civil," Ellen begged, trying to express her feelings that Miranda was in the room.

"You too, mother; you are on his side… you're supposed to be my mother. You traitor!" Mary was uncontrollable. Miranda started to cry into Ellen's lap.

"Mary, let's just end this right now, the baby is crying and upset, and this isn't the way it should be for her," Cruz said, tired of the whole situation.

"So that's it, that's all you ever cared about… that snotty brat. Well, guess what? She's not your child."

Cruz began to laugh, "You know I knew this would come up one day… I had Miranda tested when she was born."

"You what? How dare you, how dare you without my consent."

"I wanted to know since you slept around that she was my child." Mary lashed out, trying to slap Cruz beating him on his chest and back. Her tears were tears of rage and desperation. Cruz held her blows at bay, which made her even angrier.

"All you wanted was that brat; well, guess what? You're not getting her." Mary pulled the screaming child from her grandmother, grabbing the poor child by the throat. Miranda was turning red and sobbing with fear. "Don't come closer, or I'll snap her neck… I will not be bested by a snotty nose brat." By this time, the room was filled with witnesses. Cruz fought down the feeling of dread; he thought this woman was going to get her revenge on him if she had to kill her own child.

"Why are you trying to hurt her…she's an innocent child. Choke me." Cruz came closer. "Here's my neck look." He tried to pry her hands away from Miranda's delicate neck. That was turning blue from fear and crying. "I'm the one you want to hurt… feel the veins in my neck throbbing… go ahead." Mary could only stare at Cruz, who was now face-to-face with her. Miranda tried to wiggle out of her grasp. When she looked down, it was over. Cruz punched her so hard he thought he had killed her.

Mary woke up the next day with her jaw wired, eyes swollen, and a guard standing nearby. Mr. Cooper sat in the chair, waiting for her to wake up.

She tried to sue Cruz for a lot of money. But the judge was not moved by her beauty or her fake tears and motherly affection towards the daughter she tried to kill.

The only thing she walked away with was what she brought into the short marriage and any gifts he had given her. Cruz carries the wounds Mary inflicted on him like a banner of shame. The only good thing that came from the union was his precious daughter Miranda who seemed to feel the contempt her mother had for her. Miranda was three years old when Cruz divorced her mother… she hadn't seen her since.

Mr. Cooper was rich for a reason. He was a shrewd businessman making his lawyer draw up papers for him when he married her. The Will stated that if he died of any suspicious accident or untimely death, she would not get a single penny.

Mr. Cooper also had a taste for kinky sex; he made Mary perform like a puppy whenever he wanted. She obeyed, or the huffy allotment would be reduced.

Mary had no idea that her husband was going to live as long as he had. She cursed him each night that he would die in his sleep, but every morning he was up before her and out the door. He refused to give her a separate bedroom insisting that man and wife sleep together until death.

Mary felt trapped in another loveless marriage, but the money and security he provided made up for the disgusting sex he forced on her. She ruled her nest, and the servants were terrified of her. She was moody and snapped at everyone whenever she felt bored. Everyone knew there was a very dark side to the pretty mistress.

Mr. Cooper didn't care about the house or the amount of money she spent. Mary was a trophy wife, and he gave her what she wanted as long as she performed for him and was at his side smiling and looking beautiful for all the gala events.

Manipulation was a great skill for Mary as a young child. She manipulated everyone around her to get what she wanted. Everyone fell under her spell except for Cruz. She could not get him to let go of the purse strings. He fought about her spending all the time, but she missed the sex that stopped when she became pregnant. Though it was deliberate, he felt betrayed and never touched her again after that.

Cruz had only married her to give Miranda the right to inherit. Now Mary searches for sex elsewhere and never has a problem finding young men to quench her sexual appetite. Ricardo was one of her regulars. He was a scrapping young married man who couldn't keep his hands off of her. Every other Tuesday, she met one of her lovers and pretended she was spending time with Miranda.

Mary watched Ricardo as he lay sleeping after a long lovemaking session. She thought about Cruz and how her life would be if she'd only tried to make her marriage work. Even with all the drama, he was her best lover. Had she known he was going to expend his holdings by 50%, she would have held on to him longer.

She still became aroused when just thinking about him. She had to figure out a way to get back into his good graces, thinking again when William died, they could combine their assets and be the most powerful couple in the region.

A plan started to hatch in her pretty little head. She needed a good excuse to tell William, something that would allow her the freedom needed to put her plan into action.

Chapter 5: Out on the Town

Tajo found it almost impossible to be around Tressa. He was so serious around her, making her feel so uncomfortable. She tried to engage him in a conversation whenever he was around, but he always gave her short quick answers and walked away. His coldness was making her feel like an outsider. She could take rejection from the others, but he was Cruz's brother. Sometimes she would call out to him, and he would ignore her and wouldn't acknowledge her. It was racking her brain, wondering what she did wrong and couldn't remember when they had a real conversation. She wanted to confront him and clear the air. If there was something she did, she wanted to apologize so they could move on to a friendly relationship. Tressa walked upon him on one of the upper terraces.

"Tajo," she said just above a whisper.

He felt a chill rush through his body at the sound of her voice. "Oh, hi…what's up," he tried to sound cool

"I need to ask you a question if you have a minute," she sounded serious.

He looked at her, wondering what was wrong, "Sure… have a seat." She looked him in the eyes, and he almost fainted.

"What's going on, Tajo? Why do you dislike me?"

He couldn't speak; there weren't words to express the pain written on her beautiful face, he thought. "Well, that's what I want to know… I mean, have I done something to offend you? You've given me the cold shoulder, and it's driving me crazy. I love your brother, and I would love to get along with you. He always talks about you and how great you are."

"Why would you say that?" He was so uncomfortable he had a hard time looking at the expression on her face. Afraid she would see his longing for her.

"I find it hard to believe that with everyone else, you're this happy guy, and when I'm around, you just clam up and walk away. Sometimes when I try to talk to you, you ignore me. Did I say or do something; I just want to clear the air right now. Sometimes I know I can be a bit abrasive and if I have, please let me know. I don't want to carry around guilt."

Tajo tried to control and compose himself, "I'm sorry I never meant to make you feel unwelcome… it's just that." He didn't want to tell her the truth. "I have so much on my mind… this little pain in the ass follows me around, and she's getting on my last nerve, so please don't take things personally. I'm sorry for being a jerk." Tressa couldn't help but laugh. "Can we start over? Hi, nice to meet you. I'm Tajo."

She had broken the ice. Tajo started to laugh and relax around her. He had to face his dilemma, she was the woman his brother loved, and she loved him back. He tried to put her at ease. They began to talk about the beautiful countryside, and Tajo gave her plenty of childhood stories to blackmail Cruz with.

Cruz felt good to see his brother and Tressa talking finally. It was so awkward when they were around each other. Cruz was no fool. He knew Tajo fought his feelings for Tressa. "I know you two are not talking about me."

"Too late, baby. I know your whole sordid story and all your girlfriends."

"Why, I thought you were my brother. We have to look out for each other."

"Hey, don't blame me. She pulled them out of me."

"Hum, did you now…I think I will have to punish you for that," he hugged her, kissing her on the neck.

"Is that a promise?" Tressa teased.

"You bet; I was actually looking for you, Tajo. The engineers want us to meet with them tomorrow to go over the plans for the new hospital. So, what I thought was that

Tressa and Miranda could go shopping while we conducted business at their office. It's close to the marketplace… what do you think, sweet cheeks?" He smacked her bottom.

"I'd love to… Miranda needs some new shoes, and I want to get a riding outfit made for her."

"We'll leave early. The marketplace is vast. You buy whatever Miranda needs. Oh, get yourself something sexy."

The three continued to talk and laugh together late into the night. Tajo realized it would take time for him to get over his feelings for Tressa. The more he spoke to her and got to know her, the more his heart broke, knowing he could never be with her.

Early the next morning, everyone was up and ready to go. Nina and Sandra decided they also wanted to come along and get some shopping done. While Nina and Sandra rode in a car, and Miranda rode with Tressa. Cruz also included Jason and Andrew to watch over the female travelers. Tressa felt insulted and wanted to protest, but Tajo warned her not to try. It would be futile.

Miranda was so excited; she rarely got to go to the marketplace. Normally she went in one of the cars and was not allowed to do much more. The main market square was buzzing with activities. The owners had their merchandise displayed smartly in the window. Miranda wanted to jump off the horse and peep through every window.

"Are you alright, sweetie?" Tressa asked.

"I can't wait to look in the windows. Everything looks so pretty."

"I'm sure we can look in some of the stores. Wouldn't that be fun?"

"Yes, I never get to walk, Aunt Sandra is always afraid I will get lost, so I stay in the car, and she just picks up packages. I told her I couldn't wait to grow up so I could see all the pretty clothes myself."

"Well, today's your lucky day, sweetie, don't worry. I won't let anything happen to you."

As soon as they arrived, Nina disappeared. She took off and didn't tell anyone where she was going.

"Don't worry about her. She'll be back before we leave," Jason commented.

"She does that all the time… when we're finished, there is a nice restaurant across from the office. Why don't we meet for lunch around noon," Cruz suggested, "This way, we don't have to spend hours looking for everyone. You buy whatever you want and charge it to the house."

Miranda was beside herself with excitement. She pulled Tressa and Sandra from one store to another. She was a girly girl, wanting to try on heels and older girls' clothes. "When I grow up, I'm going to have two," she put her two little fingers, thinking a moment, "no, maybe three closets of clothes. Yeah, three big closets." The girls laughed

"She's a girl after my own heart; I love to shop," Tressa added, taking her hand. Jason and Andrew tried to keep their distance while the women shopped. They didn't want them to feel crowded. They went from store to store, trying on clothes, shoes, and hats. Tressa never left the house without a hat to cover her hair or sunglasses to cover her eyes.

It was such a beautiful sunny day made for walking and shopping. Miranda chattered on about the horses and how she wanted to ride as well as Tressa. Tressa found a friend in Sandra. She was sweet and was so different from her sister. They had a lot in common, clothes, furnishings, and even the same taste as men.

Sandra was a small delicate woman with long straight cherry-blond hair. Her pretty face, sprinkled with a few freckles around her nose, made her look like a southern beauty. Sandra was sweet and soothing, and her mother and Nina were loud and sometimes annoying.

Tressa ordered some riding clothes for Miranda, a pair of riding boots, and a saddle. If she was going to be a horsewoman, she might as well look like one, she said. Poor Andrew was the designated package carrier. His face turned red from all the female packages he was forced to carry. Finally, they managed to find a bench at the plaza between two vendors. One selling sweet cakes and the other fruit juices.

"Huh, this is where we usually wait. Nina should be here soon, she won't miss a meal, and if she wants to ride home," Sandra said, looking up and down the street to see if she was coming.

Tressa purchased cherry and orange juice while they waited for the men to finish their meeting. From a distance, Sandra spotted Nina running towards them, with a bunch of other people following behind. "What the hell's wrong with her?' Sandra questioned as they all watched, confused, "why is she running so fast?"

"Is someone chasing her?" Tressa strained to see who was behind her.

"Yeah, looks like trouble to me," Jason chuckled.

"Wow, she broke her record this time. Normally, it takes twenty-four hours for her to stir up trouble," Andrew added.

"Help me, somebody, help me," she said, almost running Sandra down, "they're after me," she said, hiding behind Jason. "The bitches are after me. They want to kill me," Nina said, out of breath, hiding behind Jason. Six women, also out of breath, stopped short as Tressa stepped in the middle. She stood in front of Jason, who was already taking defensive measures.

"Don't get in this, Jason. This is not your fight," Tressa warned, "do me a favor and hold Miranda," who was already starting to shake. "I'll take care of this… trust me," Tressa crossed her arms in front of them and confronted the leader. "Why are you after her?" She said in a firm, authoritative voice. The women, who didn't seem too organized, started to yell profanities at Nina. They were angry, and it looked like Nina had made a lot of enemies.

"That skinny bitch, I'm going to kill her coming after our men, stealing from their families."

Nina became brave in front of everyone. "Well, if your men are going to give me the money, I will take it," she said, cocky and arrogant.

"You're a whore! You need to be taught a lesson." Each woman outweighed her by fifty to sixty pounds.

Tressa grabbed Nina by her shirt, bawled up her fist, and punched Nina in the eye, sending her crashing to the ground out cold. Everyone was stunned.

"Oh, shit, that was sweet!" Jason said, amused and surprised, unable to stop laughing. The others joined in, amazed at what had just happened. By now, the crowd was thick.

"Look, see, I took care of it. She's on the ground out cold, and you didn't have to break a fingernail," Tressa pointed to Nina out cold on the ground, trying to avoid bloodshed.

"That's not enough yelled one of the women… she needs to have the shit kicked out of her so she learns how to leave what doesn't belong to her alone."

Tressa wanted to squash the situation, "Hey, I know what she did was wrong…. I don't even like her that much. But I won't let you beat her up… there are six of you."

"Then she shouldn't have been messing with our men," shouted the second one.

Tressa stood her ground. She looked at Nina lying on the ground and wished she could let these women beat her up. But she couldn't, Nina was young and stupid, but she didn't deserve a beaten like that. Jason started to step forward.

"Don't get in this, Jason… you're a man, and they are women. You keep Miranda and Sandra safe and out of the way. Trust me. I got this."

"Miss Tressa," Andrew said, alarmed, "you're outnumbered, and we are responsible for your safety."

"Like I said, they are women, and I've been in the worst situations. So, step back, and relax. This won't take long." She turned her attention to the angry woman, "As much as I would love to let you teach her a lesson, I can't let you do it," Tressa stepped toward the woman removing her hat and sunglasses. She could hear the murmuring from the crowd about her hair and eyes. The women began to get loud and aggressive. The crowd began to push in.

"Then we will go through your skinny ass, too," the first woman yelled.

"So, bring it on," They were taken aback for a minute but didn't want to show face with the others in the crowd. The leader of the pack swung a long stick at Tressa, but she stopped the blow. Tressa didn't even flinch as she grabbed the stick from her so fast that all she could do was look down at her hands, wondering what had happened. "Nice toy…" Not taking her gaze from the woman.

"What are you, some kind of witch?" Another woman charged at Tressa. Not wanting to hurt her, she grabbed her arm and flipped her into the crowd. She twirled the stick in her hand, hoping the others would go away. "Who's next?" The other women looked at each other and began to rush Tressa, who skillfully dodged the women trying to inflict the least amount of pain possible. The crowd roared as, one by one, Tressa smacked them in their rear with the stick and tossed them on their butts. She was busy with one woman when another grabbed her foot. She twisted her hand until she let go. When she looked up, Cruz was standing in front of the crowd with arms crossed, looking at her.

"Daddy," Miranda cried excitedly, flying out of Jason's arms.

"For some reason, I just knew you were right in the middle of this," he couldn't help but smile. Tajo and the rest of the men broke up the crowd and sent the women on their way with their wounded pride and bottoms.

"Cruz, it wasn't her fault my sister started this mess, I'm ashamed, and I want to apologize for her behavior. It was pretty bad," Sandra said, helping her sister up from the ground.

"Why are you apologizing for her? She's the one who needs to apologize for what she does. You're nothing but a troublemaker," Tressa said, scolding Nina.

"Hey, you punched me! She punched me in the face," Nina started to cry.

"You're lucky that's all you got; a black eye. Those women wanted to kill you. Come on, let's go," Sandra said, pushing Nina ahead of her, angry and frustrated by her behavior.

"No, Sandra, you're staying with us. Let your sister lick her own wounds by herself," ordered Cruz. "Jason, take Miranda and Nina. We'll get ourselves some rooms for the night. Miranda needs some lunch. Let Nina watch over Miranda, and if you let anything happen to her, you may as well be dead."

"But why, I want to go with you guys. What if they come back?"

"Then you need to learn how to fight and really fast. You got what you deserved." Tajo said, disgusted.

"Since you can't act like an adult, you can't come with us. Andrew, you stay with the girls, Jason. When you get them to settle, we'll be at the Dust to Dawn bar and grille. Meet us there." Jason smiled. He knew what was ahead of him.

"Yes, sir."

"I didn't want her stupidity to ruin our day out," he turned his attention to Tressa, "why are you going around beating up on my people," he teased her.

"Oh, your people, maybe I should have let them beat the crap out of Nina."

"It would have served her right; she's always looking for trouble," Tajo added with sarcasm in his voice. "I can't stand going anywhere with her."

"Had it been one-on-one, I would have said do your best. But they all wanted a piece of her," Tressa said, wishing it were the case.

The food at the Dust to Dawn restaurant/bar was great. After a few beers, everyone was having a good time telling jokes, laughing, and carrying on. The biggest comedian was Tajo; he had a way of telling stories about Cruz and himself when they were kids, how their mother would chase after them to beat them up. Everyone was relaxing and just having a great time.

The Dust was getting busier as the evening crowd came in for some beer and to shoot pool. "Why are you wearing that stupid hat and those dumb glasses? I like the way your shiny black hair rolls down your back all the way to your sexy bottom?" Cruz raised his eyebrows, teasing her.

"I just want to avoid trouble," she replied.

"What are you talking about? What trouble… it's just hair and eyes, baby?"

"In my hometown, it's not a big deal. They know my family and me, but outside, people stare, and there is always trouble that follows."

"Baby, I can understand the stares for many reasons. You are a stunning woman. Believe me. I would be looking really hard had I not met you like I did." The men agreed.

"You don't believe me… you want me to show you?"

"You're telling me that your hair and eyes get you in trouble?"

"All the time, and not on purpose, Cruz. I've been through this so many times, especially at a bar."

"Not here, I guarantee you. These fools won't mess with you."

"Alright, I'll show you, but… you have to promise me that no matter what you see, you stay in your seat… you got that. I can take care of myself."

"I don't like the way it sounds," Cruz laughed.

"Trust me, Jason, Tajo, keep him in his seat. I'm going to the bathroom a minute, and then I'm going to sit at the bar… just watch."

"Okay, I promise I will sit here and not get out of my chair."

"If you interfere, I'm going to be mad at you." Cruz laughed at her crossing his heart.

Tressa went to the bathroom, brushed out her hair, tossed it around for volume, and put on some lip gloss. She walked past their table toward the bar. She wore black spandex pants and a black top cut low in the front, making her breast look bigger. At the bar, she ordered a drink, and the bartender dropped his cigarette from his lips. "What did you say? What can I do for you… miss?" he whispered

"I need something strong… like you… on the rocks," she smiled, winking at him, losing track of what he was doing. Everyone at the table started laughing at the bartender and how she flirted with him. By the time she got her drink, two men were right by her side. Cruz started to move uncomfortably in his chair.

"Just sit back and enjoy the show," Jason announced to the rest.

"Hey there, sweet thing, my name is Reyes… what was your name again. I didn't get it."

"That's because I didn't give it," Tressa replied, sipping on her drink.

"Reyes, you need to step back… let Big Daddy Kevin speak to the pretty lady. Has anyone ever mentioned you have beautiful eyes?"

Tressa tried really hard not to laugh. "I'm sorry, guys, but I'm expecting someone." They continued to stare at her and make luring remarks.

"Is this your real color hair? And those eyes, are they real? I've never seen eyes that color before. I bet you like putting spells on men. What do you think, Kevin… she has me under her spell already?"

They started to get closer, and Cruz was almost out of his seat, but Jason and Tajo held him down.

"Wait on it; just watch and learn," Jason said, watching her next move.

"Hey, why are we wasting time down here? I got a nice room upstairs. We can get busy," Reyes said, rubbing his crouch.

"You guys leave the young woman alone. Don't scare off my customers," the bartender complained.

"You shut up, fat boy, let a real man handle this," he knocked the beers off the counter and laid a hand on Tressa's shoulder.

"Come on, baby. I'll show you what real men are like…" before he could finish his sentence, Tressa had twisted his thumb in such a way he was screaming for mercy. She punched him in the throat and in the groin. Kevin grabbed her by the neck from behind. She head-butted him in the nose, cracked his foot, and flipped him on his back. Both men lay on the floor in pain.

"Damn," Cruz stood over the two. When they saw who it was, they started to beg him not to hurt them. "I'm the one she was waiting for."

"I'm sorry, Sir," Reyes put his hand up in surrender," I was only playing… I didn't know she was your girl."

"She's not my girl. She's my woman. If I ever find out that you disrespected other women this way, I will throw you both out of my town… understood?"

"Yes, Sir… I'm sorry we were only playing, right Kevin." Kevin only grunted. They both left in a rush. Cruz tried not to laugh.

"I told you," She laughed.

"I don't care; I still want your hair out, no more hats, and only wear glasses when you need them. Believe me, and those two assholes will spread the word, so don't worry."

"So am I your…WOMAN… huh?"

"Yeah, you have a problem with that. You're my woman," he chuckled.

"No, I just like to hear you say that. Come on, say it again," she teased him.

"Be quiet, woman, before I take you over my knees and spank that pretty hinny of yours."

"I don't know. I might like it," He grabbed her and kissed her in the middle of the bar, "you probably would enjoy a good spanking."

"I think she can whip your ass, brother," Tajo chuckled, instigating trouble.

"Are you starting something already, little brother?"

"I can whip your ass," Tressa said, teasing Tajo, rolling up her sleeves.

"Clear the table, come on," Cruz ordered. She threatened Tajo to Indian wrestle.

"Oh, you think you can beat me… are you serious… woman, have you seen these guns?" Tajo flexed his muscles.

"Bring those pistols down here. If I can bring your hand down to the table, I'm the winner, and you have to tell everybody I beat you."

Tajo rolled up his sleeves, "If you beat me, it will go down in my book of shame."

"My bets on her. I think she can take you," Jason slapped down two silver coins.

"Oh, this is great… come on, woman, I'm embarrassed already," Tajo took his place.

"Put your pistols where your mouth is," They get in position intensely, staring down at each other.

Cruz gave them the go-ahead. She begins to strain but never loses focus. "Damn, you're strong," Tajo said, keeping his hand steady.

"Ouch…" Tressa said, causing Tajo to ease off as she slammed his hand hard on the table.

"I won!" Tressa cried. Cruz picked her up and spun her around.

"Oh my God! You cheated. I can't believe it… what a cheater! Oh my God, Tressa, you play dirty," Tajo felt foolish. She tricked him.

"You have to tell everybody I won. Those were the terms."

"You cheated, unbelievable; see, you're not right. And I will not admit you won," they laughed at the joke she played on him.

They continued to drink, tell tales and have fun by the end of the night. Tajo and Jason had to help Sandra to her room. She could hardly walk. Cruz threw Tressa over his shoulder and carried her to the hotel room. Cruz fell into his lover's arms; she was his every match, sexy, beautiful, and dangerous. He pulled her close to him, falling fast asleep.

The next morning Tressa was up before anyone. She had prepared drinks in case some people had hangovers. Tajo crawled down the stairs toward the dining area when he heard Tressa talking and laughing with the cooks.

"Damn, woman, don't you have a hangover? You drank just as much as I did?"

"Poor baby here, drink some of this and two of these… you'll feel good in no time."

"Man, this tastes horrible. What's in it?

"Stop being a baby and drink it. I can hold my liquor because I went to college. Think about it… first time away from mom and dad."

"Oh, you're a beast of a woman… I hate you."

"I know. I hate you too."

"You do. You don't really hate me, do you?" He smiled.

"No, silly, now drink it all up, or I'll tell everyone I beat you last night."

"Oh, yeah, last night… you cheated… what a cheap trick. I'll never live that down."

"I'm telling everyone," Cruz said, coming behind him.

"Your woman is cruel; she has no heart, no mercy."

"Suck it up, brother. We have witnesses remember."

The trip back home was quiet. Almost everyone was asleep beside Cruz and Tressa. They laughed at all the things that had happened the night before.

"I had so much fun last night. But I have a feeling you like to fight," Cruz said, "first, you punch Nina out… which she rightly deserves. Then you smash six women into the ground; afterward, you beat up two bums. Last but not least, you beat my brother at hand wrestling."

"I had to learn to fight. My sensei started me when I was three years old."

"Why the urgency?"

"I was born in a very secluded place called The Valley of God… it's a very secretive place with a long history of secrecy. Because I was born with the mark, I was treated special. One of the laws stated that once I turned 18. I would go outside the borders and find my destiny. But when my mother found my father again, we went to live with him. However, my father was obsessed with my training."

"What was the mark? The only mark I've seen is that cute little birthmark on your fine ass."

"The mark is not a thing. It's who I am… my color. They said I was blessed because I was one of the original people. So, I had to start my training early and be ready to take my journey like the ones before me."

"You mean there are others like you?"

"Yes, two that came before me, my father's grandmother and my Aunt Brydus, who is no blood relation but was also from the Valley of God."

"You have a very intriguing background, are your parents still together?"

My father loved my mother from birth. They were raised together but had no blood ties. He was five when she was born and loved her ever since."

"Why did they separate if he loved her so much?"

"It was not by choice. My grandfather wanted to marry her off to some stranger behind my father's family back. They didn't hide the fact that they were in love, but they were teenagers. Everyone knew that someday they would be married, no one but my grandmother knew this, but in fact, they were secretly married.

My uncle Jesse had summoned the families to the Inner Cities, but my mother was sick and couldn't make the trip, so my grandfather stayed behind to care for her. He was extremely jealous of my father's family. Mother is a very beautiful woman, and at fifteen, my grandfather lusted after her. You see, she wasn't my grandmother's biological daughter; her mother was a servant, a very beautiful woman. Who had a woman's body and a child's mind? My grandmother said that Rosa's mother had trouble during the delivery and suffered oxygen deprivation, so she never developed mentally. But my grandfather only saw a woman and raped her. She ran away after my mother was born. Grandmother said she was afraid of my mother and didn't really know what was happening to her.

Anyway, mother ran away in the middle of the night under hurricane winds and rain. She was searching for my father and became terribly lost. She was near death when a stranger pulled her out of the water and took her home to his family. They become daddy Polo and Mama Sara, my guardian grandparent, which I adore. But my mother lost her memory for ten years, and I was born in the Valley of God seven months later."

"That's amazing, but how did they get back together if she didn't remember who she was?"

"It was hard for her, and the memory loss haunted her. She didn't even remember her name...my father went looking for her. For three months, none of the family knew his whereabouts. My grandmother said that when he finally came back, he was so thin they thought he would die. The only person who was able to console him was his grandmother Nylaya. My great-grandmother said he sobbed like no one she had ever seemed. He was heartbroken and wanted to die.

It was only when Aunt Brydus set out on her journey that she met my uncle. My father's brother. They were married and had a son. When she returned home to visit her family and friends, my mother was so excited to have her back home and wanted to see the baby. They were best friends. Brydus had this pendant with the initials of her husband, my uncle, and that triggered memories for my mother… it was the scariest thing. My mother fainted. I thought she was dead. When she came, too, she questioned Brydus about her pendant. She was afraid that Brydus had married my father. But when she heard her story, she set out to find my father, her long-lost love. When my father saw us, it was so emotional watching that reunion. Everyone heard my father's screams for miles."

"They were meant to be… just like we are met to be together. Think about it. Look at the extraordinary way we were thrown together. So, now your mine, and I'm the rebound guy, and everything is cool,"

"I just love the way you sum everything up in this nice little package," she smiled.

"I know you love me. I can tell."

"You're not convinced, are you?"

"Well, I know at least that you have feelings for me. No one can be that passionate and not feel something."

"I do, and they are a lot deeper than you think. Remember, I just broke up with my ex. However, you stole my heart.

"That makes me very happy. I love everything about you, sweet cheeks. I know my family will fall under your spell also."

I hope so, but I'm worried about your brother and Nina. Do you know she has his name tattooed on her breast? I saw it when I grabbed her."

"She's a troublemaker from the door. Tajo is always running her out of his place. She's obsessed with him and is driving him crazy. I've seen him run her out of his place naked. She'll get in somehow and get undressed and wait until he gets home to start something."

"But she's a kid," Tressa replied.

"Nina is no kid. She's been having sex for years. But she wants him… bad, and he's told her in front of everyone, even her mother. He wants nothing to do with her. However, she continues to believe that someday he'll marry her."

"Really, well, she is in for a big let-down."

In the distance, they saw a car parked in the driveway in front of the main gate. "Hey, look, you have a guest," Tressa pointed. Everyone looked to see who had parked their car in the middle of the driveway. Tajo fell back to where Cruz was.

"The devil has returned," Tajo announced. Miranda stiffens in Tajo's arms. "Cruz… that's Mary's car."

"What the hell does that bitch want after all this time?"

"I'll go hide the knives," Tajo replied, convincing Mary he was looking for trouble again.

"Please take Miranda around the back, Andrew. She's afraid of her," Tajo helped her move on to Andrew's saddle. Miranda shut her eyes and lowered her head. He could feel her shaking.

"Don't worry, baby girl, I got you," Andrew held her tight. He went through the kitchen, handing her over to Ruby, the head cook. Miranda's face was pale, with a look of terror on her face.

"Oh, my poor dear, let me take you upstairs the back way. My sweet girl, I will protect you. She wouldn't be caught dead near the servant's quarters. The nerve of that woman showing her face around here after all these years; no shame, she has no shame at all," Ruby fussed.

Mary strode around the small sitting room, talking with her mother when Cruz arrived. "He's here, mother. How do I look?"

Ellen was speechless. Her nerves were twisted in knots, like a string about to break. She failed to get her out of the house before Cruz and the others returned home. "Well, mother, what's wrong with you?"

"Nothing dear, you look… marvelous like always."

Mary's heart started to race as he looked down at her. Those old feelings began to creep back in full force. He looked magnificent, she thought; at that moment, she knew her past actions made her regret not handling their breakup differently.

"What are you doing here, and who let you in?" Cruz managed to say, extremely upset, that she was sitting in his house as if nothing had ever happened between them.

"Oh, Cruz darling, stop being so overdramatic," Mary smiled, batting her green eyes at Cruz, who wasn't amused by her company.

"Overdramatic, woman. I want you out of here."

"I have a court order that says I can come and see my daughter."

"Your daughter," his eyebrow arched, surprised, "you mean the one you haven't seen in three years, and there isn't a judge on earth who would court order you to come near Miranda. So, what's your interest now in her?"

"She's my daughter. I miss her."

"Oh, God. Now you're making me sick with your hypocrisy. What do you have up your sleeves? You always have an arterial motive for everything."

Mary stood up slowly so he could get a good look at her body. She wore a tight shirt cut low in the front that exposed her breast. Mary knew she was a head-turner, always wanting attention. She walked towards him. "Does a mother need a reason to want to see her own child," she smiled.

"Mother, wow, you throw that word around freely, considering you've never been a mother to Miranda. Whatever it is, Mary. Whatever is in that twisted little mind of yours, don't count on ever seeing my daughter."

"Cruz, why can't we… be friendly towards each other? I know that I have made mistakes. I would like a relationship with my child. I'm sure she would like to have a relationship with me, her Mami," she said sexually.

Tressa walked in and stood next to Cruz. Curious about his ex, Mary dropped her cutesy attitude. She was not prepared to meet someone like Tressa. Mary's mood changed as soon as she laid eyes on her. Immediately Tressa felt a surge of hate coming from Mary. Her eyes spoke a million words without opening her mouth. "So, this is your new… friend." Mary had a hard time putting the words together. Her cheeks turned pink.

"No, she's going to be my new wife if she'll have me; next question."

"Marriage, well, I see you don't waste time, do you."

"It took me a long time to get rid of the foul stench from our lives. I don't have to explain anything to you, my life is my business, and it doesn't concern you."

She refused to acknowledge Tressa turning up her nose at her. "I hope you know I want a background check on your… new woman. I want to protect my child. She's not from around here, and… who knows where she's been." Tressa just smiled. When Cruz reached over and held Tressa's hand, Mary felt the heat rising from her feet.

"Go to hell, Mary. I never said anything when you decided to marry your sugar daddy."

"Well, I see you don't want to be cooperative, so I'll have my lawyer talk to your lawyer. I'm sure we can come to some understanding," she turned to her mother, who stood quietly listening to the exchange. "I'll be seeing you, mother. Send my regards to my sisters. This is not the end."

"I'll walk you out, dear," Ellen said with pointed nerves. Mary turned around before she walked towards her car, "tell that bitch she better watch out. She doesn't know what she's stepping into, and I sure am the right person to show her the door.

"Mary, sweetheart, don't make waves. You have a good husband and a beautiful life, don't ruin it, please."

"What's wrong, mother? Are you afraid he'll throw you out in the street? If he marries that… that thing, your ass will be on the streets. So, if I were you, I would pray that she leaves before that happens."

Cruz was not himself. He thought Mary would be out of his life forever. Now when he finally found love, she had to come around to make trouble. Tressa could see the stress around his jawline, "Sweetheart, is everything alright?"

He brought her hand to his lips, "I'm sorry, baby, I promised myself that I would not let her get to me, and she does all the time."

"Do you still have feelings for her?"

"Feelings… like hate, disgust, murder, you don't have to worry about me wanting her. I have cursed the day I laid with her. The only good thing that came from this unholy union was my baby girl. Our relationship was very brief. There was no love, just sex. The marriage only lasted a year. We got married right after Miranda was born, and soon after that, it went downhill fast."

"She is rather scary, so what are you going to do now?"

"I'm going to get my lawyers on this right away."

"Baby, you know it's not about Miranda… I bet money on it… this has to do with something else. Something she wants from you, love. Miranda is just an excuse to get back in your life as she is the only connection."

He looked at her strangely. "How can you tell? You've only met her for five minutes."

"I'm a student of psychology and sociology; we learned how to profile people in my line of work. From all the stories I heard about her, it makes sense. Now that I got to meet her… the eyes, Cruz, they tell it all. They were wide, cold, and lifeless. I can tell you that she is a sociopath. Be careful, baby, don't turn your back on her. She can kill and walk away like nothing."

"Maybe you're not too far from the truth. Tressa, I don't want you in the middle of this."

"Notice how her attitude changed when I walked in. Whatever she has planned now has to be rewritten in her thought process. If you look into her eyes, you can tell something is missing. Watch your back, honey; her claws are coming out, and they are sharp."

Tajo overheard what Tressa was saying to Cruz. He had seen something in Mary's eyes before but could never put it into words. Now a cold chill overtook him. He remembered the time Mary stabbed Cruz; he was there to take the knife away, and she was strong. She was so out of control that day that it took two grown men to pin her down. Now she's back and deadlier than ever. He wondered if her husband knew what she was up to or is he going to come up missing.

Sandra tried to coax Miranda from under the bed, "Come out, darling. She's gone."

"No, no, no, I want my daddy," she cried. Tressa stood at the door, wondering why Miranda hid under the bed.

"Sweetie, look, Tressa is here. She won't let anybody hurt you," Sandra reached under the bed to help her out. She ran into Sandra's arms.

"Where's my daddy?" She whined.

"Daddy's in his office," Sandra replied. Miranda disappeared down the hall.

Tressa was puzzled by her reaction, "What's happened to her?

Sandra gave her a sorrowful look, "Let's go downstairs. I don't want her to catch us talking about Mary. She'll freak out again." Sandra made sure the living room was empty, closing the doors behind them. "It's a long story. For the longest time, we knew Mary was not well. It's not something we like to talk about, but maybe you're about to understand who Mary is and why Miranda is terrified of her own mother.

My mother was only fourteen when she was forced to marry my father. Grandfather catered to him. He worked really hard to give them what they wanted. But my grandmother was really spoiled and selfish. Grandfather died of a heart attack at work. He was a lawyer and had a good business. Everyone loved and admired him. However, in order to provide for his family, he went into debt, leaving everyone penniless. Giovanni Cicone was my father, another lawyer. When he found out my grandmother was in financial trouble, he approached her to buy the firm. Father was a very handsome man, but he liked young girls. Grandmother saw how he looked at his mother and used her to make a deal with the devil.

Mother had just turned fourteen. She was young and fresh. So, they struck a bargain. He wanted the fourteen-year-old, but his grandmother wouldn't let him go near her until they were married. The wedding was just as simple a ceremony, just a few co-workers and grandmothers. However, instead of treating a young budding girl gently, the honeymoon became a night of horror. There were no sweet words of love or any kind of gentleness. Mother said it felt like he was ripping her in two. She was a virgin and bled everywhere. She could hardly walk when she returned. That was just the beginning. Mother got pregnant on her horror moon, she called it. Father was angry because his woman child was pregnant, but even pregnant, the strange and savage sex continued. I saw a picture of a mother when she was nine months pregnant with Mary. She was so thin. When Mary was born, he was not happy. He wanted a boy, and for a while, he was alright. He backed off of her a little, so she could take care of Mary, but even from birth, his mother said Mary was very difficult. Mary was two when I came along. Again, he wasn't happy. And that's when the verbal abuse became physical. Mother had grown into her body and lost that freshness. He ignored me, and I guess that was a blessing.

My grandmother kept her in line. She would blame her for the beatings, saying he was her husband and needed to do as he said. My grandmother was living well in a fancy home, and my father used to pay all her bills.

I used to hide in the closet; my poor mother had no one to turn to. Mary was a bully. She was horrible to her mother. If she didn't get her way, it was hell. Mary and her father had drag-out fights. I was eight when Nina came along, and so I took on the mother role. Nina was terrified of him. We used to hide and sometimes sleep under the bed because he would come into our room. Nina always slept with me. We thought it would protect each other if we stayed together.

Mary always had the best of everything. Anything she wanted, he gave her, and I found out why when I accidentally walked in on them."

Tressa covered her mouth, "They were…"

"Ah, yeah, I froze, and I dropped the books I was carrying. I was shocked. She was half-naked on the library table. He looked up at me and started yelling obscenities. I slammed the door and ran to my mother's room. Mother was covering up a black eye. When I told her what I saw, she didn't even bother to turn to speak to me. She said, how do you think she gets everything she wants? We called her Queen Mary."

Tressa was still in shock, "Did your mother try to stop him, and did he ever get after you?"

"Mother tried in the beginning. However, he broke her arm, and she spent three days in the hospital, unable to move. He came after me once, I was sleeping, and I felt him sit on my bed, I started to scream, and he left me alone. It didn't seem to bother Mary. She used sex to get what she wanted. Things changed when their father was accused of going after one of his client's daughters. His practice suffered and was losing clients. After that, he started to take on really seedy clients. Father started to drink, and when the money started to dry up, Mary became more troublesome. One evening father had two men over for drinks. Mother took us over to our grandmother's house so she could take care of her. My grandmother was sick, and I didn't want to stay home with him.

Mary stayed behind, serving them drinks. Father noticed that they were interested in Mary, and they kept on about how beautiful she was. Father asked them what they would give him if they wanted to have sex with her. They struck a deal. They dragged the screaming Mary downstairs to the basement. They raped her, and… when they were finished with her, they just laid around laughing. Mary came upstairs and got two butcher knives. They didn't see her coming. She stabbed them over and over until she got tired. Then she went upstairs where my father sat drunk and plunged the knife through his heart."

Chills ran up Tressa's spine, "Oh my God, Sandra, that's sick. How did she get away with killing three people?"

"When we got back to the house, there was blood everywhere. Mother had me take Nina upstairs to our room and lock the door. Mary was not responsive, still holding the knife. Mother pried it from her hands and called the authorities. She spent two weeks in a mental clinic in shock. When she was finally able to talk and tell her story, they called it self-defense, and her mother told them that she was being molested by her father. They dismissed the charges, and after about six months of therapy, she was released. They said she was all better, but we knew she wasn't."

"What a way to start a life. Now I see it affected Nina."

"Nina is a lot like my father. He was always chasing some young thing. I don't know if you notice that mother always seeks the company of women. I think she's afraid of men.

"Do you blame her? After living with a sadist, she was but a child, you can say, when your grandmother sold her to the devil."

"I guess you're right, and Mary, what an actress, fool Cruz, and when she sets her sights on someone, watch out."

"I understand why Miranda's afraid; Cruz told me how she tried to kill her."

"It wasn't the only time Mary went after her. I would take the baby to my room. One time as I bathed Miranda in my bathtub, I put all her little toys in the water so she could play with them and enjoy her bath. Well, I forgot her pajamas and ran to her room, leaving her to play with her toys. I was only gone a minute. I panicked when I heard the water running. I ran in to see Mary trying to hold her head underwater. Thank God the water wasn't deep enough to cover her face yet. I screamed, and she let go of Miranda, who was crying hysterically by now. She turned around like nothing, got up, and walked away. Miranda was shaking, I told Cruz, and he made sure someone was with the baby at all times. Amparo, his mother, would take her home a lot. Mary would kill her just to get back at Cruz."

"Lord, how could you stand to live with her? Someone that sick should be put away?"

"Oh, you're absolutely correct; she is very sick and dangerous. We are all afraid of her. Mother is terrified. Why do you think we don't live with her? That's why I have to get away; I don't want to live the rest of my life afraid of my own sister."

"I don't blame you; I'll make sure I keep my guard up."

Mary was furious when she left the estate. That woman was not what she expected. She thought his new girlfriend would be some bimbo with huge breasts and over-bleached hair. She scared Sandra, others she could manipulate, but this one… she was strange; she could tell by looking at her she was going to be a challenge for her. Mary raced down the road; there had to be a way she could find out who this woman was and why she was with Cruz. Her plans had to be amended. When Mary arrived home, she became the concerned mother. Worry about the welfare of her daughter.

"Sweetheart, are you alright? I have never seemed you so upset," Mr. Cooper asked. She sat on his lap, pouting like a child.

"He has this new woman, and she's really creepy. I don't trust her, and he refuses to see it. I need your help, my love; I need to use one of your special investigators to find out who this woman is before they marry. I mean, she could be a killer or something… who knows, and if she harms just one single hair on my precious daughter's head… I'll hurt her."

"Honey, I could put Clive Jackson on the case, he's my best man, and he's well-traveled."

"Thank you so much, baby. I knew I could count on you, my naughty little boy." He started to giggle like a child. "You've been so naughty today. I'm going to spank you good." She spoke to him like a mother speaking to a two-year-old.

"I think I'm going to have to be changed, too," he answered like a child.

"Don't worry, my sweet, I'll take really good care of you tonight," she whispered in his ear. He felt chills from his head to toes.

Chapter 6: The Proposal

Every day presented a new challenge for Tajo. The beautiful smoking-hot Tressa had captured his mind, body, and spirit. Almost two months of torture was enough watching the couple express their love publicly. Every time he saw them hugging and kissing, the guilt made him sick to his stomach. He was glad he had his own place, away from everyone else and away from Tressa.

Tajo walked into his veranda and stared down the main house. Belinda joined him, wearing only his t-shirt. "Penny, for your thoughts, lover boy," she kissed him, and he smiled at her.

"Not worth that much. How are you?"

"After last night, wonderful," she teased, "you know I heard about your sexual appetite, but until last night I thought it was just a rumor."

"What can I say? I'm just horny all the time," he put his arms around the pretty Belinda, but his mind is on another untouchable beauty.

"So, what are your plans, stud muffin? What are you doing today?" Belinda asked, trying to get him to invite her to stay.

"I have to go in town and put an order in for supplies to finish the housing project. I can drop you off on my way if you want."

"Sure, that would be great," Belinda was disappointed. It took her some maneuvering to get him to ask her out, and now that she was in his house, she wanted to stay. She had wanted him for years, and yesterday her dreams were fulfilled.

He was shooting pool when she offered to buy him a beer, they hit it off, and when things got hot and heavy, she suggested his place. He did not let her down, but true to his word, he made it clear he was not looking for a serious relationship. She didn't care about treasuring this night forever. Belinda heard stories about the hunky Montenegro brothers and how aggressive they were as lovers, and he didn't let her down, but she was not satisfied with just a night of wild sex.

"Tajo, will you call me? I mean… I really enjoyed our time together."

"Sure, but I have to tell you I'm going to be very busy tying up some loose ends, and then I plan on going away on vacation."

Belinda felt she was being dumped. "Tajo, can I ask you a question?"

"Sure, baby, what's up?" He said, not even looking her way.

"I'm aware you're not a happy person, you have women coming and going, and I wonder if you are capable of having a serious relationship, something meaningful and long-lasting."

He shrugged his shoulder at the question. It took him a few minutes before he answered. "Honesty, Belinda, I would like nothing better than to have a loving, passionate relationship," he pauses for a minute, searching for the right word. Belinda was a beautiful woman, and she deserved an answer. "Unfortunately, my feelings are for a woman who is unattainable, and until I get her out of my heart and out of my system. It wouldn't be fair to string another woman along and hurt her when things don't work out. I would be a hypocrite, and that's not how I want to start a relationship."

"Relationships take time to work, but at least you're honest. You don't make promises, and women know that from the door. It's just mindless sex."

"Hey, don't make it sound terrible, but it helps me forget for a moment, and it's not mindless. I enjoy it. I hope my partner does too."

"Oh, believe me, they do. I haven't heard one complaint about your lovemaking. Anyway, can you keep me in mind? I'll take whatever I can get right now."

Tajo smiled and kissed her. She melted at his touch. "Anything for a beautiful woman… how about one for the road, baby," he said, and she didn't hesitate to comply with his request.

Tajo had a successful day at the inspectors' office. All his papers were signed and sealed to get his project finished. It was still early. His stomach rumbled, craving a sandwich from his favorite bar and grille. After ordering his sandwich, he settled down with a beer to enjoy the view.

Manny, the bartender, engaged him in light conversation when he felt someone was staring at him. From the corner of his eye, he could see a shadow. He turned around slowly, nearly choking on his sandwich. Mary Cooper stood by, smiling at him like an old lost friend.

"Tajo, long time no see; what brings you to civilization." Tajo rolled his eyes and moved to a corner table. "Tajo, why are you being so unsociable," she said, trying to bat her eyes at him.

"Why are you even talking to me?" He blurted out angrily.

"Why are you so dramatic? I just saw you come in here and decided to say hello. Is that a crime?"

"Actually, it is. Now, please, I'm trying to eat. Go away."

But instead of leaving, she pulled out a chair and sat down. "Well, since you have a few minutes, I wanted to talk to you about… that woman, that black beast your brother is with at the moment."

Tajo sat back and wondered what she had on her mind. "Are you talking about the beautiful tan skin woman with the luscious long black hair and curvy hips and thighs? Who has captured his heart? Is it the very same woman that my brother is banging two or three times a night," he teased as she became extremely uncomfortable.

"I don't particularly care to know any details, but if you must know, yes, the very same one you fantasize about," she hit a cord.

"Look, my brother is happy with Tressa. Why don't you just mind your own business and let him be happy? You've moved on."

"But I haven't… I dream of him; I didn't know how much he meant to me until… he made me leave. I was sincere when I told him to give us another chance."

"Well, you sure blew that. Maybe you should have thought about it before you tried to kill your own child."

"I was hormonal; I have proof from a doctor."

"Hey, I'm sorry you still have the hots for my brother. What does this have to do with me?"

"You're in love with her. You can't hide it. It's written all over your face like a sick puppy."

"Who told you that shit?"

"You don't have to deny it to me, Tajo. I'm on your side… I know firsthand how it feels to be rejected."

Tajo was getting angry, "Let me make this very clear to you, and I'm going to speak nice and slow so that you can understand. Cruz and Tressa are crazy about each other and are planning to get married, so please don't make this about me."

She grabbed his arm, "Tajo, I'm not here to make you angry. I just want you to listen to my plan; hear me out before you tell me to go to hell."

Tajo leaned back against his chair to finish his beer, "go ahead; speak your mind."

"I'm not embarrassed to say I still love Cruz."

Tajo laughed, "You're insane and confused, that I know for a fact."

"Now, please, I realized I still loved him, but it was too late. He had already made up his mind."

"Do you think it was because he found you in bed with another man?"

"He didn't want to have sex with me anymore. What was I supposed to do? I'm a very sexual person. Sometimes I wonder if I had picked you as a lover… things would have been different. I would still be around."

"Wow, you amaze me every time you open your mouth. You and I… would have never happened. I didn't like you then, and I don't like you now."

"Sure, you say that now but then I notice how you looked at me," she tried to sound amused.

"I look at you with contempt. If you weren't a woman, I would have punched you in the mouth already. So, get to the point if you have one."

She looked around to see if people were listening, "Alright, here is the plan. I know you are in lust with this woman. I'm sure you dream of her and want to know how it feels to kiss her and all that other shit. You envision yourself making love to her, touching her. I just don't understand why you just don't go after her and seduce her.

I mean, I know you have the worst reputation with women, but you're extremely handsome, and frankly, I had considered you before your brother," she laughed, "Once, you seduced her and ran away for a short time. I know your brother will forgive you after a while. I'll get my lawyer to get visits with my daughter, and slowly I can move in and comfort him. I have learned many new ways of seduction, very effective ways."

Tajo just listened as she went on about her crazy plan. He began to realize just how far she would go to get what she wanted. Mary was truly delusional; now he understood why Nina was so strange. "So, Mary, let me get this straight, your plan is for me to seduce Tressa and run away with her for a while, so you can move in and comfort my brother. In time he would forgive me for stealing away the love of his life. Oh, and you two would live happily ever after." She sat happily as if he was considering her idea. He crossed his arms and looked around the bar that had only a few people having lunch. He tried very hard not to get loud and out of control. Mary knew just how to push people's buttons.

"I'm amazed that you haven't figured it out yet. I would rather throw myself off a cliff before I hurt or disrespect my brother or Tressa. And another thing, I wouldn't touch you or your sister if you two were the last females on this earth.

I'd cut my nuts off or do a guy before I touch any of you bitches. I'm embarrassed to even be seen talking to you, and as far as my reputation… I'm not the one who's screwing everything that hangs, and you're married. You're a cheating, disgusting slut, so don't even compare yourself to her. You are so not in her league; Tressa is loyal to my brother. They're in love."

Mary's face turned bright red, "So does that mean your answer is no?"

He was not surprised at her reaction. "The answer is hell no! Whatever feelings I may have for Tressa, I will deal with," he stood up to leave.

"I should have known you were a coward. You're nothing but a scared little boy afraid of going after what he wants. I misjudged you, Tajo," She ran after him. "You're nothing but a little boy afraid of big brother," she yelled.

Tajo turned around and glared at her with disgust, "You're nothing but poison, you and all your family, do me a favor bitch, don't ever try and talk to me again!" He crossed the street, leaving her behind, fuming with anger.

"You're going to regret not being my ally," she yelled after him. Everyone stared at her as they walked by. She composed herself and walked towards her car, regretting wasting all the time waiting for him, but she was desperate.

If her investigator didn't bring her some good news, she would have to make something up to get Cruz away from that woman.

Tajo rode his horse hard until he entered the main entrance of the estate. He slipped in through the kitchen and found Cruz in his office.

"Hey, your back; got those documents for me?"

"Signed and delivered" he hands him the documents.

"What's wrong little brother? You look angry. What's going on?"

Tajo took a deep breath. "Well, my day started out beautiful. I had this really fine-looking woman last night. Got some love before I left. Great and wonderful news from the inspectors, so what could go wrong? I stop in at Mario's to get something to eat… and then things go downhill. I'm sitting there eating a great sandwich, drinking a cold one, when guess who walks in… the she-bitch from hell."

"Not the beast. Damn, I'm sorry about that, bro; she would have ruined my day too. Huh, strange, it's not a place she would visit."

"You're right. Then she sat at my table and proceeded to tell me that she wanted me to seduce Tressa, run away with her, and then she would move in with you because she still loves you."

Cruz made a face, "What kind of drug shit is she on. Like I would even let that bitch come near my house again? Why would she ever think I consider her ever?"

"Cruz, has she ever made sense… she hates Tressa, plain and simple, so she wants her out of the way."

"But why would she think you would do such a thing? Mary knows you don't like her."

"Hey, she did it to Sandra. You know Sandy had it in for you… did she care about her feelings? Mary thinks everyone is the same."

"No, you are absolutely right. She has no rationing reasoning of right and wrong. I'm sorry she ruined your day."

"Well, I just wanted to let you know that she's up to something, of that I'm sure, so give Tressa a heads up. You know I'll be around to keep an eye on things when you go to your conference. However, when you come back, I'm going on a vacation."

"Hey, you earned it, brother. You busted your balls finishing that project. I appreciated the help."

"Well, we should be able to move people in by the end of the month."

"Beautiful, these people have been living in those broken-down buildings too long. So where are you going?"

"I think I'm going to Los Tres Rios. They have some great fishing and hunting."

"Wow, that's really far. But the area is beautiful. So, do you have plans for tonight?"

"I have someone coming over, Belinda Adams."

"She's a sweet girl..."

"Yeah, she is very sweet. She begged me to let her come over tonight… I tell you what. I hate when they beg. It's a turn-off, but I have nothing to do tonight, and she offered to cook, so I said why not."

"You've had it too easy, bro, but watch out, one day you're going to find one that will knock you on your ass."

"Man, there isn't a woman alive that can tango with El Tajo."

Cruz laughed at him. "Yeah, that's what I thought until I ran into Tressa, she is a challenge and doesn't take my shit, and I love it."

"Well, there's only one Tressa, and you needed someone to put you in your place… you can be quite an asshole at times."

"Okay, brother, just tell me how you really feel. You're supposed to be on my side," they laughed, "Make sure you see me before you leave. There are some things I need to go over with you. We'll talk about our next project when you get back from your vacation. Enjoy your dinner with the pretty Belinda."

Cruz didn't let on that he was bothered about Mary's plan. Why would she even think Tajo would seduce Tressa?

Tressa peeked into Cruz's office as he looked through a mountain of blueprints. "Hi, hot stuff. I'm heading to take a shower. You want to join me?" He smiled and dropped everything, and followed her out the door and down to their private suite.

Tressa knew he had something on his mind. Even while they kissed and made love, he was not his funny or his charming self. "Alright, spit it out. What's going on in that brain of yours," she demanded.

"We're not married yet, and already you're bossing me around…"

"Look, I've been around you long enough to know that something is bothering you, so what gives," Cruz was reluctant to bring up the subject, but she had to know.

"Tajo said something that kind of disturbed me today. Can I ask you something, even if it sounds crazy? Please be honest with me?"

"I can read you like a book. What's wrong?" She lay in his arms, snuggling against him.

"Has my brother ever. It's hard for me to even think this. However, has he ever, you know… come on to you?" Tressa shot up straight in the bed.

"Where is this shit coming from?" She asked angrily.

"Baby, don't get mad at me; I mean, my brother is a handsome dude."

"Cruz, what the hell are you talking about? Your brother barely says two words to me."

"I'm sorry! Mary approached Tajo today and suggested that he run off with you so that she can move in with me."

She rolled her eyes, "And you listen to the ravings of a psychopath, and what do you mean to move in with you? So let me throw this back at you. Have you given her any reason to believe she has a chance?"

"God, woman, I just asked you a question, don't hurt me," he started to laugh.

"Had your brother made an inappropriate gesture towards me? He would be sporting two black eyes along with other cuts, bruising, and markings along the lines."

"My apologies… I was just asking. My brother does have a way with women, and you're super-hot."

"Maybe you should stop right there before you put your big foot in your mouth."

"Hey," he embraced her, "I'm leaving in two days. Be nice to me."

"Why should I? You're talking nonsense" she rolled her eyes at him.

"I love you so much I'm even jealous of my brother. So, if I'm being a jerk, it's because, at this moment, I feel a little insecure. It's not like I had a chance to date you and develop a relationship. You can say I raped you, sure it was under crazy circumstances, but if you really think about it, you were not a willing partner."

"But you thought I was a prostitute. You didn't know."

"Baby, I found out you were a virgin before forcing myself on you… I wanted you then as much as I want you now. I could have stopped… I just didn't want to. So now that I have a chance to think about us, I can only wonder what you thought when you woke up and… I had taken something from you I could never give back.”

Tressa was moved by his admission. She played tenderly with his hair. “I was ready to fight you… when I woke up, I saw blood on my thigh. I’m in this strange bed. I flipped out and ran into the bathroom… I cleaned up and got dressed. I was ready to fight my way out of there.”

“So, what stopped you? I understand if you had.”

“When you came in the bathroom and pulled me into your arms. I was shocked, and when you kissed me, I was confused… you were so happy, and you wanted me. I didn’t have to prove myself to you. I must confess… I didn’t want this to end. You did something to me. I felt free for the first time in my life… free to do as I wanted without my parent’s influence or others scrutinizing me for being Jesse Quintanilla’s niece. I felt free, not having to act a certain way and being watched or even betrayed. Being with you, I don’t have to think about what I would do with my life. Now all I can think about is being here with you and Miranda and how much… I love you.”

He pulled her on top of him. “You love me? You never said you loved me before… It sounds so good to hear you say that,” he kissed her tenderly. “I don’t want anyone else,

Tressa. You are the air I breathe, so please forgive me if I feel insecure. I look at you, and I say to myself, damn… I'm the luckiest sonofabitch on this earth… and now you say you love me, and that makes everything complete for me. I love you more."

She kissed him passionately. "And you wonder why I fell for you when you say the sweetest things…"

"I get it from my father. He would say the sweetest things to my mother, and he didn't care who was around. He once said to me, son… speaking from your heart does not make you less of a man… but a better one."

Tressa rested her head on his chest, listening to the beat of his strong heart. "This is where I want to be, in your arms. Please don't forget that."

They made love again, but this time with a different understanding and openness that would allow the seed of love to blossom.

Tajo sat on his veranda, hoping it was his turn to find love; maybe he just didn't give his relationships a chance to grow into something special. What was keeping him from being happy and surrendering to a woman, he thought. That was something he had to understand when he went away on his soul-searching mission. He vowed upon his return he would try harder to take chances on a woman and not run like hell when she says she wants to cook dinner or see him one more time.

Tressa felt disheartened as she watched Cruz ride away with his men. When he turned around and waved, her heart swelled with happiness. She loved him so much in such a short time that being apart would be hard. She began to understand what her father always tried to explain. Sometimes love has to grow, but other times it smacks you in the face. That is how he felt when their mother was born, and he fell in love instantly.

Her heart longed for him… she busied herself with Miranda and Sandra, who made it bearable. Tressa also stayed in touch with Logan, who kept her informed about the prince and what was going on with the courts. "Logan, I have this fine man that I truly love, and I want to make plans with him."

"Wow, you really are in love, damnit. I guess this thing with Samuel wasn't what you thought it was."

"This is a whole new experience for me. It's so different. He's strong and successful. I can see a future with him. So, please tell me when I can move on without the fear of some spoiled jackass prince trying to look for me."

"Trust me. I will do my best. I can't wait for this to be over with so I can find myself a special someone. You're not the only one who wants to be in love."

"Thank God you left that scary woman you had. Now maybe you could find real love from a good woman,"

Sandra interrupted her. "Who are you talking to?" Sandra asked curiously.

"Hey, I have the perfect woman for you. She's a beauty and available… talk to him, Sandra. He's very good-looking." She handed her the phone, "he's a hottie," she said to Sandra on her way out. Sandra looked at the phone, not knowing what to do next.

Tressa searched everywhere for Miranda. Then she remembered that she wanted her to learn how to take care of her pony. From the entrance of the stable, she heard Miranda's sweet tiny voice speaking to her pony Pepe. She was feeding him carrots and brushing his soft coat. Tressa backed out slowly, not wanting to interfere; she entered the main house through the kitchen when Nina almost ran her down. "I'm sorry I didn't see you," Nina said, running out the back door.

Tressa never understood why such a pretty young woman like Nina was running after a man that didn't want anything to do with her.

Maggie poured her a cup of coffee. "That child will kill someone one day, the way she runs around here without looking."

"Heaven forbid we keep her away from her men," Polly added, laughing with Maggie.

Tressa looked confused, "I thought she was madly in love with Tajo. He's all she talks about."

They looked at each other and laughed so hard they were in tears, "we're sorry, Miss Tressa; it's just that… that child has been having sex with anything that hangs since she was fourteen," Polly said. Maggie agreed, shaking her head.

"She swears to love him, told me I better keep my hands off of him."

"Miss Tressa… Tajo doesn't want that child. He has beautiful women running in and out of his place at all hours of the day and night," Maggie replied.

"He's a handsome stud, just like Cruz. That little girl doesn't have a chance in hell with him. I can't tell you how many times he's run that girl out of his house butt naked," Polly giggled about the whole situation. "She's nasty, Miss Tressa, nasty and evil just like her sister Mary. Watch out for her. She's not to be trusted.

"I see. I'm beginning to think that the only normal one is Sandra. The mother's a little Koocoo too."

"Miss Sandra's a good girl. Your absolutely right," Maggie agreed, "it's a shame she's related to that family."

"Well, maybe she just needs to get away from them and start a new life somewhere else," Tressa suggested.

Polly stared into space, "You are right. She needs to run as fast as her pretty legs can carry her. Her family will truly bring her down."

Nina met with her cousin Leroy who was hiding by the entrance of the gardens. "What took you so long," he cried, "I'm getting bitten up and everything."

"I was busy, you jackass," Nina yelled back, annoyed.

"Well, what the hell is so urgent? You know I hate coming here."

"I need a huge favor from you."

"Well, it's going to cost you a lot," he gave her a dirty look. Every time he did something for Nina, there was drama. "I ain't doing anything stupid. You always get me in trouble."

"Look, I got money this time. I can pay you."

"What kind of money are you talking about? What does it have to do with me?"

"I have twenty-five pieces of silver."

"Twenty-five silver pieces. Where'd you get that kind of money? Who did you steal it from? Show me?"

"Hello, Mary has plenty of money. She gave it to me; see, look," she opened her backpack to show him. He grabbed the money from her.

"Right, like I'm supposed to believe that crazy Mary gave you that much money. You must think I'm some kind of fool. So, what do you want me to do for this blood money?" Nina hated to deal with her cousin, but he'd do anything for money. He could get her what she needed without a lot of questions.

"I need you to find me three or four money-starving guys to rough up someone. I mean, I need them to scare the crap out of her so she'd be so afraid and run away. You know, beat her up really bad. Destroy her in so many ways," Nina was getting excited with the prospect of hurting someone.

"Are you serious? I'm not going to jail for beating you, someone. Are you nuts?"

"Look stupid, take five for yourself and get some desperate fools that are hard up for money. Then they can split the rest. You don't have to dirty your hands at all."

"I don't like the odds. I want ten pieces for myself, and if I get three guys, I have to offer them the rest. They can split the rest between them."

"Alright, God, you're such a puss. I'll get you the rest of the money. I want to get this done as soon as possible. I don't want anyone else hurt. My family is not to be touched… do you understand."

"I know what I'm doing. You don't have to tell me how to do my business. I know just the three amigos that would do it. These clowns will do anything for money and can be talked into doing anything."

"I got a call from the tailor today; your cousin Miranda's outfits are done and ready for pickup. You can get her then."

"I get the bastards there, don't worry."

"The plan is to separate her from the rest. I know my brother-in-law. He won't let her go alone. Drag her ass into one of those dirty back alleys; beat her, do whatever it takes,"

"And who do you hate so badly, sweet cousin Nina."

"My brother-in-law's mistress, you can't miss the black hair and awful brown eyes. She's the ugliest thing I've ever seen."

"You've got to be kidding me… oh hell no. I ain't messing with that dude's woman. You see how big he is; shit, you're crazy."

"Stop being a coward… he's not even here. Cruz is miles away, and Tajo isn't around, either. By the time they find out, they'll be gone and with money in their pockets."

"Well, fifteen pieces of silver is a lot of money for these fools. Alright, I'll set it up, but if anyone comes asking, I don't know you, and you don't know me."

"I can't wait till that black bitch is out of the way."

"What has she ever done to you?"

"Tajo… he has the hots for her… I can tell by the way he looks at her. He never looked at me like that, and I want her gone, back to where she came from."

"Alright, you don't know me, remember."

Nina watched her cousin disappear into the back gate of the garden. "Let's see you fight men instead of stupid women. Adios bitch, run for your life," Nina said out loud.

Meanwhile, Miranda was so excited about her new saddle and riding clothes she begged Tressa to allow her to come along. Tressa couldn't resist the five-year-old, especially when she smiled at her.

"She can ride with me, Tressa," Sandra said.

"Alright," Tressa caved in, "Big John is coming with us… to protect us." They laughed.

"I know he's as big as a building. I don't think anyone will be crazy enough to mess with Big John."

It was a great day for traveling. The sun was shining, but there was a nice calming breeze. Miranda was a little chatterbox. All she could talk about was her pretty pony and what a great rider she was going to be.

The marketplace was busy, as always. Sandra led them to the stables behind the leather shop. The riding outfits they ordered for Miranda made her look like a professional horsewoman. She paraded around in front of the mirror, feeling like a million bucks. "I love it, Tressa. I can't wait to show off my new clothes to daddy."

"He's going to love you in it, sweetie. How do the boots feel?"

"They feel wonderful. The leather is so soft," she smiled.

"Well, the saddle fits perfectly. Are you ready to ride on your own?"

"I'm ready… Pepe is going to look like new with my fancy saddle."

The afternoon sun was overhead, and Tressa wanted to get back on the road. "Big John, can you please bring the horses around? I think we should leave so we can enjoy the daylight on the way home."

"Sure, no problem. Miss Tressa, I shouldn't be long." Big John didn't like the part of town. Every now and then, there were reports of muggings.

The girls continued to look around the leather shop, trying on gloves and other leather-made goods. Sandra whispered to Tressa, "Hasn't he been gone a long time?"

"Yeah, I was thinking the same thing. I'll go out and check. You gather our things."

Tressa didn't like the atmosphere. She walked down to the stables and realized John had not made it to the stables at all. She ran back to the store and didn't find the girls. When she asked the store clerk, he said they left right after she did. Tressa started to panic when she turned the corner behind the store alleyway. She saw Big John by the side of the building bleeding from his head. Then she heard a movement behind her.

"Thanks for coming. We've been waiting for you," a tall thin man with long stringy, greasy hair and a bad case of acne held Miranda by the arm. The other man had Sandra by the neck.

"So, I'm here. Let them go, and I'll do what you want."

"You damn right you'll do what we want bitch," the third person said. She started to laugh. He was barely 5 feet tall. "What's so funny bitch!" He shouted.

"I'm sorry, I didn't mean to laugh… it's just that. It's hard to be scared of you. Here you have a child and a helpless woman, and I'm supposed to be afraid of a bunch of cowards… please give me a break. Let go of them and deal with me, assholes. Come on, don't tell me you're afraid of a female." Tressa taunted them; she could see them getting angry. The taller one pushed Miranda aside, and she ran into Tressa's arms. Sandra stepped hard on the second man's foot and stood by Tressa, who looked as if she was ready for action. The only problem was they couldn't leave Big John behind, who was too heavy to carry. "Sandra, take Miranda and get help. I can take care of these clowns myself. Go!" She hadn't taken her eyes off the three who now had weapons.

The tall man had a knife, and he was the first one to come at her. Tressa moved to the side, kicking the legs right from under him as he fell hard on his back. She took the knife from him and threw it in the corner. The short one tried to poke her with a stick, but she snatched it from him. He just stared at her. "What's wrong short shit! Did you lose your balls too?" He rushed towards her. She quickly turned on her side and hit him behind the legs, falling to his knees. She could hear Big John waking up. The taller guy tried to grab her from behind and flipped him over on his back again. The short man jumped on her back. She grabbed him by the hair and punched him in the face sending him crashing to the ground. The third person never made a move. His feet were frozen to the ground as he watched her beat up his friends.

When the authorities arrived, the two were moaning, all busted up and bleeding on the ground. She was trying to help Big John, who was having a hard time focusing. The officers were confused about who was being attacked. They didn't know who to point their weapons at. But the young officer recognized Tressa and knew she was from Cruz's house.

"Ah, um, Miss, are you alright… these guys didn't hurt you, did they?" Tressa could only stare at the young officer. She ignored the officer and continued to assist Big John, who was finally coming to.

They arrested the two and chased down the third one. Big John was embarrassed and refused to go to the hospital. However, Tressa insisted. On the way home, all Tressa could think about was how she was going to tell Cruz she had put his child in danger. Miranda was not fazed by the incident; she boldly spoke to the officers about how Tressa beat up two crazy men. Tressa was not used to having to be responsible for someone else but herself. She questioned whether she was ready to take on the challenge of a ready-made family.

Tajo was on the phone when they arrived. He made sure Miranda was okay and then turned to address Tressa. She looked tired and stressed. Tressa wondered if he blamed her for what happened. Tajo put his arm around her shoulders. He could feel her shaking and wished he could comfort her more.

"Hey, listen, don't beat yourself up," he gave her a reassuring smile, "I couldn't get a hold of Cruz. Sometimes, when we're out in the fields, we can't get a call through for hours. How about if tomorrow early we go see him, you can explain what happened and spend some time together… I know he'd love to see you… it's been what two weeks since you've seen him?" Tears rolled down her cheeks, she tried to turn away, but it was too late. Tajo sat next to her and held her; she turned her face into his chest, crying. Tajo felt like a traitor holding her in his arms, wanting to do much more than he could. He held her at a distance so she could see his face.

"Listen to me… this was not your fault. You did everything right. Big John is feeling like shit right now because he let you down."

"Maybe I should have waited. I put both of them in danger," she cried.

"They were not in danger. They wanted you… I spoke to the officer on the scene. He said that you were the target. When I spoke to Miranda, all the man did was hold her arm and tell her not to say a word, the same with Sandra. Someone paid money… to hurt you."

"But why? I haven't done anything to anyone. I don't know anyone aside from the people from the estate. Who could hate me that much?"

"We'll get to the bottom of this, trust me. What has me puzzled is that it may be someone from the house. Cruz has to know. He's not going to be happy. But please don't worry, this is not your fault. Our women should not be afraid to walk around town. So, try to eat something and get some sleep. I'm going to stay here tonight." She hugged him while he relished the moment and broke the spell.

Nina watched from the stairs, angry; all she wanted was to get rid of Tressa. Instead of managing to put her in his arms. She felt such jealousy boiling inside of her, fighting the urge to go and push her out of the way. She had underestimated Tressa. Now she was out of money and still had the black bitch holding onto her man's arms. There was no escaping Tressa, but she also feared Cruz. If he ever found out it was her, she'd be tossed into the streets, she thought.

It was a long sleepless night for Tressa. Her brain wouldn't shut down, replaying the events of the day over and over. Miranda lay in bed with her just to keep her close. She watched as Miranda lay on Cruz's pillow with the doll she always slept with. All she could think about was the man that had her hostage and her feeling of helplessness when it came to Miranda. She was so small and fragile. Tressa fought the urge to cry every time she pictured her tiny face in his hands. It made her angry, fearing what Cruz would say.

Morning came really fast, and she finally fell into a deep sleep right before she had to wake up and get ready. Polly knocked softly to let her know it was time to get up. As quietly as she could, she left the room, careful not to wake Miranda up out of a sound sleep.

Tajo was punctual. As usual, he waited for her at the stables with a cheery smile. But she was not consolable. "Did you get any sleep? You look tired."

"Very little, I'm afraid."

"Well, it's only a two-hour ride from here, and the view is going to take your breath away." Tajo tried his best to take her mind off of things. Even at her worst, she had a way of moving him. After an hour, she began to relax and enjoy the morning ride into some of the most beautiful lands that were once a city.

"So, Tajo, anyone special in your life," he turned to her and smiled.

"No, at the moment, I'm... kind of just playing the field."

"I heard you've been playing that field a lot," she laughed.

He chuckled, "who is spreading lies about me? Don't believe everything people say. I'm saving myself."

"Sure," she laughed, "that's a good one... do you ever want to... you know, have a serious relationship, get married, have children, you know, the works."

"Yeah, I think about it, but I'm not the easiest person to live with, and I haven't met that special someone who would put up with my shit."

"Woo, okay, I heard you loud and clear," she laughed.

"I need a woman who is not so needy... who is not afraid to tell me to kiss her ass when I get out of hand."

"Well... I have the perfect woman for you... just say the word, and I'll hook you up."

Tajo laughed, "No, I don't do blind dates. I used to hate it when my mother tried to set me up with her friends' daughters… they'd always get hurt. I don't have problems meeting women; I just haven't found the right one yet."

"Oh, I notice… I've seemed you with some really pretty women. They have stars in their eyes for you."

Tajo was amused. "I know what you're thinking, that I'm this huge male slut using helpless women and breaking hearts."

"Ah, I think you do break many hearts, you're a good-looking man, and I know women throw themselves at you all the time."

"Well, at least I'm not like my brother. He wouldn't even offer them dinner. But I understand why he never brought any of his dates around… after Mary. I would be afraid to bring anyone else home. He was afraid that Miranda would get attached and then feel abandoned… you know what I mean. So, we were really surprised when he brought you home with him. We were all shocked."

"Why, because you thought I was a prostitute? He was my first love, and I'm glad things happened the way they did. I would have never met Cruz, Miranda, and you. I love it out here. Country life reminds me of my birthplace. I was a little apprehensive when I woke up in a strange bed, and there he was, so happy to see me, turning my life around."

"You are the best thing that happened to my brother."

"Thanks, he's what I needed. I had a horrible break-up and was feeling very lost. I didn't know what I wanted to do with my life. I left the agency trying to connect with my ex-fiancé. I was supposed to be planning a wedding, but something always held me back. Anyway, he… he forgot to tell me he had a son and another in the oven. God, I felt like the biggest fool. What about you? Did you ever get close to getting married?"

"I've thought of getting married, but I've got to be honest. I always thought that the right person for me was out there. I just had to find her. My brother used to say the same thing… I guess he was right. Here you are, and I have never seemed him this happy or … in love with anyone."

"I love him so much, but I don't know if I can continue to put others in harm's way. Maybe I should just leave… and take all the troubles with me."

Tajo stopped his horse. "Have you lost your mind… do you honestly think that Cruz is just going to let you walk out of his life? Please, woman… just sit back and relax. Let him handle things."

Tressa felt as if she had made a breakthrough with Tajo. He pointed to a few buildings standing in the middle of the fields. "There's his office away from home."

There was new construction everywhere she looked. Tajo grabbed her hand, guiding her toward a huge gray building. "That's where our offices are, but be careful. It could be dangerous around here sometimes. When they entered, they found a young man at the desk using the phone. He lit up when he saw Tajo. "Hey, boss, what brings you up this way?"

"Eric, I need you to do me a favor. Go into the field and get my brother; tell him it's urgent."

"Yes, sir," Eric nodded at Tressa and stumbled towards the door.

Tajo could see that Tressa was still stressed about what had happened. He tried to assure her that everything would be alright and not to worry.

Cruz was surprised and truly happy to see Tressa. He held her tight, breathing her essence. "God, I missed you, huh? Now, this is the kind of urgency I like. What's up?"

"Hey, why don't you two get a room," Tajo said. Cruz turned his attention toward Tajo, who was holding some paperwork he needed to sign.

"Don't worry, it's on my schedule," he winked at her. "Baby, you alright? You look troubled."

"Yeah, there is an issue you need to address," Tajo expressed, "Maybe Tressa can try to explain what happened since she was there."

It was hard to read Cruz's face after Tressa told him what had happened. He held her tenderly. "Did they hurt you? Are you okay?" He kissed her again.

"I wasn't hurt, but I blame myself for bringing Miranda and Sandra with me, and poor John had to go back to the hospital," she started to cry again out of anger.

"You did what I asked you. Big John is one of my best men. But someone better have some answers for me…"

"Cruz, I spoke to inspector Jong-Woo last night, and this morning, they have the three guys in custody… someone paid to have her beat up." The more Tajo spoke, the angrier Cruz became. The veins in his neck were throbbing with anger. "They each had three silver coins; they were a bunch of punks, young wannabe gangsters. They were very shocked when they found out Tressa could fight back."

"Eric, can you get inspector Jong-Woo on one of the lines? This shit is not acceptable, Tajo. Who has that kind of money around here?"

"At first, I thought it may have been Mary since she's the only one that has a grudge against Tressa. But she's not stupid. With her money, she would have contracted a professional."

"Your right but... she's the only one I know that can get her hands on that kind of money... However, I don't think it was her doing, but I can swear on my life she was behind the money. Who do we know that would like my baby out of the picture? That's what we have to find out. I have a good idea who." He was interrupted by Eric. Cruz gripped the phone with such anger his knuckles were turning white. "I just found out what happened in town yesterday, and I'm not happy about it. I want my people to feel safe walking the streets of our town. You know my family worked really hard to build a strong and safe community for our people. I want the guards to be on alert, and this is coming directly from me. I'll be damn if I'm going to have our community in fear like years ago. When and if these clowns are released. I want them out of our town. If this continues, I'm going to lock the town down, and everyone who comes in will be searched." Cruz continued to rage on the phone. Tressa looked at Tajo, distressed; he motioned to her to keep quiet. When he finally finished with the poor inspector, he picked up a paperweight and threw it against the wall so hard it shattered.

"Are we okay, bro...?"

Cruz shook his head. "I don't know, man… I'm so pissed off I could break those guys in two, and the worst part is I don't have the proof I need to grab someone by the neck. But they are conducting an investigation, and they are going to visit Mary. They will be contacting you, baby, and Sandra for a statement of what happened."

"Hey, brother, I'm sorry I had to bring you some bad news."

"I'm glad you did because had I found out later… that would have pissed me off even more. It pains me to know someone wants to hurt my baby," he held her close.

"Cruz… they were paid to beat up and… who knows what."

Cruz could only close his eyes and try to breathe calmly. "Are you going back today or tomorrow?"

"Actually, I'm going back in a few minutes. I needed your signature, and I know that having Tressa here would keep you from going crazy."

"You know me so well; I want you to take back a message to the house… I want everyone from the stables to the messengers waiting for me tomorrow. I'm going to put the fear of God into some folks. I'll be there sometime late morning."

"Alright, just don't start without me; I want to see the look on their faces when you blast them because whoever it was is going to be squirming in their place."

Tressa dreads leaving the peace and tranquillity of the outland, feeling safe in Cruz's arms. They spent such a wonderful evening together; she didn't want to face the problems that were brewing at the main house. The idea that someone wanted to hurt her in such a brutal way concerned her. Cruz was even more infuriated about the whole situation. His ability to protect his family was coming under fire, and he was not happy. "Tressa, please believe me when I say you didn't do anything wrong… you did exactly what I told you to do… Big John will recover, his ego is hurt, but this will not happen to him again."

Watching her so sad was breaking his heart, "Baby, had it been just me, it wouldn't have mattered, I'm used to fighting my way out of situations, but there were innocent people involved." She tried to hold back her tears.

Cruz held her face tenderly, trying to kiss the tears away, "Listen to me, baby, before you came into my life… all this was just something that had to be done. But you… you gave me purpose. All this… all these buildings now have a meaning for me. When I go home after a hard day's work and I see your pretty face, it makes everything worthwhile. I know what I have been missing – you. All this time, I didn't know I was missing someone to love and be loved by. Baby, I didn't know just how miserable I was. Tressa, this means nothing to me anymore if you are not here to share my life with me. I will go to the moon to find you if I have to, but I know deep inside that you were born for me, and I was born for you."

"Cruz, you always know the right things to say," she touched his face, "I love you so much. Everything is happening so fast. It's like a dream to me. I didn't know what love felt like. In a strange way, love can hurt. When we're apart, there is this emptiness inside. But when you're near me and I see your handsome face, a fire lights inside of me. These feelings are all new to me. I thought I loved Samuel, but I was always angry with him and didn't trust myself to relax and be myself. You make me feel special, Cruz Montenegro," her lips touched his, feeling strange and wonderful sensations coursing through her body.

He wrapped her in his arms, "Believe me, I will follow you to the ends of the earth. I will find you. I know that you still have business back home, and I want you to know that you don't have to do everything by yourself… I will be there with you. As soon as I'm finished with things up here, I'll be closer to home, and I'm going to be there for whatever happens… you got that."

"I got that baby," she kissed him passionately. "You're my man."

"I'm your man forever," he replied, squeezing her tight.

"Cruz, you said something earlier. You said that your family helped build this town… you seem to have a lot of power for someone so young."

"Well, my grandparents had nine sons, they had a girl, but she passed away when she was young. They were dairy farmers, my abuelito Pablo. Everyone called him Polo, he was Puerto Rican, and my Abuelita Diana was Cuban. They worked like dogs to build their business… he inherited the pig farm and turned it into a booming dairy estate. My family had horses and all different kinds of farm animals. My father used to say that Abuelito could throw seeds out the window, and they would grow." Tressa listens attentively.

After he built up his business, my abuelita lived like a Queen. Dad said she was very proper, dainty, and delicate. Hard to believe she had ten children, but she ruled. Most of the boys worked on the farm. My abuelito gave them a piece of land as a wedding present, and they built homes and worked the land. But then came the two years of hell on earth. The Dark Days wiped out most of the neighboring families. My father being the youngest had just gotten married when the devastation hit the world. My grandparents were lucky they didn't lose any of their children, but there were distant family members that didn't survive. My abuelita still cries when she remembers the suffering, not knowing if her children in Cuba had survived. It was four years before they heard from the three sons and other family members. Mother said she would light candles to all the saints she knew for news and to keep them safe.

When things began to break down, my abuelito fed his neighbors and whoever came along. He said he'd rather use his animals to feed people than watch his friends and neighbors die of hunger.

People were desperate, and after struggling to survive, they lost all sense of decency. A mob of people torched my family's farm. The very people my family helped burnt down his home and looted our homes. My family lost everything. The only thing they were able to save was some of my abuelita pictures and a memento she had at one of my uncle's homes.

They left New Jersey and traveled south. Abuelito always had money stashed away. It was as if he saw this coming. They settled here. This area was burnt to the ground. One of my uncles started to hustle. They worked like animals getting the money together and buying some land. They had years of experience in farming, so little by little, it continued to grow. My uncle Carlos and Manny went to the Inner Cities and petitioned for help. They had a plan put together, and that's how they got started. In ten years, they rebuilt their wealth and named the town El Paraiso Valley. My uncles branched out into different areas. A few of them moved back to New Jersey with my grandparents and rebuilt. My grandparent passed away five years ago; my grandmother got really sick, and she never recovered. My grandfather died of a broken heart a year later. They were married for 67 years."

"So, your parents just left you two in charge."

"After college, we worked with my dad and Uncle Rene, who became a big-time corporate lawyer. He helped write the bylaws to get our town on the map. We built a police department, and it was a lot of work, even though the hospital was new. We're co-owners and became Overlords. This gave us the power to build and establish the laws that help us to operate. Our family still owns the land. We're just caretakers. They wanted to make sure we had a legacy for our children. Four years ago, my uncle bought a horse farm. Afterward, he sold it to my parents for really cheap. They saw a great opportunity. They live around forty miles from our place.

"That's how my uncle Jesse got started. He took charge, and before he knew it, he was the big cheese. My father and Uncle Joaquin inherited a huge estate from the original owner."

"I would like for our children to live well and take it further than we have. Notice how I slipped that in there, children."

She grinned, "I heard you loud and clear."

They continued to exchange stories about their families; Tressa learned their families had similar stories about hardship and overcoming tragedies. It also helped her to understand who he was and what kind of values his family held dear.

After an intense love-making session and an intimate heart-to-heart, she realized that this was where she belonged and that no one was going to run her off that easy. She had never ran away from a fight or a dangerous situation before, making her more determined to make her life with Cruz.

Tressa stared at the man lying next to her. His muscular chest spread unto her side of the bed. She followed his muscles from his built forearms and shoulders to the rippled chest and abs. So strong, yet when he spoke to her from his heart, he turned her to mush, she thought. She kissed his lips as he reached for her, his arm bringing her into a tight embrace. Gently she moved the curls from his face. A smile formed on his face as he realized she was watching him sleep. "Come, let me hold you," he whispered as she molded herself to him, feeling so safe in his strong arms. A tear escaped her eyes as she thought about where she was three months ago and where she was now.

The main house was in an uproar when the messenger rode ahead to let them know that Cruz would be arriving any moment. She could see the tension building up on his face. "Baby, I want you to take Miranda to her room. I don't want her to hear what I have to say. She gets scared when I yell. I'll come up and get you both. I have a special surprise for both of you."

Everyone lined up in the main hall when they arrived. Miranda jumped into Tressa's arms as she ushered her upstairs away from the rest. They all lined up in two rows facing each other. Cruz on one end and Tajo at the other, Cruz's face was like a steal as he went down the line from one person to another until he stopped in front of Ellen. "Madame, where is your daughter?"

Ellen's mouth went dry. "I called her to come downstairs. I guess she must have gone back to sleep." She replied in a timid voice.

His face started to turn red with anger, "I specifically gave orders for everyone to be here. What makes her so damn special!" His voice thundered throughout the house.

"I'll get her, Cruz," Tajo said, volunteering, taking the main stairs to her room two by two.

"We'll wait…" Cruz said.

Tajo didn't even bother to knock on her door. He flung the door open. There was Nina still in bed, and she wasn't alone. One of the stable boys was in bed with her. Tajo filled a bucket with cold water and dumped it on both of them. Nina woke up choking and cussing as the young boy rolled off the side and hid under the bed. Nina's eyes grew larger, watching Tajo looming over her.

"Get your lazy ass out of bed!" He bellowed, "Cruz is waiting for you downstairs, and he is not in a good mood, so I suggest that you dress in record time before he throws you out the window… and Billy, your ass is mine when he's done."

Nina threw on whatever she could find and hurried downstairs, where the others stood waiting at attention like soldiers. Billy almost tripped down the stair not too far behind her.

Cruz was surprised to see the half-dressed Billy red in the face. "Ellen, I want to see you, Nina, and Billy in my office after this lecture… don't make me wait; I'm already pissed off," Cruz was getting angrier as he had to wait.

He ranted and raged for thirty minutes. Everyone looked at one another, wondering who was the disloyal person he was talking about was among them. Nina's knees began to shake as he looked right at her when he was talking. The silence was deafening. They were scared they were getting fired.

Nina's heart sank when Tajo escorted them to Cruz's office. She was ready to flee, but Tajo stopped her. "I just want to change out of these wet clothes," she smiled at him.

"You better not. Cruz is not playing with you anymore… you can change afterward." Nina and Billy stood before Cruz's menacing stare. Ellen stood behind them.

Cruz stood before them, steaming with anger, "How dare you… disrespect my house, have you no shame!" He bellowed, glaring at Nina, who stood pouting.

"I didn't do anything wrong," she replied sarcastically.

Cruz was shocked by her response, "Explain to me why you think you didn't do anything wrong?"

"You're doing the same thing… you're sleeping with her. Why can't I do the same?" Cruz was slowly losing his temper again.

"Listen here," he pointed at her, "and I'm going to bring it to a level that you can understand because nothing seems to get through that thick head of yours! This is my house… Tajo and I work hard every single day to keep our things… the people who work for me work really hard to keep your lazy ass clean. You don't do a goddamn thing around here!" his face inches from hers. "You're disrespectful and nasty… Do you think you can order everybody around here? Well, let me set you straight… you ain't shit here. You are here out of the goodness of my heart because you are related to my child. I am the master of this house… that woman I'm sleeping with will be the mistress of this place, and if you don't like it or whoever doesn't like it can go straight to hell." The color drained from Ellen's face as Nina stood in front of Cruz rolling her eyes at him. "Ellen, reel in your daughter. I am embarrassed to go into town and hear that she's been spreading her legs to any man, even married men. I'm not going to have it around my daughter. If you can't keep her in check, I'm going to have to ask you to leave… go live with Mary. I don't care."

"But I don't want to go live, Mary," she responded sarcastically. "I won't leave. This is my house too." Everyone looked at Nina as if she had grown another head. "Or… I'll go stay with Tajo."

It was Tajo's turn to jump all over her, "You are so damn lucky you're not my child because right now, I would be pulling my foot from your ass. I don't want you anywhere near my house. What my brother says stands. My house is his house. You disrespected this house when you bought Billy into your room… and Billy, I'm truly disappointed in you because I thought you had more sense." Billy hung his head in shame.

"I'm sorry, sirs, truly I am."

"Ellen, this is the last time I'm going to address this. Keep your child in check, or else I will. Nina, you no longer have a maid. You wash your own damn clothes, clean your own shit, and your room better stays clean. I will be watching you closely," Cruz yelled.

"But that's not fair, Mami, say something…" she turned to Ellen, who was terribly embarrassed by her behavior.

"He's right, Nina, you've had it easy… he is the lord of this house and this county, and you have been very disrespectful… it's time you grow up, child."

"Thank you… and Nina, if I find out you had anything to do with this… pack your shit and be out before I come home. Now you may leave except for Billy." Nina started to cry, storming out of the room.

"Allow me to apologize." Ellen expressed sincerely. "I'd been hoping that she'd grow up a little but your right. She is out of control, and she's been getting worst. This is your house, your town; I know what they say about her. I will try really hard to keep her straight."

"I'm tired, Ellen. You're a good woman, but your daughters are rotten, aside from Sandra. I don't want that kind of influence around my daughter."

"I understand. Believe me, Cruz, it pains me to see her throwing herself at different men."

"Listen, Ellen, I know she hasn't been easy. If she needs professional help, I will pay for it, but this has to stop before something terrible happens to her."

"That is my biggest fear, thank you; that may be an option to think about," Ellen stood outside the door contemplating what Cruz offered.

Billy shook, knowing it was his turn. He looked towards the door, hoping someone would come and save him. Cruz ordered him to sit down, "Billy… did you seduce Nina?"

Billy's eyes turned as big as saucers, and tears rolled down his face, "No sir, I swear to you it wasn't like that… please believe me."

"So, are you two dating… how did this happen?" Tajo questioned him. Billy hung his head.

"We were all hanging out by the public pool where we get together and kid around. You know, teenage stuff. Nina came up to me and told me it was my turn. I wondered what she meant at first. She said it was my turn to see what I could do. I didn't want to refuse because I didn't want her to make fun of me."

"What did you mean to make fun of you?" Cruz asked, eyebrows rising with curiosity.

"Well, a few weeks ago, she went after Jason. He turned her down because he had a girlfriend he really liked and didn't want to cheat on her. Well, Nina started in on him… she called him all kinds of names like… faggot, and little penis… she used other words. Trying to make him feel bad, but he just walked away."

"So, you didn't want the others to think you were a sissy?" Tajo added.

"Well yeah, Nina's a pretty girl. It's not every day a pretty girl comes up to me and grabs my private." Tajo and Cruz try not to laugh.

"Alright, but next time you disrespect my house, I'm going to kick your ass… you got that? And stay away from Nina. She's trouble," Tajo warned him.

"It won't happen again. I guarantee you, Mr. Cruz. Oh, Mr. Tajo… I'll have my mom wash your shirt, and I'll get it back to you."

"My shirt… what are you doing with my shirt?" Tajo asked, surprised.

Billy looked down at his bare feet. "She made me wear it… said it smelled like you, she called me by your name while… while we were doing it."

"Keep the shirt; throw it away. I don't want it… now go!" Tajo shouted.

Cruz shook his head, "Tajo, I love you, bro. But you're going to have to find yourself a good woman and get married. That girl is going to cause you nothing but trouble."

"Yeah, I've been thinking about it… I guess that's why I'm going away, just to get a new perspective on things, you know. I don't give any of the women I sleep with a chance. I just do them and leave them."

"That's because you ain't fallen in love yet. Who knows, maybe you'll meet someone at our wedding."

"So, you're going to do it? You're going to ask Tressa to marry you," he smiled.

"I got to, bro. I love her… this time apart was really hard for me. I'm going to ask her tonight… I've had the ring for a few weeks now… here, let me show you," Cruz pulled out a little red velvet box.

"Man, it's beautiful; you know she's going to cry."

"Yeah, I might cry a little myself… please be happy for me."

"I am… a little jealous but happy. She's a great woman. You know she said she had the perfect woman for me."

"What did you say?"

"Man, I'll get my own woman… you know me, I'll be checking out all the women at your wedding. I honestly don't know what kind of woman I need. I want them all."

"And you called me a pig."

"I learned from the best… you were my idol," Tajo laughed.

The evening was perfect; the cook had made a special meal for them, and Miranda joined them for dessert. "You look so pretty, Tressa. Are you going to marry my daddy," Tressa looked surprised as Cruz went to his knee, holding the ring.

"Tressa, I know it's only been a few months. I love you and don't want to spend the rest of my life without you. Will you marry me?"

Tressa put her hand over her mouth; she was speechless, even though she had dreamt of this moment, "Say yes, Tressa, please be my Mami,"

Tressa started to cry. "Oh my God, it's beautiful, Cruz… yes… I'll be your wife and your Mami, you little monkey."

They kissed as he put the ring on her finger. Tressa didn't realize she was holding her breath that entire time. "Cruz, it's huge… are you sure about this," she held up the ring to the light.

"I've been sure for a long-time baby… you're the one… the one I've been waiting for," he whispered in her ear.

Miranda hugged her neck. "Now I'm going inside… you two love birds stay here and make love," Tressa laughed.

"You know what she means, right?" Miranda skipped away and disappeared into the house.

He pulled her unto his lap. "I know we talked about marriage, but I didn't think it would be this soon. But if this is a dream, I don't want to wake up," she said, putting her arms around his neck.

"I know it's my dream come true…" It was like magic as he kissed her sweetly, running his lips to her neck and breast. "I don't want to wait too long, baby, to get married."

She could hardly think straight as his hands began to explore her body, feeling the heat rising, "sweetheart, I can't think when you're molesting me," she giggled.

"Alright, just for now," he took a deep breath, "So, ah, I want to meet your father. When things are up and running well with the expansion, we'll make a trip to your parent's home, so I can meet your parents and let them know what my intentions are towards their daughter… if that's okay with you."

"My father is really tough and very jealous when it comes to his daughters. But I think you'll pass his test."

"I hope so because you said they didn't like your other fiancé."

"My father is just like your family. They come from strong, hardworking people; my ex was a mama's boy… his idea of hard work is taking the next victim to bed."

"I want you to plan a nice engagement party so our parents can meet. I know you will love my parents and they'll adore you. They know some of your family members, Jesse and Renee."

"I can't believe this is going to happen… we married, and I don't have any doubts. I had so many with Samuel."

"Just remember this, love, you were made for me… big daddy Cruz, there's no place on earth you can't go where I won't find you."

She kissed him. "You won't have to go very far… I'll be the one sleeping right next to you."

Chapter 7: The Plan

Mary couldn't get away from her husband fast enough. The high price investigator she hired was bringing her good news, and she was in great spirits. She smiled, waiting to meet with Nina to find out where Cruz was working and how to get Tressa away from him.

Nina argued with her mother, convincing her that she needed to go to town. Her failed attempt to chase Tressa out of town didn't work, and she was getting desperate. Ellen had been watching her like a hawk. It was the first time in two weeks that Nina was allowed to take a car in town, and she had a time limit. Oscar accompanied her to the hotel room, where she was meeting Mary and her lover.

When Nina arrived, Mary was getting out of the shower. Her lover came to the door wearing but a towel around his waist. "Make yourself at home. She should be out any minute," he said in his deep voice. "Well, I see you just as juicy as your sister," he said, laughing, putting on his pants and shirt.

"You're not so bad yourself. Let me know when you get tired of the old stuff… I may surprise you." She flirted, and he roared with laughter.

"You don't have enough money, little one… and I don't know if you can handle… the big load," he teased back. "But I will surely keep you in mind if I need to take a break. Tell your sister I'll see her next week, same place… same time, and if you want to join us, I think I can overlook the extra expense."

Nina was already touching his chest and shoulders. "Well, we shall see." He touched her chin before he left. Mary finally comes out of the bathroom with a towel wrapped around her hair, covered with just a towel.

"He was interesting… what a stud," Nina said. Mary shrugged her shoulders and lit a cigarette. "He's one of my regulars… Ray is alright."

"What are you talking? He's perfect… you're so spoiled."

"I've had better… sit. We need to talk."

Nina looked at her watch, "Mom has me on a time frame since that bitched was attacked."

"You still haven't figured out how to get around the old bag. Put some sleeping powder in her gin. She'll be out for hours. Now… tell me about my man. I need to know where he will be for the next two weeks."

"He is still out of the district in the outlands with his foremen."

Mary smiled and started to get dressed. "Perfect. Do you know how long he's going to be away?"

"About two more weeks. What's this all about?"

"What about Tajo? I need to know where everyone is going to be. I have to meet with someone very special this afternoon, and this information will set everything up."

"Don't worry about Tajo. He's going on his retreat, and he's usually gone about two weeks or longer."

Mary laughed. "Everything is going as planned, little sister… this will be easier than I thought. Soon that black bitch is going to be history."

Nina got caught up in her excitement, "I can't wait. Every time I see him mooning after her, it makes me sick to my stomach. Mary, what is so special about Cruz, and why do you want him back… you have a rich husband who has one foot in the grave?" Mary looked at her sister sadly for the first time.

"Nina, I know how you feel. Remember when I said I've had better… he was my better. My husband is a very generous man, but he's not Cruz. You're lucky you haven't slept with Tajo because… at least, you don't know what you're missing. Cruz was like a drug to me. He's a very powerful lover. But he also has a very tender side, and I think that's what I remember the most, the tenderness. He has this strange way of making a woman feel wanted, and that makes you want him more, and girl, when you've had sex with him, you felt it all day."

"Wow… all that, and you can't get that from another."

"It goes a lot deeper, Nina. When he stopped having sex with me, I lost it… I was desperate. He rejected me… nobody rejects Mary. I tried to make him jealous, and he just wouldn't respond, so I tried to use my daughter. Sometimes after I have sex with my husband, I begin to remember all the mistakes I made with Cruz. I made a mistake by getting pregnant the way I did. I thought I would have his baby, and I would be able to hand the baby over to a nanny and be done with it. I didn't realize he expected me to actually mother the child. I wasn't made to be a mother, at least not at that time. All I wanted was to have lots of sex and spend a lot of money."

"But Mary, it's been three years… why didn't you try to get him back sooner?" Mary brushed her long thick blond hair; she stared into the mirror and smiled.

"Nina, you're so young and stupid. No wonder you never get Tajo… I almost went to jail. You know what they say time heals all wounds… I was giving it time, and I was alright when he was sleeping with everything that wasn't tied down, but when he bought her home with him, those old feelings began to creep up. I know the only way I could possibly get him back is if he's hurt and broke down to the point that he doesn't know what's going on."

"But you're married. How was that going to work."

"I want him as my lover, and when my husband finally passes, we can get married and make things work."

"How can you stand having sex with that old guy… he's so gross."

Mary laughed. "Girl, you don't know anything… he doesn't like normal sex, he thinks I'm this dress-up doll, and when he touches me, I remember all the money I get out of him, and I begin to fantasize about someone else, sometimes even Tajo," she teased.

"Mary, you don't really want Tajo, do you?"

"Nina, you are my sister, and I got to set you straight. He is too much for you… he is so hot I didn't realize it until I spoke to him at the bar. There is no chance in hell you will get him to sleep with you. I know women, who tried, and these are season women, women who know how to please a man and not like those little boys you've been sleeping with. He is too much man for you, sister."

"But you got Cruz. Why is it so impossible for me to get Tajo."

"Oh, my poor little sister, I admire you for aiming so high, but Tajo is a "love them and leave them type" of guy. He even has a broken heart club named after him; you're just not his type."

"I have to make myself his type; he's all I think about and want."

"Well, take a number… Nina, you go to any of the clubs on any Friday night, and you'll hear about his latest heartbreak. It's not like he doesn't tell them it's only sex with him, but they all think, just like your sister, that he will magically fall in love with you. It's not gonna happen. He doesn't even like you, Nina. You need to give it up."

"I can't, Mary… I can't give it up… one way or another, I'll get my love, and if I become addicted to him, then that would be my cross to bear."

"Well, look, you have to go. I have a meeting with someone here in fifteen minutes, and I don't want you around."

"What's it about?"

"The less you know, the better… go now… I have to get things ready."

"Alright, stay in touch," she pouted, "I have to find a way into his heart."

"Good luck, that's all I can say."

Nina left, and Mary began to reminisce. Sometimes she would have episodes where she would lose track of time. Her mind went to another place. Before meeting Cruz, she would lie on the bed looking at the ceiling. She knew about the handsome Montenegro brothers and their reputation. Sandra had a mean crush on her boss, Cruz, when she worked as his accountant. Mary didn't put two and two together until she saw Cruz at the Rio Spot. It was a night of clubbing with Sandra and some friends, that's when she first saw Cruz, and it was over for her.

He had been dating some other woman off and on for a few months. Sandra introduced them, and there was a spark from the beginning for her. She still remembered what he wore. He was so handsome women were pouring all over him. Little did Sandra know her own sister was going to pursue him until she got what she wanted. Mary bullied Sandra into getting her a job at the main house as an assistant secretary. She wore provocative clothes and was always in his face about every little thing.

By this time, Sandra got winded of what she was doing. It was too late. Mary had seduced Cruz one night when she volunteered to work late on some building plans. The next morning when she got home, they got into a big fist fight. Sandra was no match for Mary. The police had to come and break up the feuding women. Because of Sandra's injuries, she was not able to go back to work for a few weeks. By the time she was able to come back to work, Mary had cried on Cruz's shoulder about the ordeal. He let her move into one of the guest rooms. Mary and Sandra rarely spoke to each other when they were forced to work together. Everyone can sense the hostility in the air.

Mary made herself out to be a helpless victim whenever she knew Cruz was around. She would pretend to cry, and he would always be there to console her, which would lead to sex. After a while, she didn't need an excuse to jump into his bed. Whenever he didn't have a date over, she was at his door. Mary loved how he made her feel after having a hot, steamy night of sex. She didn't hold back. She used every trick in the book to keep him interested.

One afternoon when he was away, she snuck into his bedroom and put holes in his condoms. She knew that upon returning from his trip, he would be ready for a few hours of stress release. They spent the whole weekend together, barely leaving his room. She had everything worked out when she would possibly conceive.

When Cruz found out she was pregnant, she was pleasantly surprised that he was not angry. They talked about it like adults, and he said he would assume all responsibility regarding the baby. What disappointed her was that there was no mention of marriage. That's when things became strained with them. She always guilted him into what his responsibilities should be and how people talked about her being pregnant by a powerful man and not married.

His mother was opposed to the relationship from the beginning. She was always watching her and telling her what to do about her pregnancy. Mary cried almost every day at his door about marriage until he gave in. He made it clear that he didn't love her and that the only reason was to make his child legitimate. Mary didn't care; her true colors shone through once they were married.

When Cruz found out about the condoms, he was hurt. She tricked him that way. Cruz refused to sleep with her feeling betrayed. That's when she realized she had stepped on many toes and made everyone's life miserable. She was unhappy, making her the most hated person in the household. The knocking on her door brought her back to the present.

Clive waited patiently until Mary opened the door. She ushered them in. Zaim was surprised when he meant Mary; he was not excepting such a lovely woman. "Come in, gentlemen. Let's get down to business. Did you bring me what I wanted?

Zaim put the small suitcase on the table, which was full of money. Mary laughed out loud. "Well, now we're cooking," Clive was afraid of Mary. He'd worked for William on other occasions and did well, but he wanted to impress William, hoping Mary would give him a great reference.

"Everything is in place. The Montenegro brothers will be away for two weeks, so we have to jump on this opportunity right away. Timing is critical," Mary said, stressing the issue.

"I bring special greetings from my Prince. He is very excited to have his dark flower in his arms. Here is a small token of his esteem," Zaim placed a small black box in her hand with a beautiful sapphire necklace inside.

"Well, his highness has good taste. Thank him for me. I guess it's a nice gift for giving him the woman of his dreams."

"Yes, he will be very happy. He's been talking about his princess for months and is urgently waiting to make her his wife."

"I am thrilled to have a hand in bringing these loved ones together," she smiled wickedly.

"So, I have everyone lined up. We have to know what day we are going to move on. The money will pay for their silence," Clive said.

"Alright, gentlemen, she should be out to sea by the end of the week, and soon she will be someone else's headache. Mr. Zaim, please stay out of sight. You shouldn't have any trouble docking. My husband owns the place."

"Very good thank you for all your help, Mrs. Cooper. If you're ever in my part of the country, please don't hesitate to drop in. You are most welcome." He bows and leaves Clive and Mary to tie up loose ends. She throws Clive a part of his cut.

"You'll get the other half when that black bitch is at sea." She said, watching him put his money in his suitcase.

"It was a pleasure doing business with you. I will make sure everything goes as planned."

"Good, I don't want any mistakes. Now I have to put phase two into play, and I'll have Mr. Montenegro front and center for months dealing with child custody issues. I will act surprised and be extremely supportive over his loss.”

“Oh, so you have it all figured out?”

“I know Cruz; he’s very passionate and forgiving. He’ll moan over her for a while, and then his sexual appetite will kick in, and I will make myself available to him once more.”

“You must care for him a lot… he should appreciate all you are doing for him.”

“He will, but right now, I have to go back to my sugar daddy husband. I’ll slap him in the ass and dig in his pockets. Clive, when all this is done, I don’t want to see you in this town. You’ll have enough money to start a new life elsewhere.”

“Oh, I intend to be out of here as soon as this goes down.”

“Good that we’re clear on what our roles are.”

Chapter 8: Time to Go

"I can't stand it anymore. I've got to get out of here," screamed Nina slamming her mother's bedroom door; Ellen followed her right down the hall. "You heard what Cruz said. You are to stay close to the estate until they find out who was behind the attack on Tressa and Sandra."

"Why do I have to suffer because of them? I wasn't the one attacked… I'm suffocating, and you're choking the life out of me."

"You need to start listening. Do you want to live in the streets once again? I guess you don't remember the tiny one-bedroom apartment. You're a spoiled young girl, and one day your mouth will get you in trouble."

"Mother, your so damn old fashion. I'll never forgive you for not letting me say goodbye to Tajo."

"Nina!" She shouted, "when are you going to get it through your head that he doesn't want you around? His house is off limits; do you hear me!"

"I hate you, mother… Tajo will be my husband one day… and… and when we're married, I'm going to put you away in an old folk's home where you won't be able to spy on me ever again!"

"Grow up, child. You're living in a fantasy… just stay away from him before he starts to hate you."

"Never, he will never hate me, I'll be eighteen soon, and he'll see me as a woman and not a child," Nina screamed at the top of her lungs, running outside where Sandra and Tressa were making wedding plans.

"It's your fault!" She pointed at Tressa, "I wish you never came here… you're the cause of all my misery," she screamed.

"Maybe another black eye will cool you down."

"I'm not afraid of you… Mary will take care of you," she ran off, disappearing into the stables.

"What was that about," Tressa asked curiously.

"I don't like the way that sounded. I think I'm going to tell Cruz when he comes home. I think my sister knows more than she's letting on."

"I'm so happy we can talk. I don't think Nina and I will ever be friends. How did you deal with it all these years?"

Sandra tried to smile, "No one knows the hell I been through all my life… I'm always apologizing to them. It's embarrassing. Why do you think I never had a man in my life? The minute they meet my family, they run for the hills.

I love my mother, but she has always been afraid of Nina and Mary and lets them do what they want, even if it costs us.”

“Hey, you deserve to be happy too. I hear that Logan is crazy about you,” Tressa teased. Sandra blushed at the sound of his name. “He really does like you, Sandra. Logan is very patient and sensitive.”

“He’s amazing. At first, I was so nervous, but the minute he opened his mouth, I felt as if we’d known each other for years. We had such a good time. Tressa, I’ve been thinking of leaving in a few months and moving closer to where he works. Do you think it’s too soon? Am I tired of waiting for happiness? I think I just need to go get it.”

“Well, I think Logan is the right guy. I’ve known him for years. We went through training together, and I was there when he went through his breakup, which was ugly. He was too good for her, so I’m glad he found someone who can return his love. You two make a great match.”

“I’m not a rebound girl, am I?”

“No, his relationship with her was over a year and a half ago. She just had a baby from a married guy. It was an ugly mess.”

“Yeah, he told me about her, stating he dodged that bullet.”

"It's strange how life takes us in different directions. I came here to be with my love, and you found love where I used to live."

"It's time for me to go. I can't wait."

"He's coming to the wedding. Said he wouldn't miss it."

"Yes, he told me. We are planning on spending a few days together, meeting halfway. Tressa, I know if I stay here, my family will suck the life out of me. My sisters are…very selfish."

"Sometimes, you have to put the past behind you. You and Logan make a wonderful couple. I think you're going to be very happy with him."

Sandra spoke to Logan almost every day. Their relationship was blossoming, and Sandra turned into a confident young woman. She even changed the way she dressed and the way she spoke up for herself.

It was almost a month after the attack when an investigator called Tressa for an interview. Sandra took the message. Tressa went to visit Cruz and was on her way back. Sandra was excited about meeting Logan the next day.

"I can't wait to see you again."

"Don't worry, baby. I'll be in town tomorrow morning. How about dinner? I have to meet with some people during the day. I miss you. I have made wonderful plans."

"I miss you too, Tressa, and I have to see an investigator. Do you have a pencil and paper? I can give you the address in case you finish early. You can meet me there."

"Perfect, baby, I have a surprise for you."

"The address is 2745 Madison Road. It's one of the new buildings. The office is on the second floor, suite 205."

"Great, I may have some information on Tressa's case… we got some word that the prince went back home… I'll fill you in tomorrow, and honey… I love you."

"I love you too… I can't wait to see you," her heart was racing when she hung up the phone. "I love you more," she whispered, not believing her good fortune. Someone loved her, not Mary or anyone else. But she smiled, remembering how wonderful it felt to be in his arms. Tomorrow couldn't come fast enough for Sandra.

Tressa was happy to hear that everything was finally coming to a close. She wanted to put all the craziness behind her and start a great life with Cruz. Every time they said goodbye, it pushed her into a state of sadness.

Sandra was beside herself, knowing she would meet Logan for an early dinner. "How do I look," Sandy asked, watching for Tressa's reaction.

"You look beautiful. He's a lucky man."

Sandra blushed, "I have a confession to make. I didn't like you much when you first came to live with us. I'm sorry, and now I feel like a fool. Had it not been for you, I wouldn't have met this wonderful man who has changed my life. Can you forgive me?"

"Don't be silly. I'm glad we became friends. Now don't forget to invite me to the wedding."

Big John was still on the injured list, so they took Eddy and Ramon. Cruz was worried that there was still trouble looming on every corner.

The building was in a newly built plaza not too far from the courthouse. It was very elegant, with beautiful stained glass windows and marble-looking floors. A pretty receptionist greeted them and instructed them where to go.

"Wow, they did a great job on these buildings," Tressa said. The second floor was divided into offices and meeting rooms. Eddy and Ramon refused to let the girls out of their sight. Another woman escorted them into a very expensive office with a water fountain and flowers adorning the large center table. Eddy and Ramon were asked to wait outside the room in the hallway. A gentleman dressed in a gray sports suit welcomed them cheerfully, making them feel comfortable.

"Thank you for coming, Miss Quintanilla. I'm LT. Roger Gates." He was surprised to see Sandra. "And you are?"

"I'm Sandra. I was there with Tressa when this happened. I can fill you in before the attack." He seemed a little nervous.

"Alright, why don't I take Miss Tressa's statement first, and then I'll be out to get yours. I… I'll be out for you, Miss Sandra. Please sit and make yourself comfortable." He acted strangely. Sandra watched them disappear into the inner office.

Tressa sat in the very comfortable chair while Roger sat behind the huge desk. I'm waiting for my secretary to come in. She's going to take notes for me." They waited a few more minutes for the secretary when she noticed he was beginning to sweat.

"Are you okay, Lt. Gates?" She frowned.

"I'm alright would you like some water?"

"Yes, thank you," Tressa drank the water, and finally, the secretary came and sat next to her.

"Okay, now we can start," Lt. Gates, the secretary, nods at him. Tressa began to tell him what had happened when she began to feel dizzy. Her mouth started to feel dry, so she asked for another glass of water. "Are you alright, Miss Tressa?" Lt. Roger asked. When she stood up, Tressa fell back. The secretary caught her and laid her down on the sofa. "Do you know what you're doing?"

"It's just a sedative. I took it from the doctor's medicine cabinet."

"Where are the guys," Roger asked nervously, scared to death.

"No worry, they are being taken care of… it's the girl we have to do something about."

"That wasn't in the deal. Where are they…" the door opened, and a man in a turban and Mary Cooper entered the room. Tressa was out cold.

"You don't look so tough now, do you," Mary laughed, "what a loser, nobody messes with me bitch."

"There's a problem… she didn't come alone. There's a Miss Sandra in the other room." Roger said, sweating profusely.

"Well, well, well, so my backstabbing sister came along for the ride. Sorry, Mr. Roger, she's your problem now."

Sandra sensed something was wrong. Then she peeked outside the door; two men were nowhere to be found. She heard a strange noise and other voices coming from the other room. "I did not sign up for this, Mrs. Cooper. I will not be responsible for your sister."

Mary came dangerously close to Roger. You do as I say, or… you will be facing many years in prison… you got that. So, handle the bitch."

Tressa was smuggled through the back elevator and out to the shipping area. Sandra knocked on the door at first and then tried to open the door when Roger and the secretary confronted her. She fought for her life, remembering some of the defense moves Tressa did her practice over and over. The office was a mess as she used whatever she could to defend herself, but the two overtook her, and after being beaten, she was drugged and tied to a chair.

"Is she dead?" Roger was scared and only wanted to get as far away as possible.

"I don't know. I'm not sure how much I gave her… let's get the hell out of here before we are discovered."

Logan looked at his watch once again and thought maybe he misunderstood where they would be meeting. When he questioned the receptionist, he began to worry.

"Miss, did you happen to see two young women come through here today?"

"Why yes, earlier today… I thought they were here to rent some of the offices on the second floor."

The blood drained from his face, "What are you saying… they were here to speak to an investigator. They came to give their statement?"

The receptionist looked bewildered. "I was told they were coming to check out some of the offices."

Logan started to panic. "Okay, did you see them leave?"

The receptionist is baffled. "Come to think about it, I didn't… and I've been here all day; my backup never showed up. I would have seen them leave.

"Call the police now!" Logan took the stairs to the second floor finding the office suites open. He pulled out his weapon and slowly began combing the area; nothing was out of the ordinary. Logan went from room to room. There was a strange eeriness and a faint odor he was familiar with but couldn't put his finger on. He opened the other doors, following the scent. Pushing open another door, there was evidence of a struggle. The room was dark, but the place was a mess. He heard soft, muffled sounds coming from the corner. Logan felt for the light and couldn't find it. When he opened the door to the inner office, he found Sandra tied up to a chair bleeding from her head. "Oh my God, baby… please hang in there," he cried, checking for a pulse and removing the tape from her mouth. Sandra took in a deep breath before she passed out.

Felix's hands trembled as he called to Cruz, who was still in the outlands. He heard his cheerful voice at the other end and wished he wasn't the one who had to give him the dreadful news.

"Hey, what's up?" There was a silence on the line, "Felix, is something wrong… has something happened to Miranda?"

"I'm sorry, sir," Cruz felt a chill rush through his body, "Miss Tressa is missing, and Sandra is in the hospital in critical condition." Felix heard the phone drop. His men could only stare at Cruz's reaction anticipating the bad news.

"What happened…? Cruz," Ruben asked, trying to snap him back, "What's going on?"

"They've taken her…"

"Taken who Cruz talk to us?" Ruben asked forcefully.

"They took my woman… Tressa is gone. They finally did it."

"Shit, man, what do you want us to do?"

"I got to find her… bring her home," tears rolled from his eyes, "I knew I should have kept her here with me."

"We're here for you, man. I'll gather the crew."

"Thanks, Ruben… I have to go." He was still in shock.

Cruz and his men traveled down the dangerous trails in the dark. When they arrived home, the whole house was in an uproar, and poor Miranda was hysterical. When she saw him at the door, she ran into his arms. "Daddy, they took her. They took Tressa," he hugged her tightly.

"I know, sweetheart, we'll get her back, I promise." Cruz was exhausted, and he needed his brother. Tajo had a way of keeping him calm and not allowing him to go to extremes. The hospital was full of police and agency employees trying to put together what had happened. When Cruz entered Sandra's hospital room, her mother, Ellen, was crying, holding her hand, and Logan was giving orders on the phone. Logan walked toward Cruz, extending his hand. Cruz could hardly recognize Sandra, who lay so still in her hospital bed. A lump formed in his throat.

"How is she?" Cruz asked barely above a whisper.

"She's better; they stabilized her. Let's talk in the next room,"

"Where is my woman, Logan? Who's responsible for taking her?"

"I got as much information from Sandra as much as I could. She feels responsible because she took the message. According to the girl at the front desk, some strangers were looking for offices the day before yesterday. They wore turbans and spoke in a different language.

They told the receptionist that a young lady matching Tressa's description was coming to look at some offices to rent. They were waiting inside for them," he turned his face for a second.

"Sorry when I saw her like this... I... I didn't think she was alive," he cleared his throat. They were not expecting Sandra to come with Tressa. They anticipated the two men, but Sandra was a surprise. They identified themselves as officials. Sandra said there was no struggle; she heard a woman laughing, and it gave her chills because she sounded like Mary. That's when she became alarmed and opened the door to the office. A man named Roger and another woman were waiting for her. She fought them as best as she could. The office was a mess... and the two guards were found drugged in the back alley. One of them almost died. Apparently, the water was laced with a strong drug. They did not know how much to give a person." Cruz ran his hands through his hand, frustrated and feeling helpless.

Investigator Jong-Woo joined them. "I'm sorry, Cruz, we're doing all we can to piece together what happened and where to start."

"Don't bother to search here," Logan added, "she is far gone… we know for a fact that she was boarded on a vessel eight hours ago, and they are out to sea. However, we know who and where they're taking her. We have contacted people on the other side to assist us."

"Well, that saves me from beating on some people. I need to know where they're taking her… I'm going to get her back. She is my life, and I promised her I would go to the moon to find her if I had to."

"Cruz, why don't you let the experts handle this? They know what they're doing," Jong-Woo suggested, wanting to stop him from interfering with the investigation

"Screw that shit. The experts couldn't keep her safe. They were supposed to be watching out for this prick. I'm going after her and the son-of-a-bitch who took her, and I'd like to see who's going to stop me. I have my own means of transportation, money, and manpower."

"You have to see my boss, Mr. Lee. He knows everything about this Prince and his homeland. I want to stay with Sandra for a little while."

"I understand. I have to gather my forces. There will be hell to pay." Cruz wasted no time gathering his crew and heading toward the agency. Mr. Lee paced the floor of his office for hours, waiting to meet with Cruz and his men and getting his approval to set sail. Because of the kidnapping, all ports leaving the coast had been closed until further notice. Everyone leaving would have to get special permission from the coastal department.

Cruz has his men and vessel ready to leave, but the only person missing is his brother. He wished that Tajo was coming with him. But he would speak to Mr. Lee to give Tajo special permission if he wanted to follow and needed help. Lee watched four men walking towards the building from the gate. When Lee saw Cruz, he was surprised he was not expecting such a strong man with such a forceful character. "Well, I had no idea Mr. Montenegro was such a big... powerful fellow."

"Yes, he's here and not too happy," Logan explained.

"He's not going to punch me out or anything. Let me know so I can take my glasses off."

"Calm down, boss. He's anxious to get on his way. He needs that clearance."

"Show him in. I have enough to deal with without having to worry about a mean-ass boyfriend, too," Mr. Lee tried to sound helpful.

"Mr. Montenegro, I've heard so much about you." He extends his hand. Cruz took his hand reluctantly. "We have a lot to go over before you ship out."

"All I want to know is if I have clearance because whether or not I do, I'm leaving this afternoon, with or without permission. I'm tired of the bull shit and the runaround." Cruz's demeanor went from angry to calm and still.

"I have clearance; for you and your brother… Cortez Montenegro is that correct."

"Yes, my brother will follow me when he finds out."

"Mr. Montenegro, I understand your frustration, but we are doing all we can to retrieve Tressa… she is like a daughter to me. We have people in place to assist you… Logan, can you fill us in,"

Logan laid out a world map. "It is a long trip to Saudi Arabia since the international transporter has been destroyed for years. We have tried to repair it, and we have been unsuccessful. Air support has been out of the picture for over 50 years. So, there is only one way out and back, and that is by sea. This is where one of our agents will contact you. Drew will be looking for the Lucky Lady. Make a stop in the city name Jedith - a seaport that has been renamed. Now this area was heavily devastated during the Dark Days. It was so bad that they were still burying people five years later. However, the good news is you will not be noticed. It is a merchant port, and anyone with gold is welcomed. If they ask you what is the reason for your visit. You can tell them that you are interested in trade. Believe me. They will treat you like royalty."

"Where are they keeping her? How will I know?"

"Our temporary headquarters is in one of the major cities. I'm hoping that she is being kept at the main palace. However, it's hard to know until you meet up with Drew. By now, he'll have enough information to pinpoint where she is," Logan hoped the information he gave him would give him some hope.

"Alright, I'm out of here… is there anything else I should know?"

"The waters are dangerous. We cannot patrol the waters like we used to. We have recently begun to build arm forces again. So much technology was destroyed during the Dark

Days. The transporter was obliterated by fanatic groups who claimed they were helping humanity by blowing shit up. So be very careful. We don't have ways to monitor things from here."

"Mr. Cruz," Lee said with great concern, "We're doing all we can to retrieve her safely."

"My last question to you, Mr. Lee, is why, if your agency knew their intentions, how they could be granted permission to cross our borders… who fell asleep?" Lee rubbed his chin, his face drawn and tired.

"The breach did not originate on our side. Whoever assisted them had lots of money and power to make someone look the other way. This was a well-planned kidnapping, and it came from your side of town."

Cruz was stunned. He tried to keep his composer, "You mean to say that someone in my territory made this happen?"

"Someone wanted her out of the way really bad. We didn't even know where she was staying until recently when Logan went to see his girlfriend. This took weeks of planning."

"They could see the tension building up on his face. "Then I apologize to you and your agency, and I truly appreciate your help. I will find out who is behind this when I get back… I promise you."

Chapter 9: At Sea

For days Tressa lingered in and out of unconsciousness, unable to focus on the shadowy figures. Voices and fussing were going on around her. On occasion, she tried to hold her head up but fell back into a sea of blackness.

"Miss Beauty, please wake up. You must eat something," Batula shook her.

Tressa woke up with a massive headache; the sun coming in from the window intensified the pain. She felt her stomach turning, looking for something to puke into. The pain in her head intensified with every bout.

Tressa tried to open her eyes slowly and surveyed the room. It was richly decorated with deep reds, brilliant yellow, and purple pillows and rugs. The bed she lay in was also made in reds and browns. Tressa laid her throbbing head back on the soft pillow fighting with her brain to get control and focus. A young girl came to her bedside with some water and painkillers. Tressa snatched them from her and swallowed them quickly. The pain was so dreadful she couldn't even speak.

The young girl covered her back up, and she fell fast asleep. Tressa tossed and turned in the huge bed fighting some unknown people in her dreams. Batula, the servant girl, tried to wake her up. "Miss Beauty," she shook her again. "Miss Beauty, it's time for nourishment. You haven't eaten in days. You need your strength." Tressa heard this tiny voice from far away. She tried to focus on the girl trying to remember where she was.

"Who are you…?" She said, trying to cover her eyes.

"My name is Batula, and I'm here to serve you… I have some special American-made soup for you that will help you get your balance back."

"Something tells me I'm not in Kansas anymore… where am I?"

Batula smiled at her. "You are so lucky… we are on the way to see the great Prince Harden; he is very handsome and wants to crown you, Princess Beauty."

Tressa was finally able to focus on the pretty, young delicate girl. "Please, Miss Beauty, eat something. It was made especially for you." Tressa laughed at her predicament. She took the bowl and bread away from Batula and was able to get it down without running to spit it back up.

"Batula, I need you to get me someone in charge… like, right now!"

Batula was wide-eyed. "I do not know who is in charge."

"Well, get me, someone you think may be in charge. I need some answers right away… please."

"I will do what I can; you eat, keep up your strength." Tressa ate the chicken soup and the bread. They had her in fancy clothes and shoes; the room was set up for a Queen. A middle-aged gentleman came to her door. He wore the custom turban and beard. He bowed when he approached her.

"Miss Beauty, I am here at your service. I am Zaim. What are your pleasures." Tressa tried to stand next to him, and he put his head down.

"I am here against my will. I demand to know where I am being taken."

"Miss Beauty, I…" she interrupted him.

"I am not black beauty. She is my sister," he was shocked.

"But I saw the pictures, could there be two of you…" she folded her arms and looked at him sternly.

"My name is Tressa; we are identical twins."

Zaim's jaw dropped. "I… I'm sorry, Miss Tressa… for the mistaken identity. I am but the messenger."

"I demand you take me to shore where I can get transportation back home."

"We should be arriving in a day or so. I'm sure the prince will rectify this mistake. Please accept my humble apology."

All of a sudden, Tressa doubled up in pain. She started to perspire and cried out. Zaim called for Batula to assist him. Tressa was awakening again to the soft voice of Batula. The doctor took some blood and tried to assure her she would be alright. Batula pressed a cool towel against her forehead. "You passed out, Miss Tressa. The doctor will find out what it was they gave you. He is my father and very good at his job." Tressa tried to smile, but she felt so weak. "You sleep… I will be here in case you need me; I will take care of you, Miss Tressa, I promised."

It seemed like she had just closed her eyes when she felt Batula's nudging her to wake up. "Miss Tressa, I have some clean towels for your bath, a toothbrush, and all kinds of toiletries."

"A bath that would be heavenly," she stretched in bed.

"Good, I will run your bath. Breakfast will be here soon. You must keep up your strength; father will be in with your test results." Tressa did not miss the worried look on her face. "He was very concern about the drugs they gave you to make you so sick."

Tressa eased herself into the steaming tub of scented water. "Batula, how long have I been traveling?"

"We have been at sea for seven days; we should be seeing the coast by tomorrow."

"Seven days. How the hell, Batula? What is going on?"

"You were in and out the first three days. We were very worried. You slept so deeply my father ordered an IV, and he put something in it to revive you."

"That's probably why my head hurt so much when I woke up."

"Yes, my father said you would suffer a terrible headache." Tressa laid back in the tub. The soothing water helped her relax. Tears formed in her eyes, falling into the water. All she could think about was how worried Cruz must be. He didn't know what had happened or where she was. The tears turned into deep sobs, "Miss Tressa please, what's wrong… what can I do to help you?" She looked over at poor Batula and tried to force a smile.

"Have you ever been in love, Batula?"

"I know a little about love… I think?"

"I have a man at home… you see this ring" she touched the pink stone.

"It is very beautiful."

"He gave me this ring with the promise that we'd get married and have a family," she let out a deep sob, "he said he would find me wherever I am... but he doesn't know where I am. He'll never find me, Batula... I love him so much." Batula couldn't help but shed a few tears herself; the man she was going to marry was the prince. Batula was promised to the prince when she was four. She only begged her father to let her go with him because she wanted to see her competition.

"Miss Tressa, you do not want to marry the prince?"

"Batula, I don't want to marry anyone but my fiancé... he is tall and perfect, strong and powerful... and sweet and gentle at the same time."

Batula looked away, "He sounds like you two were made for each other."

"I thought we were, but now... an ocean separates us... and I miss him so much."

"Come, let me help you out and get dressed. Things will work out, I promised."

Batula watched as Tressa ate with great sorrow. She felt terrible that she was the one giving her the drugs. Now all she had to do was get her and her lover together so she could see her way to the prince the way it was promised.

Meanwhile, Cruz kept his men on high alert. They had just passed two vessels destroyed by fire and saw some dead bodies scattered in the water, one of them was a child. Everyone was ready to fight. Cruz took twenty of his best men; they were fully armed and dangerous. But he couldn't help wondering how Tressa was, what he wouldn't do to hold her in his arms right now. Ruben stood next to Cruz as he stared out into the water. "I was wondering if you took a few minutes to eat… cook made some smoking chilly."

"I'll have time to eat later."

"Cruz, you have to keep your strength up. You are no good to us if you are too weak to do anything. She's going to need you strong… how about some food."

"I guess you're right; I need to stay strong to break somebody's neck."

"Pablo is on the watch out; you know him, and nothing gets by him. Let's eat downstairs; I could use a second bowl."

Cruz didn't realize how hungry he was, attacking the food, "That was a great cook, and the cornbread hit the spot."

"We have a good plan, boss. We'll get her back," Nester said, trying to assure him.

"Yeah, because I'm not leaving until I have her back in my arms where she belongs. I will take that place apart piece by piece."

"You're not alone, Cruz. We got your back. She is one of us now. They had no right to take her."

"You know, all I could do was think about what Mr. Lee said; someone with big money and power did this… who do we know has that kind of money and power.

"Mary… Mary's husband has the money and power."

"No, you're wrong, he has the money, but she has the power. She uses it very skillfully."

"Ug nasty…"

"You got that right." The siren alerted them trouble was coming. Everyone rushed to the top of the deck with their weapons in hand. Pablo pointed in the direction where a small vessel was approaching them at full speed. They didn't seem to make any attempt to stop, slowing down and flood lights brazen. Two half-naked women stood on the deck waving a white flag. They started to dance provocatively and waved, flashing their breast.

"They were decoys. Someone's coming from behind," Cruz said as they positioned themselves for an attack. Two other men were quietly making their way onto the yacht.

Skillfully they managed their ropes and weapons as if they had done this a million times. The women continued their exhibition, trying to keep the attention on them, but Cruz's men were not impressed by the women and stood their ground.

Cruz and Ruben waited in the shadows patiently until the two men stretched their legs over the side. They high-fived each other as they pulled out their knives, ready to take over the vessel. All they heard was a click as Cruz and Ruben carefully pushed their high-power weapons against their temples.

"Drop it, you piece of shit! You are trespassing, and I am trigger-happy. I will splatter your brain all over the place!" Cruz urged the younger man. They may have been father and son.

"Cruz, with one bullet, I can blow both their brains out; just give me the order."

"Let's get the others on board," Cruz and Ruben roughly ushered the two men to the stern.

"I told you this was a mistake," the older man argued.

"Shut up!"

"When I want you to talk, I'll ask you, so shut the hell up!" Cruz yelled. Ruben got on the loudspeaker. "We have your friends. Now you have a few choices. You can come aboard quietly. Two, we can kill your friends and blow your asses out of the water or… I think you ran out of choices."

"How many," Cruz urged the older man.

"I ain't telling you nothing," they must have been at sea for a while. Their teeth were green, and their complexion was dry and leathery from the sun. "You got to the count of three, you son-of-a-bitch, and your brains will be part of my deck," Cruz pushed the gun hard against his temple.

"One… two…" he pushed the gun against his head.

"Alright, six, there's two more." the man pissed himself. Cruz shouted out orders.

"Get those bastards on board. We'll hold court to decide what we will do with them."

"The women came on board kicking and screaming, but the teenagers didn't make any fuss. They were all the same, weather-beaten missing teeth, and angry. They were taken below to a holding area tightly bound with weapons drawn on them at all times.

"So, who are you, and why were you trying to commandeer my vessel," Cruz said, lighting up some cannabis. "Somebody better say something, or this is going to be a long night, and I've got nothing but time."

"I think this is the leader," Ruben pulled the young man by his musty shirt. "God, you stink like shit… are you the brains of this operation," Ruben pushed him back down and pointed his gun at his head.

"I'm in charge… this is my family. We do what we have to do to survive," the older man cried, afraid they would kill his family.

"Oh yeah, then how about working hard to make a living instead of killing people," Ruben implied.

"They wouldn't give up the goods, so we… fought them, and they lost… it's the way things are," he answered sarcastically.

"Well, I guess the tables are turned now. You lost…" Cruz closed the distance between them.

"What are you going to do with us," cried the younger woman.

Cruz crouched down to look her in the face. "We're going to extend you the same mercy you gave to the people you left dead in the water; we saw the child's body. So, you tell me why we should treat you any differently," he stood up. "Well, I hope you are comfortable. This is where you will spend the night with my good friend, trigger-happy

Harry. He'll be watching over you." Harry was like a statue holding his rifle in place.

"Tomorrow, we'll let you know what we're going to do with your sorry asses. Let's tie them to the wall." The women began to struggle as Pablo slammed them against the wall. Harry and Pablo took turns guarding the prisoners for the night.

The ship Tressa was docked in a private docking station. It was a long exhausting trip that seen to go on forever. No matter what she ate or drank, her stomach was not reacting well to the food. When they reached the palace, they carried her under protest, too weak to fight the six men who tried their best not to touch her in those prohibited places so as not to dishonor her. She was ushered into a very beautiful room, just like her cabin. The suite was splendidly decorated with beautiful rich green, gold, and red colors. The bed was a double king with beautiful sheer curtains draped around it. Again, masses of pillows of different sizes lay carefully along the walls, and a large round glass table by the open panel doors led into a large terrace and swimming pool.

Tressa's stomach was raging. She would get bouts of pain and sometimes puke her guts out. Servants paraded in with dishes of fruits and drinks. The large glass panel doors let in just enough breeze to keep her comfortable. A few hours later, Batula came to visit dressed like a queen. Her eyes were made up, and the red silk dress gave her cheeks a beautiful glow.

"Batula, I didn't recognize you at first." Batula embraced her and motioned her to sit down at the table.

"I have a confession to make… if you hate me, I understand. But please hear me out before you… decide you don't want anything to do with me… I have it coming. My name is Zarya. I have been betrothed to Prince Diya-al-Din since I was four years old. We are not only betrothed but also childhood playmates. My father and the previous King were very good friends. My father was and still is the physician at court."

"But if he's betrothed to you, why am I here? I understand they can have multiple wives, but bringing me here is crazy."

"Please don't judge us too harshly. We are supposed to be married in two months. You would be wife number one; therefore, you would be queen if his brother King Amir-Al-Mirza died. I would be the second wife with little say-so, so you see how important it was for me to be the first wife."

"I'm not following you, Zarya. What does this have to do with me? I'm not marrying the prince under any circumstances."

"I know that now, but at the time when I heard of the plan to bring you here, it was devastating to me… please forgive me, Miss Tressa; it was I who made you sick. I was riddled with jealousy," she started to cry. "All my life, I was told I would be the first wife. I trained with the best to someday be queen, and then you… you were bought in and ruined everything I ever dreamed of. All my hopes were gone.

I begged my father to allow me to go with him as your servant," she put her head down. "I am ashamed, Miss Tressa; I let my feelings almost commit murder," she began to sob. "This is not who I am. When I saw you lying there hopeless and how exquisite you are, I began to understand why you were so attractive to my Diya-al-Din. You look like a queen, and I couldn't deny the world someone, as amazing as you." Tressa looked at her and started to laugh. She laughed so loud tears rolled down her cheeks. Zarya sat wide-eyed confused.

"I'm sorry, Zarya. As crazy as this sounds, I understand. Please be my ally. I don't want your Prince, I have my own, and I miss him terribly."

"Then you forgive me… please say you do because I like you so much."

"I forgive you for trying to kill me… what else can I do."
They laughed.

"I will use all my powers to get you to your loved one. The prince is anxious to see you. Do not be afraid of him, for he is only a child. He is my age, but I see he has big hopes. You're an outsider, and he must wait thirty days before he beds you… however, he may not want to wait… you are very alluring, and his sexual needs may oversee our law. But I think you can handle him… I will sleep here with you in case his lust brings him to your bed tonight."

"He may find something else besides lust if he comes to my bed at night." A servant girl knocked softly, brought in water to wash their hands, and whispered in Zarya's ear. "Come, he is asking for you. I will wait for you outside his suite."

The prince had two guards standing outside his door. When she arrived, the guards lowered their heads, trying hard not to look at her. They opened the double doors into a room fit for a King with massive columns and expensive décor everywhere.

"Ah, my beauty, we meet at last," he welcomed her holding her hands in his. "You have no idea how long it's been for us to finally meet. Please have a seat." He motioned to the servants to pour some wine. The prince was very young; he was tall, thin, with not a single hair on his face but a dusted mustache.

"I wish I could say the same, Prince Diya-al-Din, but I was bought here against my will and wish to be returned to my home."

"I knew you would say that, Miss Beauty. I hope that you will give me a chance to win your love. I will treat you like a queen. All you have to do is ask for anything. Whatever you want, it will be placed at your feet," Tressa tried not to laugh. He was so young, and she didn't want to crush his spirit.

"Prince Diya-al-Din I am an American citizen. Our countries are not on the greatest terms. You are jeopardizing your relationship over this. Where is the King? Does he know about this?"

"Ah, my brother the King is on pilgrimage. He is not expected for a month. By that time, we should be married and hopefully expecting our first son." Tressa was stunned by his naivety.

"Prince, I am not going to marry you… I am promised to another and have had many steamy sexual encounters with him. I love him… he is a man, big and strong we were together the night before I was taken. I could be carrying his child right now," the prince was not moved. It was as if he didn't even hear her.

"Miss Beauty," she interrupts him.

"Prince Diya-al-Din, you do realize you have the wrong person. I am not Black Beauty; she is my sister… so you see, it was all an innocent mistake. Now, if you let me go on my way, this can all be forgotten," his eyes turn big as saucers.

"Your sister? But are you not the one in these pictures?" He showed her the blow-ups of her pictures taken in the motel.

"Yes, that is I … but the fighter is my twin sister Yadira… we're identical twins. I'm Tressa."

"Oh my…" he took a deep breath.

"Beautiful twins… side by side… how delightful could that be."

Tressa stood up abruptly, "Now hold on… we are not your playthings. Maybe that's how you treat your women here, but we are American women, and you're pissing me off."

"Please, Miss Tressa, you should be honored. You are signaled out to be part of this royal family… why are you so angry."

"Angry… I'm beyond anger. I demand you call the US ambassador; I am being kept here against my will."

"Please, Miss Tressa, there is no need to involve anyone else in these matters. I assure you that after a while, you will begin to enjoy me as much as I'm going to enjoy you."

"You're a boy. I've been with a man, a big strong man. I doubt you can do anything for me," She shouted at him.

"Please, Miss Tressa, do not let my youth misguide you. I have been schooled in the art of lovemaking for many years, and I can assure you I can please you as well as your… other lover. Once we have been together, you will forget about the other… man."

"I seriously doubt that. Please don't be offended if I leave," she walked towards the doors, and he followed and blocked her exit.

"I have not permitted you to leave."

"And I'm not asking, so please, I'm trying to be nice; get out of my way."

"Miss Tressa, you are so beautiful. The color of your hair and eyes brings back memories of my people. You are a jewel. My people will worship you like a goddess. Even with all the anger inside, I cannot resist wanting to hold you," he tried to embrace her, but she pushed him away.

"Prince Diya-al-Din, please don't add rape to the charges already against you. I am not feeling well, and at this moment, I am ready to puke all over you, so please stand aside."

He grabbed her hand, "I understand, my sweet. I know this journey was hard on you. I will come to you soon," he kissed her hand.

"I was drugged and almost died. Prince, all because of your lust…" she opened the door and found Zarya waiting at the end of the hall.

"How did it go," Zarya has a hard time keeping up with her.

"He's impossible. I couldn't get through to him. He didn't hear a word I said. What part of no is so hard to understand?"

"Yes, I understand when he was making preparations and negotiating about you. My father tried to get him to rethink his actions, but he would not listen to reason. However, I heard from some of the servants that the King was on his way. He received a message from your ambassador and is on his way to clear up the matter."

"That's wonderful news; maybe he can talk some sense into his head. I want to go home. I don't feel well."

"He is older and much more rational and hates scandals and international problems."

"At last, maybe he could see the huge mistake this is. I don't want your man Zarya, and I don't want to be queen."

Meanwhile, Cruz allowed the prisoners to clean themselves up and eat. He and Ruben stayed up most of the night, trying to figure out what to do with them. The prisoners were all frightened, looking at Harry for sympathy, but Harry just gave them a cold stare. Ruben and Pablo lined them on deck with their hands tied behind their backs. In the sunlight, they were even more frightening.

"Well, I talked it over with my boss, and we decided to set you free," they smiled at each other.

"I don't know why he didn't go with my idea," Pablo announced casually, "a firing squad would have been faster, and it's what they deserve, bastards."

"Please, we've learned our lesson; no more piracy for us, I swear," the older man begged.

"Yeah, like I believe that... we have decided to free you all on the small island of Mort. It has plenty of water and food. However, you have to make friends with the natives."

"We can do that. We can be very friendly," they all agreed.

"It's your necks. I wanted to do the human thing. Those cannibals may not be as friendly and hospitable as we were," Pablo was trying not to smile.

"Cannibals, now wait a minute, you can't leave us there; that's criminal," the younger man whined, panic-stricken.

"You should have thought about that before you started your life of crime and killing people… don't worry, we'll give you a knife. You can use it for one, to defend yourselves, or two, to build a raft and get off the island before they smell you and want a late snack." Ruben added "other than that, you're shit out of luck… let's get them off our vessel they are stinking up the place."

Cruz was on the radio talking to Tajo when Ruben walked in laughing. "Listen, take good care of Tressa's sister. I don't want her getting on my case because something happened to her later brother."

"I got this, brother, she is a pain in my ass, but I can handle her, no problem. Over and out."

"Is everything okay?" Ruben asked.

"Yeah, apparently, Tressa's sister stowaway on Tajo's yacht, and he's not too happy about it."

"I would be pissed too. She can't be no more than fourteen. Tressa said her parents were separated for ten years, and they had more children after that."

"Man, what does that remind you… you know he has this magnet for young chicks, you know Nina and her stupid little friends all have a crush on Tajo."

"How can I forget… my poor brother? So how did it go with those assholes?"

"It went well; Pablo said they were crying when they kicked them out of the boats. Wait until they find out the island is deserted."

"Serves them right for killing those people. I hope they rot on that island. We have to get back on course."

"Yip, we should be docking in three days."

"I can't wait to get her safe."

Tressa continued to have bad headaches, and once in a while, she would throw up. Zarya continued to apologize. "My father said it should be out of your system by tomorrow. I am so sorry."

"I'm tired. I need to rest. I am going to sleep on this side of the bed… if it is alright with you." she laughed.

"This bed is so big it can sleep ten people. I can't keep my eyes open, Zarya."

Zarya kept the two panels open to get some nice cool air flowing through the room. She watched as Tressa slept soundly. She was so beautiful it was only natural for men to lust after her brown eye beauty.

The room was pitch-black when Zarya felt a pair of hands reaching under the covers for her. She screamed and slapped him in the face. When she reached for the light, it was the prince's surprised face she had slapped. He was surprised to see Zarya instead of Tressa.

"Diya… how dare you come into a ladies' room like a thief," she jumped all over him "wait until your mother hears about this."

"I'm sorry… I came to see Miss Tressa… please don't tell my mother."

"Shame on you, Diya… get out!" she pushed him towards the door. Tressa laughed at the scene he was on his knees, begging her not to tell his mother.

"This is pure comedy… I couldn't write this if I tried," the two stood in the middle of the room, screaming at each other.

"What are you doing here? This is not your place," he rubbed his face from where she slapped him.

"Miss Tressa asked me to stay with her, and I'm glad I did… you sneak… keep it in your pants."

"What do you know? You're just a girl."

"And you're just a young boy lusting after a woman… go Diya, you've already made a fool of yourself tonight." The prince left reluctantly.

"Bravo! Now that's entertainment." They both laughed.

"Do you see what a child he really is?"

"How did he manage to get me here?"

"Money can buy you anything, and I believe from the talk I heard that he had help from the other side. I believe it was a very powerful woman. She made way for us to dock in private… it was a very scary place."

"Did you get a look at her?"

"I saw her from afar. She was very attractive, loud, and vulgar. Do you know her?"

"Unfortunately, I would love to forget her. Zarya, do you think we'll get another visit from the prince tonight?"

"I don't think so, he knows I'm here, and I will not change it."

The next morning Tressa was feeling a lot better. Zarya opened the window panel doors to let the sun in. The pool looked inviting as she stooped down, feeling the silky water with her hands.

"Tressa, would you like to go for a swim? I can get you something to wear,"

"The water does look tempting… I think I would like that." Zarya bought her a few bathing suits for her to try on. The pink bikini fit her like a glove. The top enhanced her full breast.

"Wow, if I were a man, I would go crazy with lust too. You look fabulous,"

Tressa jumped in the soothing water. The silkiness felt wonderful as she swam a few laps back and forth. "Why don't you join me," she called to Zarya.

"I must go and see about the events of the day. I have some towels for you. Relax, I won't be long… you enjoy your swim." Tressa welcomed the warmth of the morning sun; she laid on a water mattress allowing the gentle motion to rock her back and forth.

The King had breakfast out on his terrace when he looked down and saw Tressa in the pool below. "Musa, bring me my binoculars…" he smiled as he focused on Tressa's body, "Musa, is that Black Beauty?" His servant agreed.

"Hum, no wonder my brother took such a chance… Musa, I shall wear my finest to meet my lovely guest. Oh, and sent in my barber. I must look my best. Inform my guest that I shall be expecting her in two hours… I shall enjoy this meeting greatly."

He couldn't take his eyes off the brown beauty as the water glimmered off her full breast. He focused on her beautiful full lips and the curve of her delicate neck. He watched her long black hair cascade down her back, resting below her wonderfully shaped firm hinny. The King felt a stirring in his groin as he let the lens zero in on her shapely thighs and beautiful legs.

Tressa let the water drift her into a dream world. She dreamt Cruz was waiting for her, and they were riding into the outland together, making love under a tree and planning their wedding. Tressa was annoyed when Zarya woke her up abruptly. "Miss Tressa, please come quickly; the King has summoned you."

"The King is here?"

"Yes, and you can't keep him waiting," Zarya laid out Tressa's outfit. A sheer white wrap with a gold sash and a pair of white and gold high-heel sandals.

"Isn't this a little too much? You can see my breast. This is very low cut."

"I'm sorry you are a little bigger than most of the women here. I'm sure he will not mind."

"Zarya, I want to talk reason with him, not seduce him."

"The King loves beautiful things and beautiful people… his two wives always look wonderfully dressed when they are in his presence. Come and sit while I do your hair. You should wear it down naturally. It is beautiful the way it falls in soft curls. Your makeup must be flawless… when we go before the King, it is customary to look your best." Zarya applied her makeup with precision. All that was left was the screening veil that wrapped around her hair. Zarya stepped back to admire her creation.

"You look like a goddess. Let me bow to you," Tressa's stomach started to turn again. I will walk you to his Highness's Suites," Zarya was more nervous than she was, "I've only been in his Highness' presence twice. Okay, are you ready?"

"I'm ready. Wish me luck," When Zarya opened the door, Musa was waiting to bring Tressa to the King. Musa led her down a bunch of hallways. The further they walked, the more elegant the furnishing was up the stairs and down another hallway. They stopped in front of huge double doors. When the guards opened the doors… she couldn't believe the elegance and the richness when she entered the oversize rooms. The King sat on the terrace. He stood up when she walked into the room. "My eyes have not gazed upon such beauty," he rubbed the hair on his chin. She was not expecting such a young King. He was tall and well-built, with brilliant green eyes, thick eyelashes, and a well-groomed goatee. She held her breath. He was a stunning man.

"At last, we meet Black Beauty…" he kissed her hand, "Musa pours Miss Beauty some wine. This is truly an honor. Come sit with me." Tressa didn't know how to address him. He had totally taken her by surprise. He couldn't take his eyes off her. She knew she was in trouble when he licked his lips seductively and saw the spark of lust in his eyes.

"Your pictures do not do you justice, my sweet… I am one of your greatest fans, Black Beauty."

"Please, your Highness, you are confusing me with someone else. Black Beauty is my sister…"

He was surprised. "There are two of you. Are you not the woman in the pictures," he showed her the pictures from the hotel naked as the day she was born.

"That is me, but my sister is Black Beauty. We are twins. My name is Tressa, so you see… your brother has the wrong person."

"I believe he has the right person. The woman in the picture is the one he fell for, and I can see why." She tries to conceal her disappointment, "come walk in the garden with me. It is one of my favorite places when I visit this palace… it was my mother's masterpiece." There were flowers and plants of all colors and shapes. They stopped by a half wall that separated the garden and the terrace.

"Here, that is where I laid eyes on one of the most beautiful women I have ever seen," he pointed to the pool where she had swum a few hours ago. He comes closer to her. His nearness makes her uncomfortable. "I couldn't take my eyes off of you, Tressa," his lips came closer to her face; she could feel his breath against her cheek.

"Your Majesty, please, you must release me. I am promised to someone else."

He was not moved. "Tressa," he whispered, "How can I let you go when you belong here… with me. I felt it when I laid eyes on you. The stirring in my loins is no mistake, not for just lust."

Tressa was stunned. "Your Majesty, I am an American who was ripped from the man she loves. I demand to see the US Ambassador."

"I have spoken to your ambassador, but I am King, and this is my empire… I do as I please, Tressa, and you are what

I want." He played with her hair, "Your hair is like silk. And your beautiful brown skin is so soft and smooth," he couldn't resist touching her shoulder, "You will be my Queen," he kissed her should and neck." she pulled away from him.

"You have a Queen… in fact, you have two wives… can a King have two Queens?"

He pulled her close to him, holding her firmly by her waist. "I am King; I can release my wives if you agree to be my wife and my Queen," he grabbed her and kissed her passionately. She could feel his manhood pressing against her thigh and pushed him slightly, needing air.

"Majesty, I came to speak some sense into this whole situation."

"How can I make sense of anything when I have you so close," he pulled her roughly, pressing her closer, kissing her again, making his intentions known to her.

"Please, Majesty, I'm getting sick. If you don't want me to puke on you, let go of me right now," he released her watching her go pale. She rushed to the closest bush to throw up.

"Are you ill, my Queen?"

"I was drugged and poisoned; the drug is still in my system." He caught her before she fainted.

Musa was surprised to see the king carrying Tressa and laying her on his bed, "What happened, Majesty?" He asked.

"She's sick, have someone take her to her room," he caressed the side of her face. "What a tragedy. This is what we looked like many years ago. Look at her, Musa. She will bring color back to our people."

"But, Majesty, there is no guarantee."

"I have no doubt that one of her offspring will produce an heir. It starts with a woman like this one who possesses such beauty." He pushed her hair away from her cheek. "I will make her mine Musa; she will be my greatest conquest."

Chapter 10: The Fight

King Amir-Al-Mirza and his younger brother argued bitterly about Tressa. There was no compromising with the King.

"You cannot give her back. She is mine… I have paid a great price to bring her here," the prince whined.

"Our relationship with America is weak. You have created a scandal Diya-al-Din and an international breakdown of our two countries," bellowed King Abdul–Jabbar.

"Since when do you care about the Americans? I will marry Tressa. She will be my wife."

The King towered over his younger brother. "You will do as I say, Diya, you are scheduled to marry Zarya, and you will marry her as planned. Leave the matter of Miss Tressa to me. I will deal with the consequence you have put us in."

"You are sending me away; you cannot keep her from me."

"Little brother, you forget that I am King; you will do as I say… your servants are packing your things as we speak… you will leave within the hour." Prince Diya-al-Din stomped his feet before he fled out of the King's quarters. King Amir-Al-Mirza smiled at his progress. He wanted his brother out of the picture if he was to woo Tressa. Though he didn't foresee him as the competition, he would have been in the way.

Tressa woke up back in her quarters. Zarya was close by with pain medication for the massive headache.

"What happened? I saw the King carrying you, which was very unusual."

She got up abruptly. "Your sensible King... couldn't keep his hands off me... he kept kissing me. Luckily I got sick, and well, here I am. God, what is wrong with these men? Why can't I have a decent conversation without them trying to molest me."

"Do not judge them so harshly. They see you, and they remember our ancestors. We were once people of color, all beautiful shades of brown. Our eyes were like yours, dark and mysterious. Your color makes them want what once belonged to us and what they long to be once again. They believe they can restore that by probably having children with you... children of color."

"But my color genes don't come from my mother. It was my father and great-grandmother, and she was from her father, so there's no guarantee I will have children of color. And there hasn't been a male born yet that I know of."

"The world is changing, Miss Tressa; you may well be the first woman to bore a son with the great markings… the color of great Kings and Queens."

"Zarya, I just want to go home… make love to Cruz and see my family, ride my horse, get married and have a lot of sex with my man."

"The King has commanded you to eat dinner with him tonight…"

"I can't… I don't have the strength to deal with him… it takes all my control not to hit him. If I do, it would be my life… so all I can do is push him away. Do you know he said he would release the other Queen so he can marry me and make me Queen… is that crazy?"

"That is not good, Tressa. You will surely die. I know the Queen. She is very jealous. When he married his second wife, it was a terrible ordeal. The King put them side by side until they came to terms with the situation. You are an outsider who insults them as women of power."

"I wish I knew what to do… if I could only keep my stomach from turning and my head from pounding, I could think. Zarya, what would happen if I refused to dine with the King?"

"He would take it out on the servants, royalty is very spoiling, and even though he is a young King and new to the throne, he still demands respect." Tressa paced around the room, knowing the evening would be a repeat of this morning. She sat outside, trying to wrap her head around what was happening. If only she could get the word out to the agency about where she was. The King had seven other palaces, and she didn't know which one they had her captive. She touched the ring Cruz had given her; the pink pear-shaped stone sparkled on her finger. "How am I ever going to get back to you, my love," she said to herself. Now she had a lustful King, a crazed Prince, and soon two very pissed-off wives against her.

Cruz had no trouble docking at the port. After showing them the proper documentation and paying a fee, they were more than accommodating. Drew had been waiting patiently at one of the Inns that faced the docking station. It was a dive, but he could watch as boats came and went out. When The Latin Queen docked, Drew wrapped himself in the native cloak and turban and headed towards the docks. The lights were dim, but he could make out the beautiful streamlined Yacht. Tressa was his dear friend he had known for years, and he would do anything for her.

"Cruz, a man named Drew is asking permission to come on board," Harry notified him.

"He's here already? Please bring him on board."

He was tanned from the sun. "Cruz, my man, I've been waiting for you," he extends his hand to Ruben.

"This is Cruz…" Drew looked up to Cruz, who towered over him.

"Sorry… I wasn't expecting a… tall guy with… a built… like you… I'm sorry. I'll explain later."

"Don't worry about it. Is there any news… do you know where she is?" Cruz asked, anxious.

"Yes, my friends, I know exactly where she is down to the suite where they are holding her."

"Well, I thank you for your help. Lee said you were the best… can we offer you something to drink," Cruz said, smiling for the first time since they left.

"Yes, my friend, I am a little parched," Ruben poured his wine as the three sat down to see their plan.

"Have you seen her, and is she alright," Cruz wanted so much information at once.

"As far as I know, she is well, for now, but there is much to tell. According to idol gossip, the prince who paid so much money to smuggle her here has been sent away by his older brother, the King. It seems that when the King laid eyes on the lovely Tressa, he decided to risk everything and keep her for himself."

"You got to be kidding me? How do you know all this? Have you been to the palace?"

"I don't have to be at the palace to know what's going on. The gossip train runs through here rather quickly. My friend, when you have so many women who are lonely and desperate for male companionship, it's very easy to get all the information you want… they are very willing, and Black Beauty is a celebrity. News traveled very fast that Black Beauty was in town, AKA Tressa."

"I'm confused… who is this Black Beauty… and what does she have to do with Tressa," Ruben asked.

"Why would they think Black Beauty is Tressa?"

Drew was surprised, "How long have you and Tressa been together?"

"We were together five months."

Drew laughed, "Oh my, have you been kept in the dark? Apparently, you have been sleeping with a mystery woman. Didn't Tressa tell you she had a sister?"

"Yeah, so what… she said she had a younger sister."

"Um, classic… Tressa's younger sister is 5 minutes younger than her. They are identical twins right down to the beauty mark on those fine asses."

"Holy shit… you're kidding me. Why didn't she tell me? Why would she keep that a secret." Cruz asked, amazed.

"Believe me, it was not intentional… all their lives, they got so much unwanted attention, and everyone wanted to put the twins in this cookie-cutter mold. They grew up resenting anything that had to do with their identity, that's why Tressa would say she had a younger sister, and Yadira would say she had an older sister. It was a joke between them, and a lot of people were the brunt of that joke. Black Beauty is Yadira, and that's why they were very confused. But the girl in the pictures is Tressa. On her last mission, her identity was compromised by a peeping tom, some young punk taking pictures. He followed her to her room, cracked open the bedroom window, and got our girl in all her wonderful glory."

"How do you know about the beauty mark on her behind," Cruz asked, crossing his arms seriously.

"Hey, big guy… let me explain myself. You know, when you're young, we do stupid shit; you remember when we were young? I went to school with the hottie twins. That's what we called them, actually Logan and I. Tressa and I came from the same school and went through the academy together. The girls were always athletic, so a few friends got together one day and decided it would be cute to poke a hole in the girl's locker room. And there they were, the two hottest girls in school history, in the buff, anyway that's how we found out about the beauty mark, and boy did we get in trouble."

"Well, I can't say I wouldn't have done the same thing," they laughed.

"So, here's the deal, she is at the main palace, which is a day's ride from here. Tomorrow morning, we need to get some supplies and clothes so you can fit in. I have paperwork saying that you are merchants looking for a place to open a restaurant. I can only take one other person. Too many of us will arouse suspicion that we will go in and sneak her out."

"So, we're going to go in and take her back… that easy?" Cruz questioned his plan.

"I have connections, my friend. The only thing that would change our plan is if he…he, you know… beds her."

"You're kidding me… I will kill him," Cruz's anger showed on his face.

"I understand your anger, but he is the King. He will force himself on her, and who will question it? Look, when you first met Tressa, what did you do?"

"Our situation was complicated."

"Complicated… brother, all I'm asking you is, did you get hard."

"Yeah, and I forced myself on her… I wanted her," he looked down. "It's not something I'm proud of, but I didn't know who she was."

"I understand, Cruz. You just have to look at her and know she is desirable. We, men, are horny all the time; by their law, they are supposed to wait thirty days but think about it… if you were King, would you wait?"

"I will kill him as sure as you're sitting here drinking my wine. I will put a knife through that prick's heart."

"I know you're angry, but please don't blame her if he rapes her… it happens."

"I don't want to think about that… I just… want to hold her and make sure she's alright."

"Another thing… I don't think you know this, but I spoke with Lee yesterday. They caught the people who drugged her and smuggled her onto the prince's vessel. The drug they used was very powerful and lethal. If left untreated, she can die… it works like a virus in the system, and if she hadn't been treated, it would shut down her major organs, and she'll die."

"This is a lot to take in, my man. How am I supposed to deal with all this?"

"One thing at a time, my friend. She has time. The good thing is the poison works slowly, so as soon as we get her, a physician is waiting with an antidote at the American embassy. Don't worry, Cruz, we'll get our fine lady back, trust me…"

"You're all I have right now; I have no other choice but to trust you."

"Good then. Will have her back before the end of the week."

Cruz went back to his room and banged his fist into the wall. He remembered the last time they were together and how much he wanted her to stay with him. He grabbed the nightgown she left in case he missed her. It still smelled like her; he pressed it against his face, closed his eyes, and envisioned those sweet moments they spent before she left. He picked something, slamming it across the room and into the wall. A knock interrupts his thoughts.

"Cruz, may I come in," Ruben asked. He knew his mental state.

"Sure, come in," He could tell Cruz was upset.

"Hey buddy, I know what you're thinking, and Drew is right. Think about her feelings if she's forced and how she's going to react if she sees you with a murderous attitude," he took a deep breath.

"I'll be okay, Ruben. Once I know she is not harmed, I can put everything else out of my mind… I just wish I had five minutes alone with the bastard. I'd snap his neck… but I'll be alright. Once we're on our way tomorrow, I'll be fine. In the meantime, I need you to get with my brother and have him stand back. I don't want him caught in the crossfire if we encounter any trouble. Just tell him that we have located her and we're on the way to retrieve her… please don't give him any details. I'm taking Harry with me because I need a levelheaded person to stay here and run things while I'm away. I trust you and know you know how to handle yourself."

"Thanks. I appreciate your confidence in me. You try to get some rest. You have a long day tomorrow."

Zarya helped Tressa dress for dinner, she wore a rose color dress that didn't do much to hide her curvy body, and the neckline was so low she was afraid her breast would pop out any minute. "I can't wear this. Everything is showing everywhere," she tried to pull the dress up. "How am I going to fend him off if my dress is busting at the seam."

"I'm sorry, Tressa; this is the biggest dress I could find."

"I just won't go, I know he's going to try something, and I can't assault the King, and he's so damn handsome."

"Yes, he is very handsome. He works out every day. But you must go. He has summoned you… look, I have this shawl. Drape it around your shoulders… I have sent word to the Queen… I should receive a response tonight, so cross your fingers, and please be careful."

Musa knocked on the door of her suite to escort her to the King. He wore a sad look on his face knowing what the night would bring. She hesitated halfway. "Musa, I know he is your master, but I cannot do this with him."

He nodded, "Miss Beauty, if I may address you that way. I have served my Lord for many years. He is a good master. Please understand; that you are not just an ordinary woman to him. You represent the future."

"But Musa, I can't lay with him. I belong to another."

His eyebrows go up, surprised, "I see. I imagine he already knows this. Hum, that creates a problem for you. I know this, Miss Beauty; my master is used to having women flaunt themselves at him. No woman has ever challenged him. He does not take challenges well, especially from…a female. Challenge him with your reproaches. He would not know how to handle it."

"Thank you, Musa. I appreciate your help."

The light was dim, and the room had a scent of spice in the air. The King was dressed splendidly in Black and silver.

"You take my breath away, Tressa. You get more beautiful every time I see you. Come and sit. I had the cook make special American food. I know you would love it."

Tressa ate very little. Her stomach was still giving her trouble. The King spoke about himself. However, her mind wandered to another place. She tried so hard not to cry in front of the King, but all her emotions were coming to the surface. By the look on his face, she knew what was coming next. "Come, my sweet, drink some wine. The night is young and made for lovers."

Musa had the dinner dishes replaced with another set of clean wine glasses and opened another imported bottle of wine. He poured her another drink. "You ate very little, my Queen."

"I'm not feeling well. Remember what happened earlier."

"Well, tonight it is just the two of us, you and I… come and sit outside. The cool air will do you some good." He led her by the hand outside by the waterfalls. "Tressa, I will not mix words with you. I want you tonight; let us make sweet passionate love, my sweet." Tressa shook her head no; he pulled her off her feet into his arms. "I command it," he kissed her with great passion, holding her so tight she could hardly breathe.

"Your Highness, I'm turning blue." he picked her up and carried her to his bed. She wiggled to free herself from him, but he was too strong.

"Tressa, I can make you a happy woman. Please let me love you. Let me lose myself in your arms, my sweet," he kissed her, forcing her lips open. The more she resisted, the more excited he became. He used his leg to spread hers, pressing himself against her; his lips caressed her breast.

"Would you take me by force… is this the way a man behaves? You dishonor me," She managed to turn her face

"It is not my intention Tressa."

"You dishonor me if you take me by force… is this the only way you can bed a woman?" The King stopped and rolled off her. He sat by the edge of the bed, frustrated as Tressa tried to catch her breath.

"This is not how I behave towards women, Tressa, because I don't have to force them. They come willingly," he managed to say.

"Why do you treat me so disrespectfully? Is it because I'm American? You can take what you want from me, and I'm supposed to be grateful." he got up and poured himself another glass of wine.

"Tressa, I'm sorry you feel that way," he said angrily. She left the bed and stood by the door in front of the waterfalls trying to catch a whiff of cool air. He cannot help but watch her in the moonlight, the way it made her glow."Tressa, I can't help the way I feel."

"But you don't care how I feel… I promise to another, my heart belongs to him."

"I can make you forget him if you let me," he said, frustrated.

"He was my first… please just let me go," she pleaded.

"I cannot let you go, Tressa, but I want a willing lover." She was not getting through to him.

"I tell you what, Tressa, I'm a reasonable man. I have been known to make certain wagers in the past…I will make a deal with you. Can you fight like your sister?"

"We have similar styles of fighting. Why?"

He smiled at her wickedly, "If you can beat my champion... I will set you free, but if she wins... you stay with me and be a willing lover. I will do whatever it takes to keep you, my love, no woman comes close to your beauty, and I shall be the envy of all men. There will be images of you everywhere. Do you agree to my terms?"

Tressa was stunned, "I have to fight my way out, and if I decline your offer."

"Then tomorrow, you will be mine. Willing or not... one way or another, I will have you, Tressa. I am willing to set my wives aside to make you Queen. You should be honored, my sweet."

"Is it not your custom to wait thirty days to bed an outsider," she said, trying to buy some time.

"My love, I am King. I do what I wish. And my wish is to be deeply in your arms and my seed in your belly. I am a masterful lover, you will not regret opening yourself to me, and I shall be your servant between these walls." He pulled her, pinning her against the wall. Tressa puts her hands between them. "This is not an easy decision for me, letting you walk out of here without tasting your sweetness, making you regret you gave yourself to another." Tressa struggled against his advances, his lips kissing her neck and breast, prying her legs apart, wanting Tressa, regardless of her feeling.

"Stop," she tried to push him away, trying to breathe, "please, I can't live with myself if I can't come willingly." He stopped. Pulling away from her was not easy for him.

The King laughed, "Of all the women in the world, the one I want has morals. What is your answer."

"So, who is this champion you wish me to risk my life to fight?"

He kissed her tenderly, "I'm surprised at you, Tressa, working for an agency that confesses to knowing all sorts of international secrets. I'm amazed that you don't know that Rozalina Chernavin has been living in our country for the past two years. She was the only one your sister did not beat and is in exceptional shape. So, my future wife and Queen, do we have an agreement?"

Tressa felt her stomach that was still doing flips, "I believe I have no choice in the matter. Is there any other way I can convince you to let me go?"

King Jabba finished his drink. "I could say be my lover tonight, Tressa, and tomorrow I will set you free… but then that would be a lie. Because I have a feeling once I taste your essence, it would be almost impossible for me to let you go."

He kissed her neck, and she turned her face away from his attempt to kiss her. "I am a patient man to a point. I can't say for sure if I can wait thirty days until your next flow. Servants have a way of gossiping, but I tell you this… you will be with a child soon, and I wouldn't want controversy with my first-born son of color."

"Your Highness, you have an advantage over me, for I am not well, and Rozalina is a worthy opponent. You are a handsome and desirable man, but my love belongs to another, the King of my heart. I will take your offer. When do you foresee this event taking place?"

"Musa." He appeared out of the shadows. "Get me my publicist; get him out of bed. I don't care. Black Beauty has agreed to demonstrate her fighting abilities. I'm sure she will put on a great performance." Musa looked at Tressa strangely before he left.

"I'm sorry I have to promote you as Black Beauty. You have a big fan base," he held her hand to his lips. "So, my dark beauty, you have until the day after tomorrow to prepare."

"One day… you're giving me one day to prepare… how fair is that?"

He laughed, "I know I have the advantage, my love, but I have other matters to attend to, and your ambassador has been at my heel. The sooner I make you mine, the sooner I can get him to back off."

"You're Highness; at the least, give me a place to work out and practice."

"Sure, my love, I am not that unreasonable. We have a fully functional gym and workout department downstairs." he drew her into his arms."And since I will not call for you tomorrow, I want to remind you why I am so generous and understanding." He crushed her to him, kissing her feverously and burying his mouth in her breast. "Leave," he says in a low and sultry voice. "Leave before I change my mind."

Tressa was furious when she reached her room, screaming at the top of her lungs. "OH MY GOD, is this nightmare ever going to end."

Zarya came running out of the adjacent room to assist her.

"I gather it did not go well, but I did not expect you to come back at all," she said, surprised.

"Help me get out of this damn dress! I almost did it... I almost punched him. I had to insult him to get him to let me go. Now I'm involved in this fight for my freedom... he wants me to fight his champion."

"Oh no," Zarya cried, "Rozalina Chernavin is a brutal competitor."

Tressa smiled, "She's a puss," Zarya was shocked. "Rozalina is just a bully, and that's why people are afraid of her unless she has improved her skills are lacking."

"But your sister lost against her."

"Yadira didn't lose to her. It was a draw… and she was the reason my sister left the circuit. They wanted her to throw the fight. Her manager paid lots of money for Yadira to lose, but she refused, and they considered it a draw only because she held back."

"But that's terrible. Can you beat her… she's built like a man."

"My sister lost faith in the organization. I remember that day… father and I were in the locker room. When the fight was over, my sister punched out her manager and his bodyguard. That was the last time she stepped in the ring. My sister and I have similar styles of fighting. We both trained with the same instructors."

"I am glad to hear that because the crowds from my country are huge fight fans. They love a good match."

"Now, if I can only keep my stomach from doing flips."

"I will have my father look in on you, get some rest."

***

Cruz laughed when Drew pulled up in his vehicle, "What the hell is that?"

"What's wrong? These are the best wheels, man," Drew jumped out of his jeep.

"It looks like a pieced of shit," Cruz laughed.

"Hey, don't talk about my Suzy like that. She may look like shit on the outside, but she's all balls on the inside. Anyway, you don't want to bring attention to us. We must blend, my brother. However, it's probably going to be hard with your muscles in the way.

It was barely dawn when the three made their way toward the palace. They stopped only to eat and buy clothes that would help them blend with the rest of the people.

Once the sun was overhead, they had to make more frequent stops to rest and eat. "We can stop here to eat and rest, and this is the halfway mark… they know me, and here the food is very good," Drew said, paying someone to park his jeep. Cruz was curious about Drew's relationship with Tressa and their involvement.

"So, Drew, how close were you and Tressa?"

Drew smiled; he knew what he was getting at, "Relax, big guy, I had my heart set on her sister. Yadira was my kind of girl… she was hot, sassy, and drove me crazy. I had such a crush on her. The twins were like celebrities. Everyone wanted to hang out with them and be them, and of course, we all wanted… to at least get close enough to kiss them… but daddy had other ideas.”

“Well, do you blame him? I have a daughter, and I’ll be damn if I let some punk suck up on her.”

“Yeah, I understand, but that logic goes out the window when you’re a horny teenager. Yadira was the first girl I ever French kissed. Her father allowed the girls to attend a boy-girl party. A group of us were in the backyard playing games and eating; we all went to the same school, and everyone knew I was crazy about Yadira. I used to carve our names on just about every tree. Anyway, we were playing truth or dare, some stupid game. I was only there because she was, and I wanted to be close to her. They wore white tops and blue shorts, showing off their beautiful brown legs. We were only thirteen. She was taller than me and just started to fill out. So, there they were with their perky young budding breast. She is standing there looking mean as ever, arms crossed. My true question was how often I masturbate a day or dare kiss the girl of my dreams. So, I went for the kiss. I got in front of her, ready for my peck on the lips, when she grabbed me by my shirt and gave me the tongue lashing of my life.”

They roared with laughter. "I nearly pissed in my pants, everybody started laughing at me, I turned bright red, that girl scared me for life." they continue to laugh.

"Tressa never talks much about her childhood, and it concerns me because Yadira is on my brother's vessel."

Drew smiled, "Well, I hope he has some big balls because she's no joke. Tressa is the sweet one… I mean, I love her, and I think I'll always be in love with Yadira. However, my balls aren't big enough to handle that ball buster. Hell, she kicked her ex-fiancé through a storefront window and sent his ass right through it… landing in the street… headfirst all busted up and shit, then she throws the ring at him, walked right over his bleeding ass, and went on with her business."

"Damn, my poor brother. He's going to hate me."

"I doubt it… he's probably under her spill… he's probably carrying around the biggest boner for her. She's absolutely infectious… bold, and daring. On the other hand, Tressa was mysterious and scary to a point. She never let on about anything. For instance, no one but some close friends knew that when Yadira was sick, Tressa took her place in the arena."

"That's cheating," Cruz said.

"Well, yes and no, the audience paid good money to see a fight. People naturally assume that since she wasn't fighting, her sister was a better fighter… Tressa is one of those fighters that will play with their opponents. She lets you think you have the upper hand, and then she moves in for the kill. She humiliates her opponents, and she looks good doing it. I've seen her in action over a dozen times with both males and females, and if there is a person you want to go into battle by your side, that's Tressa. Now, on the other hand, my girl, she's a killer, has no mercy on you… when she's in that arena, she will beat you into the ground quickly."

"I should warn him. My brother is a hot-headed fool. Hum, on the other hand, he needs a ball buster. Women have come too easy for Tajo. He has this rebel Indian blood in him and, believe me, has women hanging from his shit all the time, fighting for him. Women, he doesn't even know, fighting to take his ass home with them."

"Well then, she's not for him. She is either first or not at all. Yadira doesn't play second fiddle to know one. She'll tell you upfront it's me or the highway. You ain't having it both ways."

Harry noticed unusual activities were going on outside the tavern. While they ate, people were running in and out constantly. "Hey, what's going on out there? Are they giving away something?" Harry asked; he couldn't understand the language.

"I'll go find out. You guys pay the bill. I'll be right back." There were over fifty people shouting numbers at one person, excited. Cruz and Harry finished eating and paid the bill before Drew sat back down.

"Is there something we should be worried about?" Cruz asked; Drew sucked down the last of his drink.

"No, nothing that concerns us… they are taking bets on a match."

"Oh, really, someone we know." Cruz was kidding.

"Actually, Black Beauty is fighting tomorrow night, aka Tressa… your woman."

Cruz almost choked on his drink, "Oh hell no, and this doesn't concern us. What kind of shit is that? Let's get the hell out of here and get my woman. I've got to get out of this damn place."

"Hey, don't worry… will be there sometime tonight."

***

Tressa looked at her engagement ring, she had to take it off, and it was killing her to do so. She put it by her bedside and covered it with the pink shawl she had worn the night before. The boxing gloves Zarya brought fit her perfectly.

"Tressa, I have your trainer ready for you... you look nice. Was the sports bra good enough? I had them all over the stores looking for the right size."

"It feels good, nice, and tight... can't have these babies going all over the place when you're fighting."

"I admire you, Tressa. You look so calm. I would be terrified if I had to go against Rozalina."

"Rozalina ain't shit. She's a bully like I said yesterday," Tressa wrapped her fingers. "If you bet against me, you'll lose your money."

"You are so sure of yourself; I don't understand."

"Zarya, I have been training with some of the best teachers since I was four. My sister and I practiced almost every single day until we were eighteen. If I can stand on my own against Master Lee Chang Sue, who came all the way from China to train the Quintanilla Twins, I can take on the Russian puss ass. My sister and I studied and trained with him for almost ten years... If I can't beat that wanna-be, then he did us a disservice. Master Lee Chang Sue worked us hard. We spent many a day after school, during the summers on weekends. When we could have been dating, we were in that dojo. No less than six hours a day. To be honest, I don't like her. She talked a lot of crap to my sister about the draw and beating her. My sister would have to slaughter her on the first round… that no-talent fool. Yadira told her that she would have a showdown if she ever met up with her. So, I can do it for her."

"I had no idea. Please forgive me for doubting your abilities. She is so big, and that is why so many will bet on that alone. The odds are against you, Tressa."

"That's what I'm counting on, especially the King," She smiled.

"Oh, I almost forgot to tell you… Queen Dikranouhi will be arriving today… she is Black Beauty's biggest fan and knows your situation. The King will not take another lover when the Queen is in court. She asked me if you would meet with her."

"I'll probably be in the training room all day; I need some weight training, and I am sparring with some boxers."

"She would not mind at all. She sounded very excited when I spoke to her."

"Sure, I would be honored."

The King waited for her outside the women's locker room. He looked so different in his dark blue sweat suit. Had he not spoken to her, she would have passed him by.

"So, my soon-to-be Queen, you look stylish in your workout clothes."

"And you look normal without your kingly clothes."

He laughed out loud, "I hope you slept well, my love?"

"Very well… thanks for asking."

He came closer to her, "I must confess I had a hard time falling asleep… I still had the taste of your sweet lips on mine; it took two bottles of wine to help me forget that I was a fool to let you leave last night. My body still aches for you, Tressa, and seeing you in that outfit arouses me even more."

"Majesty, I have a lot of work to do. You gave me such little time."

He pulled her to him by her arms, "You took your ring off," he grinned.

"I can't fight with it on."

"You may as well keep it off. You'll be in my bed soon enough, and I assure you he will be but a faded memory."

"I doubt that." He grabbed both her arms crushing her against his chest.

"Forget all this nonsense… come to me, my love; you will not regret it," he kissed her again, forcing her to submit to his will.

"Majesty," he was interrupted. He loosens his hold on her.

"This better be good for interrupting me," the messenger put his head down.

"Majesty… please forgive my intrusion… Queen Dikranouhi has arrived and is requesting an audience with you. She wants to meet the famous Black Beauty… she is a big fan." He smiled at Tressa.

"I will see her later. Right now, I do not wish to be disturbed." Tressa tried not to smile."The gossip train runs very quickly in these parts," he grabbed her again, forcefully pinning her against the wall. "This does not change anything… after the match, I will send her away, and you will be at my side to do as I please." He tried to kiss her, and she turned her head to avoid the force of his kisses. "Tressa, you reject me now. But soon, you will be begging me for kisses. That you can bet on," he grabbed her hair and kissed her, forcing her lips apart. She could feel his arousal mounting. When he let her go, she rubbed her arms to get the blood to circulate again. "One way or another, you will be mine; have fun trying to beat my champion," he walked away laughing.

Tressa worked out hard with the weights; ran five miles on the track… she waited for Hamden to help her with the heavy bag. Tressa took her time stretching every limb and ensuring she was warmed up properly to avoid injury. Hamden helped her bandage her hands before putting on her stretch gloves.

Rozalina towered over her, laughing. "Tressa Quintanilla, so we meet again. It's been a long time. But this time, I will have you where I want you instead of on the sidelines with your smart mouth. So now you're Black Beauty," she laughed out loud. Rozalina was a big strong woman with bright red hair. She had green eyes and a small scar above her eyebrow. Rozalina loved piercings and tattoos and wore them proudly.

"I see you finally found a home Rozalina. How much did your manager pay the King to let you stink up his country?" Hamden was surprised that Tressa stood to Rozalina; she was much bigger and scarier.

"I see you haven't lost your smart mouth."

"And you haven't lost your bright personality, and I can see your drones behind you, your crew of wannabe fighters. How much do you pay them to hang around you?"

"Don't hate Tressa. You may be pretending to be Black Beauty, but you ain't her, and you'll never be like her. You see, while you've been running around playing, I spy I've been perfecting my God-given talent. I'm in the best shape I ever was. So, when I beat you into the ground, Black Beauty's name and reputation will be finished."

Her intimidation did not move Tressa. She continued to kick and punch the long bag. "Oh, is that supposed to scare me," she hit the bag harder, "Are you working out here? Cause you're messing up the air."

"Funny, no, I have my own state-of-the-art gym... my place makes this look like a high school gym. You see, the King and I; we have this special connection... so when he told me to fight you, I couldn't wait."

"You're such a liar; you'd be shitting in your pants if Yadira was standing in front of you right now. You were always afraid of her." Tressa saw the change in Rozalina, turning pale at her statement.

"I... was never afraid of her... you're always running your big mouth."

"Look, bigfoot, if you're not working out here, maybe it's best you're on your way. You believe what you want if that allows you to sleep at night. The fact stands that my sister would have kicked your Russian ass."

"We fought fair and square, and it was a draw."

Tressa squared off at her. "That was no fight, and you know it. Your manager paid the officials to change the play score… my sister is a professional and street fighter. She would have torn you apart. Your manager knew that. If she took your broke ass down, his meal ticket would have been gone."

Rozalina turned red. "I will show you who's broken down… I will tear you apart tomorrow night… you never step foot into an arena, so I have an edge on you."

She was so loud that others stopped what they were doing. "Look, Sasquatch beat it; you are bothering me… and take your goons with you… we'll see who'll be kissing the mat tomorrow… if I were you, I'd be afraid… very afraid."

"You always did have a big mouth… but I will accept your apology after our match… and the King will get what he wants… another whore."

Tressa laughed at her. "You're jealous…what's wrong? He hasn't buried his salami in you… shame on you; now be gone. You're embarrassing me."

Rozalina was becoming defensive, and she was losing the control she thought she had."I always hated you, Miss Tressa Quintanilla… but tomorrow, I will take great pleasure in bringing you down… and you will become the King's whore, and I will rub it in your face every single day."

Rozalina couldn't get out of there fast enough. She thought that since it was Tressa, she wouldn't feel that familiar twist in her stomach. But if truth be told, her sister scared her opponent with the intimidating look and aura she expelled. For a minute there, she thought she saw the same twinge in her eyes. She had to shake it off. A few rounds in the gym will do the trick. Rozalina looked back and wondered if Tressa knew whether she had won or lost. The King had no intentions of letting her go. She smiled, wishing she was a fly on the wall when the King took back his offer.

"Hamden," Tressa yelled, "Hold that bag like you have some muscles," she punched the bag a few times.

"I'm confused… aren't you afraid of her? She scares me?"

"You know, if you don't hold this bag like you have something behind you, I'm going to hurt you. Why should I be afraid of big foot," she continued to kick the bag.

"I don't know. She defeated all the others she fought here," Tressa kicked the bag really hard, and Hamden flew across the room.

"I told you to hold the damn bag," she helped him up.

"I'm sorry…"

"Lean into it…" She punched and kicked the bag with great fury.

"I can't do this anymore… I'm black and blue," Hamden whined.

"You're such a puss… who's my sparring partner."

"Yes, I gotch you ah, two women, they are kickboxers."

"Hamden, you little shit… I need men so I can get practice… bring the women on but find me two men."

"Ah, you want them both at a time."

"Bring them on, baby…"

The Queen watched from the upper booth. Now she understood why her husband was enamored with the dark beauty. She was too fast for the two women; they retreated and wouldn't give her the practice she needed.

"She is very good, Zarya. Take me to see her." Zarya waved to Tressa. The Queen was in her splendor, dressed as richly as the King. Tressa customarily saluted her. They sat on one of the lower benches.

"Miss Tressa, it is an honor… I know your situation… I am sure you will bring great honor and triumph to your sister's name. Let me also give you thanks for not sleeping with my husband."

"I'm so sorry; I know it must hurt you to hear such things."

"You're not the first, nor will you be the last woman he takes a fancy to. However, I could understand why... did he offer the queenship."

Tressa turned her face from her, not wanting to see the hurt on her face, "Yes... your Majesty, I just want to go home to my family and my man... The King offended me, but I managed to fend him off."

"He could put me aside. I still haven't given him a son. I guess the two daughters don't make up for a son."

Tressa started to laugh, "How typical. He is blaming you instead of himself for having lazy male swimmers," they all laughed.

"My husband doesn't make mistakes, my dear. However, it is not that easy to set the first wife aside, but I'm glad you turned down the offer. Now can you kick this bitch's ass!?" The Queen said forcefully. "I can't stand her; she takes too many liberties with my husband."

Tressa smiled, "Are you a betting woman, your Majesty... I hear the odds are against me."

"I have laid a lot of money on you... and now, since I've seen you at practice. I may up the stakes. The King always bets on his champion. I hear it's a nice sum."

"Well, it serves him right... for being an asshole. He has a beautiful wife and wants more. Shit, I could have been home right now if it wasn't for him. I'm sorry, I know he's your husband and King, but I came so close to punching him. Had it been my sister, his nuts would be in his throat," they roared with laughter.

"I would have loved to have seemed that... I love him... but sometimes he can be very hurtful. "

Well, it's been a pleasure meeting you, Majesty. I assume you will be keeping your husband busy tonight."

"Don't worry, my dear, he won't bother you as long as I'm in court... and I plan to keep him very busy tonight... Tressa, I'll do what I can to get you back home. The ambassador has asked for an audience with the King, and he can't continue to deny him... good luck Black Beauty; my money is on you." The queen held her hand; it is not normal for royalty to touch an outsider. Zarya and Tressa watch the beautiful Queen make her way out of the gym.

"She's really a good person... you look tired. I'll ensure you have clean towels and food waiting for you."

"Thank you, Zarya. You've been a good friend."

Tressa sparred with the two until they gave up. They were tired and couldn't give her what she wanted. It was getting late. The lights were out as she dragged herself into the locker room. She looked at the wall mirror and started to cry… her face was flushed from her workout. She needed a massage tomorrow to work out her muscles, wanting everything to be over so she could see her family and be in Cruz's strong arms. Her stomach was still giving her trouble, having to throw up a few times.

Tressa turned off the last few lights making her way to her room. She passed guards at every door, wondering if they would stop her if she just walked out. She thought about it but was too tired; without transportation, it would be impossible to get away. The lights in her room were off when she opened the door.

"Zarya, are you here?" She walked towards the windows and opened the curtains letting in some light. The bed looked so inviting. Sitting on the edge, reaching for her ring to put it back on, she lay on her side, letting the lights from the window bathe her face. She felt Zarya sit at the edge of her bed behind her.

"Is that the way you treat the ring I gave you," she froze when she heard the familiar voice. She let out a scream. Cruz quieted her with a kiss "have you forgotten me already," she jumped over him.

"Oh my God, it's you. It's not a dream," she touched his face.

"You two are making too much noise," Drew and Zarya came out of the other room. "Drew! Oh, Drew, you bastard, you found me," she hugged his neck.

"Oh, you don't think we would leave you here."

"I can't believe you came for me," she started to sob, burying her face in Cruz's chest. "Please, God, don't let me wake up if this is a dream," she clung to Cruz.

"Guys can you give us some privacy," Cruz said, coming up for air.

"We'll be in the other room… there's food and drink. Come on, Zarya, let's leave the love birds alone." Cruz lifted her face to his, kissed her cheeks and lips, letting out all the passion he was holding inside for her. "All I could think about was getting you back… holding you again, and never letting you go." Tressa could hardly talk. She was overcome with emotions. She sobbed in his arms. He felt her body tremble, holding her tight. "Baby, we're going to take you home. I won't leave you."

"I can't believe you came for me," she cried.

"I told you I'd follow you to the moon if I had to."

"Kiss me, baby, make love to me," she said, holding him tighter.

Cruz laughed softly. "Baby, I don't think we have time."

"No, you can't leave me… let's go now… what's the plan."

"Hold on, sweetheart… let me just get Drew… he can explain the plan."

Drew sat on the bed eating chicken. "Tressa, unfortunately, you're going to have to fight. There is too much activity going on. I have a plan… Harry and I will be your bodyguards. Cruz is going to be in your corner assisting you. As soon as they pronounce you the winner, you do your thing. Parade around shows off a little as you woman do."

"So, your confident I'm going to win."

"That bitch has nothing on you, baby. I've seen you in action, anyway, win or lose. You're coming with us tomorrow night. It's all arranged. Once we get you back to the locker room, we'll smuggle you out of the kitchen exit. There're masses of people outside the gates. Once they open those gates, there's going to be some commotion. We'll be long gone before they find out you're missing. One of our undercover agents will be waiting outside the side door from the kitchen with my vehicle and some clothes for you to change."

Tressa hangs on Cruz, not wanting to let him go. "Give us a few hours, Drew, please," Cruz begged.

"Hey, we got to go. We have to get back."

"Please, one hour at least, come on, bro," he begged; Tressa was too upset and emotional.

"Alright… one hour, then we have to go. Zarya is filling me in on what's been going on… one hour, so whatever freaky shit you're going to do, make sure you're done in one hour… Uno," Tressa couldn't stop crying.

"Baby, you're scaring me… tell me how your feeling," she blew her nose and lay back on the pillow.

"I'm alright… just a little sick in the stomach," he touched her belly tenderly, kissing it, moving his hands to her breasts. She removed her sports bra. The feel of his touch made her come alive. He kissed her tenderly at first, but all the weeks of wanting gave into his passion, and she returned his eagerness as she pulled him inside her.

"If I die tomorrow, I want to go happy, knowing you still love me and… you still want me as much as I want you," she whispered between kisses.

"God, Tressa, an hour is not enough time to show you how much I desire you…"

"Don't worry, I'll let you make up the rest later," she teased. Tressa's heart was beating as fast with each touch. He knew just how to wake that passion within her. She tried to squeeze the tears that threatened to fall. She matched his ardor with the same intensity. Tressa held onto him, not wanting to let go, as they exploded into ecstasy. "Please don't leave me," she said, breaking his heart.

He felt her body tremble underneath him. He caressed her face. "Baby, you'll have to let go for a minute. I don't want to crush you," he rolled off her onto his side and pulled her into his arms. "I'm coming back for you, my love… trust me… I didn't come all this way to leave empty-handed," he kissed her shoulders.

"This has been such a nightmare," she cried.

"Baby, please tell me the truth. It doesn't change how I feel about you… did the Prince or the King force you to…you know?"

She giggled."They tried, but I almost puked on the King, and Zarya smacked the prince. Baby, I'm so glad you're here. The King and I have this agreement… if I win this match, he's to let me go…if I lose, I will go to him willingly. But win or lose, he has no intention of letting me go."

"You know I will kill him… I don't care if it starts an international war."

She faced him, touching his handsome face, "Don't get angry, my love… I just want to get out of here… see my family and marry you if you still want me."

"Are you crazy…? I didn't come all this way to say goodbye. You're stuck with me, woman."

"I'm going to give you my ring. I can't wear it while I fight. Keep it safe for me."

They were interrupted by Drew. "Time to go, lovebirds, show time tomorrow," he reminded them.

"Drew, I hate you right now," she yelled.

"I know, baby, but you'll have plenty of time to get your freak on later," he kissed her, "you better win; I got big bucks on you."

"You bet on my woman," Cruz said as he finished getting dressed.

"She's a cash cow… I'm no fool, and the odds are great."

Drew had to pull the lovers apart. They clung together until the last minute. Tressa watched as they jumped the wall that separated them. She stared into the darkness and couldn't help and wonder what he must have gone through to come for her.

"Thank you, Zarya. I know you can get in so much trouble."

"Oh, Tressa, if you only knew how boring my life was until you came along. I am having the time of my life… but now I must take care of you. You must eat something to keep your strength. I also have big bucks on Black Beauty. After some food and a nice hot bath, you will be good as new."

"I'm already good as new Zarya. He gave me the strength I needed."

"Tell me, Tressa is their other men… as handsome, and you know, sexy. For a minute, I was afraid everyone in the building heard you two."

"I couldn't tell you I only have eyes for him."

They managed to get to the jeep without being detected, "So you feel better now that you've seen her," Drew teased.

"I'll feel better once we're on our way and we leave this mess behind."

"Tomorrow is going to be crazy… I can't wait," Drew was high with excitement.

"You're looking forward to this fight, aren't you?"

"When my girl was fighting at home, I wouldn't miss a match… you'll see what I'm talking about tomorrow… the way they fight is more like dancing… they make it look so easy. Their whole demeanor changes, and the intensity it's a thing of beauty."

"Did you forget she's sick…"

"I know, and I think the King is using that to his advantage, but no worry, you'll be in her corner. If she gets sick, you can stop the fight."

The King was not happy that his Queen ruined his plans, but she kept him very preoccupied all night, and to make things worst, his second wife arrived that morning, and everyone wanted to see the fight. The King summoned Rozalina to his chambers. She was always so nervous when she came before him. Rozalina was in love with the King. For two years, she'd held the hope he'd show her even the slightest affection, but being in his presence gave her a special feeling.

Rozalina put on a lovely dress and some make-up and tried to do something with her short hair. Her anger flourished when she learned that the King wanted to bed Tressa. Here she was willing and ready for his advances with just a hint of encouragement that would last for a lifetime.

Musa ushered Rozalina into the king's rooms, leading her to the terrace where he took his lunch. "Roz, you look lovely today… tell me you are feeling like a winner."

"Your Majesty, I'm here for you to command."

"Good… I'm counting on you to defeat that… that woman who makes my blood boil with passion." Rozalina felt a rush of jealousy growing inside of her. She came closer to him, wanting to touch him.

"Majesty, but you are married to two very beautiful wives. What place could she have here?"

The King touched her chin, and her eyes lit up. "You will help me bring her into my bed… she will be my Queen, my greatest conquest." Rozalina's smile faded. She wanted him to see her craving for him.

"I will do my best, your Majesty… she has never fought in an arena like this one, and she is ill… it will be an easy defeat in more ways than one."

"Good, I have money riding on you, Rozalina; please don't let me down… sit and have some lunch with me, my champion. With my two wives in court, I have to be respectful; once you have defeated her, I will send my wives away and deal with the legal work afterward. And you, my dear, ask me for anything, it doesn't matter what it is, if it is in my power to give it is yours," she smiled, she didn't have to think too long for all she wanted was one night with the King.

"That is most generous. I will let you know."

"I drink to my champion; you are my driving force behind getting what I want. She is what I want, Roz. Did you ever want something so badly you would do anything for it," he said, turning his focus toward where he saw her swimming. Rozalina wanted to yell at him. She would dream of him touching her, making love to her, especially when he came down to watch her train. He would correct her moves, and his touch sent chills throughout her whole body.

"I could only imagine, Majesty," she said sadly.

He turned quickly towards her, "I'm so sorry, here I am talking about my desires when I should be focusing on you, my dear," he came close to her, inches away from her lips. "This will be a glorious day for you." She closed her eyes, expecting a kiss on the lips; instead, he kissed her forehead. Her face flushed with embarrassment wanting to grab him and kiss him. To show him that under all the muscles was a woman full of great passion.

"Will your wives be attending?" She asked, recovering.

"Yes, they are both here and will be sitting by my side."

"They must hate her Majesty, knowing you desire another."

"I know how to handle my women, Roz; they would try to make trouble. But not even my people will reject having a woman who was the glory of our culture, a true color, as Queen. He walked over to the balcony to gaze into the city. "Tressa represents the beauty of our people. I touch her silky skin, look into those brown eyes, and lose myself."

Rozalina fought to keep her feelings to herself, but her heart broke into millions of pieces. Listening to him speak about another woman. How could he not see how much she loved him? Her spirit screamed in silence. Love me too, she thought to herself.

He turned to speak to her, "Are you alright, my champion? You look worried."

"Oh, no, my King, I was just thinking about what you were saying. I never understood the fascination men have about her. I know that her sister was very popular with the males."

"Everything about her fascinates me, Roz, that snappy mouth of hers. I know she is a passionate woman just by the way she challenges me. But enough about Tressa, think about what I said. Anything you want is yours once you defeat her.

Crowds poured into the arena wanting a good look at Black Beauty, fighting to get a seat inside. Many others would have to rely on watching the match on the screen. Tressa went through her routine. She sparred with a few other people fighting before her match and got in a great rubdown. She was nervous and didn't know where the guys would meet. Zarya was always a good source of information, but she hadn't seen her all morning.

The servants bought some food and drank, arranging everything nicely on the terrace. Musa ran after them carrying a bunch of 8 by 12 photographs taken the day before, posing in a single-leg stance. "Miss Tressa, I am sorry to bring this to you late, but the King has many fans that favor you. Could you autograph a few of these promotional photos?"

Tressa looked at the older gentleman whose eyes were always downcast. "I will under one condition that you sit down while I sign them."

He cracked a smile for the first time since she met him, "As you command, Madame."

Tressa got a tickle signing her sister's name to her photos, "Musa, how long have you been with the k ing?"

He paused a minute as if calculating the years in his head. "I believe the King was five years old when I was assigned to him… I know you must think terribly of him. But he's a good master. Sometimes I think he could make better choices.”

“Don’t we all,” Tressa replied, signing the photos.

“Miss Tressa, if I may speak my mind.”

“Of course, Musa… you have my permission,” he looked down at his hands, eyes always downcast.

“I have great admiration and respect for you. I am well aware of the desire the King has for you, and it is genuine. I had never seemed him like this before. You stood your ground… the King has never been rejected before. Nevertheless, he was wrong to try to force you. However, I can understand why; you are beautiful, intelligent, and loyal to your true love.” he smiled. “Can you make one out to me… to a great admirer,” she signed it Black Beauty but also signed her name underneath.

“I will treasure it forever.”

Zarya busted into Tressa’s room while she was trying to relax. Her head was pounding again. Zarya was so excited she flushed.

“Have you seen Cruz? I’m worried sick. No one has said anything to me about what’s going on.” She closed her eyes, “my head is pounding. Zarya, talk to me, tell me something,” she laid on her back with a cool towel over her eyes.

"Everything is wonderful. Drew is very good at what he does. He has talked the Queen into letting one of her ladies be used as a decoy… let me see if I remember his message… tell Tressa that when she goes back to the locker room, take a left instead of a right, and there will be a girl dressed like her with the same robe. She will go into the locker room and lock the door behind her. In the meantime, you will sneak out through the kitchen. Someone will be waiting with transportation."

"Have you seen Cruz and Harry? How are they going to get in?"

"They are already inside. They've been using your big guy to prepare the arena for tonight."

"Oh God, I wonder how he managed to be at my corner during the match. I'm sure the King had someone arranged for me."

Zarya laughed, "I think he got sick, so Drew volunteered. Cruz told the coordinator he was experienced, so there is nothing to worry about. Now I'm going to get my father to see about those headaches."

Tressa felt wonderful after her nap and whatever Zarya's father gave her helped the headache and stomach. She put on her sports bra but needed something showy… choosing a white tank top and a pair of black silk gym shorts. Her black and silver hooded robe had a fancy BB; it was large enough to cover her whole body. She began stretching exercises wanting to be limber before stepping into the ring. In one hour, she would be before a crowd of people hungry for blood. She knew her opponent would not have mercy on her, and she was not about to let her have the upper hand.

Tressa was nervous as she stretched and warmed up her limbs. She heard a door open behind her. "Zarya, can you call the masseuse? I could sure use a massage."

"Of course, my sweet, anything for you." The King smiled as he watched her face go pale.

"Please forgive me, your Majesty. I was expecting someone else."

"I'm sure you were my love… I came to wish you well. I was reported that you were sick," she smiled and continued to stretch as he spoke.

"You have wonderful spies, your Majesty, but I assure you I am well enough to put on a great show for you and the others."

He closed the distance between them, "Tressa… I can stop this… just say the word and come to me, and I promise I will make you the most beloved and happy…" he held out his hand "come to me, my love."

"Majesty, please don't make this more difficult. I will fight for my freedom."

He pulled her into a stolen embrace, "Tressa, you strong-headed woman, every time I see you, my heart and loins ache for you." The King kissed her hungrily. For the first time, she feared she might be unable to stop him. She could feel his manhood press hard against her, and the more she struggled, the more determined he became, moving his kisses to her breast as his hand cupped her bottom.

"Your Majesty… please, I beg you not like this, let me go," tears ran down her cheeks. A knock interrupted him, and he became enraged.

"Your Majesty, it's the Queen. She has urgent news," He loosens his hold on Tressa, who was feeling the pain of his embrace.

"Tell her I will be there shortly!" he bellowed. "You, my dear, have not seemed the last of me. The next time we meet, not even Allah will save you," He kissed her forcefully before he left.

Tressa stumbled into the bathroom, throwing up. She washed her face and sat on the edge of the bathtub crying emotionally. She was exhausted, feeling shameful, as if she was betraying Cruz every time the King kissed her.

Harry and Drew ushered her to the locker room. Tressa seemed preoccupied and wanted this day to be over. "Tressa, the place is packed to capacity, but this is good for us… we'll be able to slip out of here easily. Now your man is going to be assisting you, taping up your hands and loosening you up, and you can't be doing any kissy, kissy shit."

She laughed at his antics.

"How are you feeling?"

"I'm feeling good… I had some rest. I'm ready."

"Good because you need to beat the shit out of that bitch… she's been on all sorts of interviews talking trash about you and your sister. It's pretty bad stuff, but that's ok because the odds are getting better. And I heard through the gossip train that most people are coming to see you. Your picture is everywhere; kids are even stealing it off the poles and billboards."

"Well, I'm ready. Wish me luck." He kissed her cheek.

"You got this, baby," he smacked her bottom for luck. "Harry and I will be waiting for you to walk you to the arena."

Her face lit up when she saw Cruz. He shot her a wink. Cruz helped tape up her fingers and stretched her legs and limbs.

"God, woman, if you only knew what I was thinking, you would have slapped me by now," they laugh. She gave him a quick kiss.

"Sweetie, I want you to promise me you're not going to run into the ring for any reason. I would be highly pissed if you did."

"Baby, I," she interrupted him.

"I know what I'm doing. I've done this before."

"I heard." She gave him a surprised look. "I promise, baby, remember, win or lose, you're coming home with me tonight."

The stadium was packed; there was very little room to move anywhere. The Tressa match was the second on the playlist. She paced back and forth until it was her turn. She could hear the cheers, boos, and shouts from the fans.

The announcer came on the air and stated it would be a full-contact fight with no limits. Rozalina had her four bodyguards and two assistants with her. The crowd clapped and cheered for her as she lifted her arms toward them. She had her assistant bring down four people and give them boards so they could hold. She proceeded to break the boards showing strength. The crowds were impressed with the exhibition as she continued to parade herself around the arena. Rozalina showed a great deal of power and strength.

When the announcer called out Black Beauty, it sounded like a roar of thunder. Everyone stood up and applauded and chanted beau-ty, beau-ty over and over as she danced her way into the arena, waving her arms towards the crowd. Cruz and Drew took their place in her corner. When she took her robe off, the howling and whistling turned into a frenzy as she displayed her Kung Fu moves and flips, showing off her skills. She went to her corner and grabbed the dragon's swords demonstrating her fighting skills. With swords, all one could hear was the swish sound as she waved them with grace and self-control, flipping and landing on her feet.

"I didn't know she could do that," Cruz clapped, amazed and proud.

"Oh, she looks good. I thought I should stand with you if you decide to run into the arena when she gets hit. You remind me of a mother hen," Drew laughed.

"Hey, this is all new to me, so back off," he teased.

"That's alright. I can explain what's happening, so you don't get freaked out. Rozalina looks really good. She actually looks better than in the past."

"Is that going to be a problem for Tressa?"

"Relax, buddy. Tressa has so many years of experience with Rozalina. She doesn't come close. I bet money that Rozalina is shitting bricks right now. She may be strong, but Tressa has speed, and she's used to making those acrobatic moves."

The referee brings them to the middle and motions them to start. Rozalina starts strong with offensive moves. Tressa blocks moving back and standing out of the way. For a few minutes, all Tressa does are defensive moves. The King smiled as he sat between his two wives.

"Why isn't she striking back?" Cruz felt the tension and was concerned that Tressa was not well enough to fight.

"Watch and learn, grasshopper. There's a motive to her madness," the crowd groans as Tressa is hit in the stomach and falls back, but she quickly recovers. The same pattern continues for the next few minutes; Rozalina keeps attacking aggressively, and Tressa blocking stoutly.

Rozalina is taller and bigger. Tressa anticipates her moves, twists, and turns quickly, which frustrates Rozalina. The Queen begins to worry, and the people who have money on Rozalina cheer for their champion. Once again, Tressa fell back. By now, Rozalina is showing signs of fatigue; her face is red and slowing down.

Tressa sat in her corner, noticing the look of concern on Cruz's face, "Baby, I can stop this any time."

She gave him an encouraging smile, "Sweetheart, I'm just getting warmed up. I have to give the crowd something."

The referee brings them back to the middle, and Tressa gives Rozalina that look… the look she had been dreading, the one that scared many opponents to be in the arena with Black Beauty… her brown eyes piercing hers, Tressa cracked that familiar smile.

"It's my turn bitch," when the referee gives them the go-ahead, Tressa didn't waste any time springing into action. She threw a few combinations of kicks and blows that shook Rozalina, some landing on her face and chest. The crowd became live with shouts and whistles. Tressa bounced back and forth like a master making each blow and kick count. Rozalina gets knocked down with one of Tressa's flying house kicks; she is having a hard time recovering and is bleeding from the bridge of her nose.

The King sat straight in his seat, realizing his champion would lose. His wives, on the other hand, cannot contain themselves.

The referee brings them back to the center. Rozalina is breathing heavily; they cross their hands to wait for the referee.

"This is for my sister, bitch," Tressa was relentless. She attacked so fearfully that Rozalina could only put her arms up to block. The King shook his head, stroking his goatee with disappointment.

Drew couldn't help but shout. he jumped up and down, punching Cruz playfully in his arm. "I told you she was good. Come on. Baby, finish the bitch!" He yelled.

The crowds stood to their feet chanting BEAU-TY, BEAU-TY. It was deafening; shouts and whistles and cheers. Rozalina and Tressa squared off again. This time Tressa was the aggressor. The last kick and series of punches knocked Rozalina down, and she didn't bother to get up. Her assistant checked her and gave them the signal she was done. The crowd went crazy as their roar surged through the arena. Tressa faced the crowd and bowed to them. They became louder. Again, the referee waited until the crowd settled down before he made the official announcement.

"Ladies and gentlemen, I give you the winner and world champion BLACK…. BEAUTY!" The crowd continued to cheer and chant her name. Cruz picked her up and paraded her around the arena as she waved and threw kisses to the fans cheering crowds.

The King came to the platform to congratulate her and give her a winner's medal. Cruz put her down and took his place back on the sideline. The King bent down and whispered to her as she lowered her head to receive her medal.

"This is not over, my dark beauty. You will be my Queen… count on it," The King said as he slipped the medal around her neck. She just winked at him as she waved to her fans.

"Please don't tell me that's the King," Cruz asked Drew, surprised.

"That's him. Why? Is the green eye monster coming out," Drew replied, grinning.

"In spades," Cruz replied, gritting his teeth. He wrapped her in her robe, waiting for the bodyguards to usher her through the crowd. People reached out to touch her as she exited the stadium traveling toward the locker rooms. A group of people tried to follow them, but Harry and Cruz held them off as Drew threw a black burka over her, and the decoy took her place, locking herself in the locker room. Drew pulled her along through the dark alley by the side kitchen. Harry and Cruz follow close behind, making sure no one follows them. The kitchen was so busy no one noticed as they slipped through and out the back where the jeep was waiting. Harry jumped into the driver's seat as Cruz held onto Tressa. The four disappeared into the darkness.

They drove late into the night with only the moonlight to illuminate the way, determined to reach the halfway destination before they stopped to rest. Cruz had reserved a suite before they left with some food and drinks. Tressa was still pumped up from the fight and the fresh night air. She needed something to bring her down. Everyone was celebrating except for Cruz.

"What's wrong, baby… why aren't you happy?" Tressa said, teasing him.

"It's the big green monster," Drew teased him laughing and chugging down his drink.

"Don't tell me you're jealous?" she said in a teasing voice.

"That was a good-looking man, all tall and handsome what I'm supposed to feel knowing you were alone with him."

She gave him a hard look, "Yeah, I was alone with him," she put her drink down and confronted him, "in fact, he was on top of me," she yelled.

"Oh, you're just pushing my buttons, aren't you," he replied.

"Nothing happened... you know why... because all I could think about was getting back to you, you idiot," she yelled at him.

"Yeah, you idiot, that's what she said," Drew pointed to her, trying to make light of the manner.

Drew made him laugh. "I'm sorry, it's just that every time I think about him touching you, I just want to break his neck... you forgive me?" Cruz said in his pitiful voice. Tressa cut her eyes at him. He pulled her into his lap.

"It's hard for me to stay mad at you. You're so damn cute," she said as he lifted her in his strong arms and kissed her.

"I can't help it. I'm a jealous son-of-a-bitch. Did he hurt you, baby," he nuzzled her neck.

Drew laughed, "Okay, Harry, it's our cue to leave. We can take up this fight later when we're all rested. We have an early day tomorrow," Drew was already loaded.

Cruz held Tressa in his arms, relieved she was finally safe with him. But early next morning, he was alarmed at how hot she was. When he tried to wake her up, she was not responding. He knocked frantically on Drew's door. When Drew finally opened the door, he knew there was something wrong.

"Tressa is burning up with fever. I can't wake her. I have to find a way to get her fever under control," Drew dressed up as Cruz spoke to him, not wanting to waste any valuable time.

"I'll get Harry to bring up some ice. There's a wagon station not far from here, I'll try to get a hitch for her, and we've got to get under the embassy's protection."

"It's the virus, isn't it?"

"I'm afraid so, but the good thing is that it's not as far as the docks... we'll figure something out."

The next morning the ambassador waited patiently for the King to resume court; so far, he had waited three hours. The young receptionist smiled as he paced back and forth. He had learned the King was very disappointed when he realized that Tressa had escaped. Finally, the double doors opened to the Kings receiving chamber. The King was dressed in all his finery, wearing his signature royal blue and silver. He motioned to Ambassador Inglewood to sit and share some lunch with him. Inglewood bowed to the King and joined him at the table.

"Ambassador, it is a pleasure to see you again. To what do I owe this pleasure too."

"King Abu, you are looking exceptionally well this afternoon. You know why I'm here, Tressa Quintanilla, aka Black Beauty. That was quite a fight last night. I must say she is just as good as her sister.

"Extraordinary is more like it. I had no idea that Tressa fought with such skills, or else I wouldn't have made that wager with her."

"Tressa is on an even plane with her sister, the true fighter Black Beauty. I must say I enjoyed myself immensely. I, too, made a substantial amount of money. But we both know why I'm here… I came for Tressa; I know she is being kept here against her will." Musa poured them tea.

The King sat back and sipped his tea casually. "She is not here. I had the palace searched from top to bottom. I was informed that she left after the fight," the King could not disguise his displeasure.

"I see you are upset, but can I have your word that you will not pursue her?"

"Ambassador Inglewood, I would pursue her to the ends of the earth had I not received news from my wife that she is with child. As you know, I have no sons and don't want to cause my wife any undue stress. In the short time Tressa was here, she… she got under my skin. I would have done whatever I could to keep her."

"Majesty, you are not the only man who has fallen for the Quintanilla Twins. Many hearts are broken each day by the thought of being with any one of them. Mine included."

"I see. She would be treasured in my country. Can you only imagine a son, a natural-born son? It would have been my greatest triumph. To help restore color to my people. However, there is more to the sultry Tressa. When I held her, I felt like a King."

"I know, but she doesn't belong to you or me, so do I have your word that you will not go after her."

The King looked away from him, "You have my word, but if we meet again, things would be much different."

"Thank you. I'm hoping she will contact us. I must be on my way Majesty. It was a pleasure to see you again; I wish you a healthy son and many more."

Chapter 11: Home Again

Drew found the neighborhood doctor to look in on Tressa, who was lying on a pillow of ice. Cruz rubbed her hands and arms, never leaving her side.

"Can she be moved, doctor? We have to get her help?"

The doctor took her pulse and temperature. "Well, her fever is down, and her heart rate is normal with the injection I gave her. It should last a few hours."

"Thank you, doctor. We have to hitch the wagon to the Jeep. Cruz, let's get some pillows and blankets so we can get out of here. I called the embassy. They are on alert." Cruz picked her up and tried to make her comfortable. They had lost valuable time, and Drew was concerned they would run into resistance along the way. They were stopped at various checking points, but because Drew knew the language, they were easy to convince.

In the process, they hid Tressa's hair, for if they had discovered who she was, it would have alerted the king of their whereabouts. The roads were hot and dusty, full of travelers carrying all their belongings. The country was progressing in its recovery but still had a long way to go to regain the beauty and power it once owned.

The embassy was a massive white building heavily guarded by American soldiers, cameras, and a high-voltage wired fence. It took them twice as long to finally arrive at the embassy. Upon their arrival, her fever had spiked again, but the medical team was ready for her to take action right away.

Cruz and Drew sat helplessly, waiting for any news. He sent a message to his brother that they were at the embassy and he could turn back if he wanted to.

Cruz paced back and forth, praying they got her in time and not knowing how much damage was done. Drew, who usually had so much to say, found himself without words to comfort the worried Cruz. They saw nurses and doctors run back and forth for hours, but no one had any news. Finally, after four hours, Dr. Jordan Smith joined them in the waiting room with an update. "Please have a seat, gentleman." He looked at his pad. "She is finally reacting to the antidote… there were some other drugs in her system that weren't giving us a clear reading. So, we had to find out what these other drugs were before we tackled the virus. Anyway, she is doing well right now. Her fever is down, but she's going to have to stay a few days so we can monitor her. To ensure the other drugs in her system don't cause the virus to mutate. But as of now, she is doing well." Cruz and Drew took a deep breath, able to contain themselves. They hugged each other and were finally relieved that she was out of the woods.

"Can I see her… please?" Cruz asked, still upset she was in danger of losing her life.

"We gave her a strong sedative. She'll be out for a few hours."

"I don't care. I just want to be there when she wakes up… hold her hand, just be near her."

"Sure, but she needs to rest; that bug they injected her was dangerous, and her body was working overtime just to fight the damn thing. Give us some time to get her settled into her room."

"Thank you, doctor." Cruz had a tremor in his voice due to hours of waiting and traveling.

"Come on, bro, we need some drinks and relax," Drew suggested. Their nerves were on edge. Harry, who was normally serious and quiet, cracked a smile joining the festive outcome. Cruz got a chance to speak to Yadira, who spooked him because she sounded so much like Tressa.

"Are you alright, bro? You sound tired," Tajo asked.

"I am tired, but I can't think of myself right now… please Tajo, take good care of her sister. I don't think her parents know their other daughter is traveling with you."

"She's a pain in the ass, but I'm taking good care of her… in more ways than you want to know."

Cruz laughed. "God, that's what I was afraid of… remember, don't want two angry people at the wedding, be careful."

"I understand my reputation does precede me, but… she's a ball buster, and I love her, just like you love Tressa."

"Good, I can't wait to meet her. Take care, my brother. I'll see you back home."

"Give Tressa a kiss for me… over and out."

After dinner and a few drinks to relax, he got to see Tressa. When he entered her room, it was cold, and the lights were darkened. All he could hear was the beeping sounds of all the monitors attached to several IVs monitoring her vitals. He almost started to cry when he saw her lying helplessly. Her beautiful black hair framed her delicate face. Long dark eyelashes fluttered as she slept.

He moved the chair closer to her bed to hold her hand and kiss it. "Baby, please be alright. I can't wait to have you home with me again. I promise I'll keep you safe," Cruz sat watching her until he fell asleep. He laid his head on the bed next to her jumping up every time a nurse came in to make sure she was alright and to put more medicine in her IV.

Then he felt her hand playing with his hair. He sprung up from his nap.

"Baby, how long have you been here?" She smiled at him. He took her hand, kissing it.

"I don't know, a few hours. How do you feel, baby?"

"I feel like I was hit by a truck… how did I get here?"

"You had a high fever brought on by the virus."

"What virus… how did I get a virus?"

He realized she didn't know she had a virus running through her body. "Sweetie, the people who kidnapped you injected you with a virus. It was not intentional. They thought it was just something to put you out for a few hours. Thank God it was a very slow-spreading bug, but had it not been treated, it would have killed you in the long run."

Tressa was still confused. "I had no idea. I know Zarya tried to poison me when she thought I was trying to take her prince away; she even confessed."

"That must have been what they found in your system. But the doctor said you are doing well, and they just want to monitor you for a few days."

"I can't wait until I'm home and plan our wedding."

"It's still on schedule. I'm not pushing it back… I don't want to wait," he kissed her. "I did manage to speak to your sister; she is driving my brother crazy… he is in love with her."

Tressa started to laugh. "I told him I had the perfect woman for him, and he didn't want to hear it, and look, they're together after all. I think Tajo would be good for Yadira; she needs a strong egotistic male."

They laughed.

"Tajo needs a woman that will challenge him, and she's given it to him in spades," he kissed her forehead.

"Baby, I love you so much… but… I can't help thinking I've caused you so much trouble."

"Sweet cheeks, stop talking… you are my life now… you and Miranda and any other babies we have together. Mr. Lee broke the news to your parents. They were not amused. Tressa, I want to ask your father for your hand in marriage… I'm sure they are not happy with how things are, but I'm hoping I can make it up to them and prove I have honorable intentions toward you."

She touched his face. "Relax, baby. Daddy will love you… he's a great man, and he wants to see me happy."

"I know your father. We've had meetings together with your uncle," he laughed. "But he doesn't know I violated his daughter."

"My father is very protective, but it's my mother you have to worry about. However, I think you'll win her over with your good looks and charm."

"God, I better brush up on my charms. I'm going to need help."

"You'll do fine. I've only had one other real boyfriend. Samuel and I went behind my parent's back when I was in High School, but it was just like carrying my books. Sneaking kisses, stupid stuff."

"Why do your parents dislike your ex so much?"

"They didn't initially; my sister and I were sixteen when we finished school. I went to college and majored in phycology. I went right from graduation to the agency, and I was lucky because I could go to school, on my missions, and sometimes tour with Dad and Yadira. So, my relationship with Samuel was pretty much long-distance. There were rumors even in school that Samuel was seeing other girls, but I never caught him. My father heard Holly was having a baby and wouldn't name the father, and all eyes pointed to him. He swore he never touched her, and I guess I wanted to believe him."

"So, you were never intimate with him?"

"It's not that I didn't want to have sex. It was that deep down inside, I didn't trust him. He made this huge deal about it, but I just couldn't."

"Why didn't you go into the fighting circuit like your sister? She has a huge fan base."

"You have to understand that we've been in the public since we were eight, not so much here but abroad. I competed until I was sixteen and stepped in for my sister when she was sick. But we just wanted our own identity. Especially my sister, I was the good girl who never gave my parents any trouble, unlike Yadira. She gave my parents enough drama for both of us. Yadira was tough in the ring. She was out to hurt someone. The match between her and Rozalina was like a slap in the face. Rozalina was terrified to fight Yadira, and she truly was no match for her. But our manager and Rozalina's trainer made some last-minute changes, so Rozalina would come out looking like it was a draw. My sister beat the shit out of her. Anyway, that's when she threw in the towel. She was twenty-three and decided to open her own school."

"And you stayed with the agency?"

"Totally, my parents didn't like my choice of employment. That was one of the reasons I resigned. I also wanted to see if Samuel and I were ready for marriage."

"I'm glad you quit the agency, so I can understand your parents' anxiety about you working there. So, the number one question is… are you going to be happy being a normal housewife and mother?"

She looked at him and smiled, "I'm ready to be with you and Miranda. I love you so much I can't see myself without you."

Cruz held her tight, "All I want to do is take care of you, baby. Once you're feeling better, I can rest again. I will take care of you, my love."

"Thank you for loving me," she replied, resting in his arms, feeling safe and secure.

Tressa continued to improve within a week. She was feeling her old self again. The crew celebrated offshore, cutting up and exploring their surroundings. Cruz went shopping for Tressa, making sure she had the best furnishing and food for the long journey back home. Drew visited daily and informed them that the king would soon be a father again. However, he was furious that Tressa beat his champion and fled in the middle of the night. Drew also found out that he had no intention of keeping his word about letting her go. He just wanted to get her in his bed.

Cruz took care of Tressa with love and care but clearly struggled with the fact that someone tried to hurt her, and the guilty person or people were still at large. He feared that they would try again once they got back.

Tressa allowed herself to be cared for by Cruz. He would carry her upstairs on deck in the evening, and they would gaze into the moonlight, drink some wine, kiss and make out like teenagers, only stopping when it got too heated. Then they would continue in the privacy of their cabin. Cruz couldn't get enough of her, but he held back because she was still recovering, and didn't want to overwhelm her with his lust. She sometimes cried when he sang to her as he held her in his arms. Closing her eyes and wondering how things would be if the king's plan for her had gone through, she would have been a prisoner to a lustful king.

She didn't want to think about the pain and suffering had he succeeded, had she been separated from Cruz forever. She felt so safe in his embrace that it scared her, she had never needed to feel safe, and it frightened her at times just how much she loved him.

The journey back home was smooth. The weather cooperated, and Tressa recovered fully. Tressa was nervous about introducing Cruz to her parents, calling them when they docked to inform them they were on their way.

The first person to meet them at the door was her grandmother, Alexandra. She had a very dramatic personality. "My darlings, oh my dear," she hugged Tressa tightly. "And you must be Cruz, oh my God, how handsome and so… tall, feel those muscles," she teased him.

Tressa introduced Cruz to her parents, and she did not expect the warm welcome he received. Her father shook his hand and spoke to Cruz as if they were old friends.

Audrey took her aside in her bedroom while Alex chatted on and on, entertaining the men in the kitchen. Audrey cried as she held her daughter in her arms. "I thank God each day you are safe. Your father saw red… and then Yadira decided to jump on some godforsaken boat to find you. We didn't sleep for days."

"I'm alright now, Mami. I… have to admit I was scared, and for a while, I didn't know what was going on or if I would… see my family or Cruz again. It was crazy. I had no idea so many people were involved in my rescue."

"When we found out, I was beside myself, and your father went crazy until he found out that Cruz and Drew had rescued you. It was like this calmness washed over him, and he turned and said to me, 'she's in good hands, honey, don't worry'."

"Mami, I felt so alone, and when I heard his voice, I couldn't stop crying." She began to cry in her mother's arms.

"I couldn't believe he traveled all that way for me… I love him so much."

"Now you understand what I was trying to tell you. When a man can back up his words of love, then you know the truth. The depth of his love and how far he'd go to protect the one he loves. Your dad searched for me for years, almost killing himself, and he never gave up. She held Tressa at arm's length. "So… what are your plans?"

"Well, Cruz is going to ask for my hand in marriage." They heard shouts from the kitchen.

"From the sound of that, he already did. I can hear from here."

Alex insisted on a toast. She gathered everyone in the living room and poured wine to toast the happy couple. "I am thrilled to have our esteemed family joined together. I give you my wholehearted blessing," Demi announced.

Tressa was pleased with the outcome. She was amazed at how relaxed and comfortable Cruz was; even her younger brothers played with him and followed him everywhere. Her father took Cruz to show him around the house, and his man cave as the women poured over the different wedding dress pictures. Tressa was her old self again, recounting her ordeal with the king and prince. They were fascinated to know that Yadira still had a strong fan base.

It was their last day, and early the next morning, they would head home. Audrey had a wonderful meal ordered for that night. Roasted chicken with all the fixing. After dinner, the men gathered in the family room to discuss new projects they were working on when they heard Tressa's name being called outside.

Samuel was yelling for Tressa right in front of the house. "Tressa, get out here right now!" he ordered.

Demi was enraged, "I will knock that punk on his ass."

"Oh God, when is this going to end," Tressa said, clearly upset. She went towards the front door, but Cruz stopped her, holding her arms. "It's just Samuel. I'll get rid of him… I'll be right back."

He refused, not letting her go. "No, I will speak to him," he said seriously.

"Baby, it's my problem. I don't want you involved."

"Too late. It became my problem the minute you agreed to be my wife," he said in a low and angry voice.

She started to protest, "Cruz, I know what he wants. I'll make him go away."

"Do you have feelings for this dude? If you step out that door, I know you are not ready to get married."

Tressa was stunned. "How could you say that after all we've been through?"

"Then I guess we haven't been through enough since this fool calls for you, and you go running. You're my woman Tressa, and you're not invincible… I wear pants in this relationship. I will handle this," he was getting angry.

"That's my man. I'm right behind you, son… Don't worry. I got your back," Demi shouted. "Kick his ass, son."

Tressa looked at her mother for support. "He's right. It's time you stepped aside and let your husband-to-be handle him."

Tressa ran upstairs to her room, frustrated. Audrey laughed as she peeked out the front window. "Mami…," she yelled down the stairs. "You don't know what kind of temper Cruz has. I don't want my man in jail for hitting Samuel… he has a bad temper when it comes to me."

"That's alright, sweetheart, that's why daddy's with him. He'll bail him out."

"Daddy doesn't like Samuel," she whined.

Audrey smiled, "Neither do I, let the men take care of men's business… the question is can Samuel take a punch from Cruz." Tressa slammed the door behind her.

Samuel continued to shout out her name when he saw Cruz; he shut up quickly. He looked over at Demi, ignoring Cruz, who stood right in front of him with his arms crossed.

"Mr. Quintanilla, I need to speak to Tressa. It's very important."

"If you have anything to say to my fiancée, you have to go through me."

"Your fiancée… who the hell are you?" He pointed at Cruz, looking at Demi.

"Don't look at him. Talk to me, douchebag. I don't appreciate you calling my woman out in the street like she's a common whore. Now, I'm only going to say this once. Tressa is with me now. I love her, and we are getting married very soon," he tried to keep himself composed.

"That's impossible. Tressa has always been mine, Mr. Quintanilla. We're engaged, and she loves me," he shouted. "You have no right… she's mine," he charged at him, but Cruz grabbed him by the shirt, pulling him off his feet. Tressa held her breath, watching from the window of her room.

"You are too light in the ass to come at me… Now, if you don't want me to beat you down, leave and stop disrupting the Quintanilla home." When Cruz let him go, he fell back.

"I can't let her go… she's all I ever wanted. We have a history together," Samuel pleaded.

"Samuel, be a man for the first time in your life and leave. Tressa and Cruz are lovers, they're getting married, and I have given them my blessing." Samuel wouldn't accept that Tressa has moved on and doesn't love him. He continued to yell her name and paced back and forth.

"I was her first… I made her a woman… she will always be mine," Samuel sneered at Cruz.

Cruz has had enough. "You're a liar; with all due respect to Mr. Quintanilla, you were not the first. I wish we'd waited, but it happened. If you are man enough to come at me… bring it."

Samuel was frustrated. He started to get angry and kept on pacing back and forth. "This isn't over, you may have her now, but I know she loves me." He ran down the street.

"Wow, that was interesting," Cruz said. He turned to Demi, who was clearly enjoying the interaction.

"Now you know why I didn't want her to marry him… he has no backbone. Come on, son, let's go down to the bar. I'm thirsty."

Tressa ran down the steps to her mother, "Where is daddy taking him."

"Relax, he's probably going to the bar to show him off… I have never seen your father so happy about someone you brought home."

Tressa ran to the window every five minutes to see if they were on their way home. Finally, after two hours, she watched them come up the driveway arm and arm. Her father comes bursting through the door first. "Tressa, get your ass down here. Your dad has spoken." Audrey laughed as she watched Tressa cut her eyes at her father and Cruz. They were laughing so hard they couldn't help themselves.

"You, my dear… I just introduced my new son to my friends," he chuckled.

"Daddy, are you drunk?"

"Your dad is fine. He's having fun," Cruz said, defending him.

"You… I ain't talking to you," she pouted.

He held up his hand, interrupting what she was going to say, pulling her towards him. "We need to talk," Cruz ushered her to the kitchen.

"You tell her son, I got your back," Demi laughed. "He's the man."

"Don't you ever do that again? If I tell you I'll handle it, then that's all you have to know?"

Tressa rolled her eyes at him again, showing her displeasure. "You're so pig-headed. I know how hot-headed you are… I didn't want you to go to jail because of him."

"I'm only going to ask you once… do you have feelings for this guy?"

"I will slap you if you ask me that one more time." Her parents had their ears pressed to the kitchen door.

"I'm waiting for your answer," he asked forcefully.

Tressa sighed, but he wouldn't budge. "No, I don't love him, and I don't think about him in any capacity," she looked away. "We had our season of puppy love, and it's over. Plus, I couldn't be with a man I couldn't trust. That was what kept me from committing to him."

"Good… then I don't have to kill him," she tried not to laugh at him. He drew her close, kissing her tenderly.

Demi chuckled, "God is that the way you two fight?" He said through the closed door; they joined them in the kitchen.

"I can't help it, Daddy… he's so damn cute." Demi winked at her.

"And charming…" Audrey added.

"So, daddy, you like my choice... so you'll be even happier when I tell you that Yadira's involved with... his brother."

Demi was confused. "Who's your brother?"

"You've met before. Last year, he presented Jesse with the plans for the aqueduct. Jesse was very pleased with it."

"That's your brother Cortez... oh my God, those plans were genius."

"Yadira. Our Yadira," Audrey was amazed. "About time... after Danny, I didn't think she could trust anyone." Demi walked toward the kitchen window, turning away from his family.

"Dad, are you alright?" Tressa put her arms around him.

"Sir, I assure you he has honorable intentions towards her. He's deeply in love with her," Demi started to get emotional and pulled out a handkerchief.

"Daddy, Yadira's a grown woman."

Audrey went to comfort him. "Honey, what's wrong... you were perfectly happy with Tressa's choice."

"No, please, Cruz, don't confuse my reaction. I always knew that Tressa would find a good man once she let go of Samuel, but Yadira... she's always been so bull-headed and defiant. I always thought she would pick someone I hated just to spike us," he smiled. "I'm overwhelmed."

"Well, Daddy, I let her give you the details, but I can assure you and mother that they are very well-matched and very much in love."

"Cruz, you and your brother have made me extremely happy."

"Thank you, Sir. I'm sure he'll show up at your doorstep one day soon."

Demi pulled Audrey into his arms, "Sweetheart, do you realize we are going to have some beautiful grandbabies," he hugged Audrey as they joined in the laughter.

Chapter 12: The Wedding

There wasn't enough time in the day for Tressa to finish all the wedding preparations, so Cruz's parents insisted they help with the wedding arrangements. Tressa was nervous about meeting Cruz's parents for the first time. She dressed Miranda in a lavender summer dress and fixed her hair in a becoming style.

"I look beautiful," Miranda said, admiring herself in the mirror.

"You sure do, like an angel. Now, remember to stay away from dirt. I want your grandparent to see a lovely princess."

"I promise," she smiled.

Tressa changed her dress several times before she settled on a blue spaghetti-strap summer dress and black strappy sandals. She didn't want to be overdressed or wear something inappropriate to meet her soon-to-be in-laws. Cruz laughed as he watched Tressa fuss with the straps of her dress. "Baby, do you think is it too much... my breast? Maybe I should change?"

Cruz stood behind her as she looked in the full-length mirror. He pulled her close, kissing her neck.

"Baby, your breast look lovely… yes, sweet cheeks, believe me, I'm an expert on them. You're going to look sexy and hot in whatever you wear," he pulled her dress up, teasing her, "what else are you wearing under there."

She slapped his hands away, "Nothing you should be interested in at this time; your parents should be here any minute," she cried.

"Hey, I'm always interested… my parents can wait… if," she interrupted him.

"You better stop it," he continued to tease her.

"Maybe I should put you on a sex diet. I'm sure you can wait six more weeks," Tressa remarked.

Cruz was in no mood to listen as he pulled her closer. "You wouldn't do that to me, would you? That's cruel and unusual punishment… so be good to me, baby," he pouted like a young schoolboy.

"Get away from me, you pervert," she giggled, pushing him away playfully, "go downstairs and make sure everything is ready for lunch. I'm sure your parents will be hungry and thirsty when they arrive."

"Alright… but no sex diet…" he said reluctantly.

Amparo didn't know what to expect; she prayed for her new daughter-in-law not to be like Mary. It didn't matter whether she would be pretty or not; she should love her son and granddaughter.

"Sweetheart, you have to calm your nerves. I'm sure she's a very nice girl... she is related to Jesse Quintanilla. I am ecstatic; such a fine man and family," Cheo said, wanting her to relax. "You have been twisted in knots."

"I know, my love, it's that... I don't know if I can bare another Mary. She was so over the top; I still have nightmares."

"Sweetheart, whatever you do, smile at the girl and don't make her feel uncomfortable. You can be too critical at times... your expression tells it all."

"I will try my best, I promise."

Tressa ensured the house was spotless and decorated the entrance and main rooms with a beautiful flower arrangement. Cruz met his parents at the door.

"Carino, how is my son?" Cruz bent down to hug his beautiful mother. "You look wonderful. I think love agrees with you," she said, looking around to see if Tressa was with him.

"It does, Mama. Come on in; Tressa will be right down."

Miranda ran down the stairs and into her papa's arms. "My princess, you've grown; look at you so beautiful," he said as he picked her up and hugged her tightly.

"I miss you too, papa."

"Why don't we go into the dining room? Tressa has some refreshments waiting for us."

"The place looks wonderful, son. It has a woman's touch… I can't wait to meet my new daughter," Amparo was amazed at the warmth the new décor brought to the surrounding.

"I know she will be just as charming… look how adjusted my little princess is," Cheo said, twirling her around like a ballerina.

Tressa was beaming when she finally joined the others. There was an awkward silence.

"Mama, Papa, this is Tressa, my future wife." Tressa didn't know what to do. They just stared at her.

"I want to apologize," Amparo said, finally breaking her trance, "I wasn't expecting… one of the famous Quintanilla twins to walk in," Amparo broke into a big smile and hugged Tressa tight so long she didn't know what to do.

Cheo took his turn, shaking her hand and giving her a bear hug, "Please forgive us, Miss Tressa. We were expecting someone different." He held her hand and kissed it. "We are honored to meet you."

"Cruz has told me such wonderful stories about his family; I couldn't wait to meet you both."

"The pleasure is ours, believe me," Cheo chimed in as they laughed, finally relaxing and enjoying each other's company.

They had a wonderful lunch after the awkward first impression. Now it was time for the secret meeting of approval. Cruz was confident that his parents approved of his choice. But he wanted to get their firsthand opinion. While Tressa attended to the dinner menu, Amparo corned her son outside.

"How could you do this to us, son?" Amparo cried in an alarming voice.

"What… Mama, I was sure you'd like Tressa."

"Like her, I love her… but she's like royalty, son. I was unprepared and might have acted like an idiot."

"She's right, son. That was a terrible first impression on our part. I'm not sure if we can ever recover." Cheo added, "I was expecting a sweet, beautiful woman. Instead, this gorgeous, stunning creature walked in, and we were speechless."

"Please, you guys can relax. Tressa is a sweet, down-to-earth person, and I want you to be comfortable around her."

"Well, we will try, but it's not going to be easy… wow… I can't wait to tell everyone. I'm so proud of you, son," she reached up to hug him.

"Well, hold on to your panties, Mama, because your other son is courting her twin sister and is very serious."

Amparo was shocked, "My Tajito, your brother?" She had a hard time comprehending.

"Yes, the one that came from your womb… remember the wild one."

Amparo was speechless. "My wild boy… in love," she smiled, "did you hear that, Cheo."

"Isn't she the fighter… ah… beauty something?" Cheo asked.

"Yeah, the very one. Black Beauty, he's over there right now… He missed her so much that he couldn't stand to be away from her. But don't tell him I told you; you know how he is."

Amparo started to get misty-eyed, remembering how hard it was when Cruz married Mary and thought he'd never be happy. She knew deep in her heart that she had great children. "We did good, Cheo… we raised two fine boys, and now God has rewarded us with wonderful daughters; we are very blessed," she kissed him.

Tressa enjoyed her time getting to know her soon-to-be in-laws. Amparo was accommodating and always had wonderful stories about the boys and the rest of the family. Everyone was busy planting flowers, cleaning, and ensuring they had enough tables and flatware for the wonderful wedding dinner. Amparo and Cheo took advantage of the wonderful weather and took Miranda shopping.

Cruz enjoyed his alone time with Tressa. Pretty soon, his parents would be going home, and he would have a hard time convincing her not to put him on a sex diet until the wedding. The cook made them a special lunch as they sat together, teasing each other playfully on the terrace, discussing some last-minute changes when Sandra interrupted them.

"Cruz, someone is here to see you and Tressa."

"Who is it?"

"It's Mr. Bronson and … Mr. Cooper, Mary's husband."

Cruz led them into his office. By the looks on their faces, it was serious. They greeted each other politely and sat down.

"Mr. Montenegro and Miss Quintanilla, I represent Mary Cooper. As you well know, Mr. Cooper is very concerned about his wife." Cruz could feel the heat rising in him, which did not go unnoticed.

"Cruz, we've known each other long," Mr. Cooper looked down as if embarrassed. "I am truly sorry for my wife's part in Tressa's abduction."

Cruz interrupted him. "She was the mastermind behind the whole ordeal."

"I'm sorry to say I'm learning more and more about my wife's illness."

"What illness?" Cruz asked curiously.

"She's been in the hospital under doctor's care since the day detectives came to question her. She had a major breakdown and has been under suicide watch ever since."

Cruz was not moved. "Mr. Cooper, I've always had great respect for you, but please don't ask me to have any sympathy for the woman who was almost the cause of my fiancée's death. Who tried at one time to strangle her own child… as you well know, she was not allowed near her?"

Mr. Cooper was shocked, "Well, that's a new twist to my wife. I didn't know… I am truly not looking for sympathy, just a little understanding. I… I am pleading for my wife… I know there are many charges against her. The most damaging charges are coming from Miss Tressa… I am pleading with you. I know my wife has many mental issues. One of the doctors informed me. Under hypnosis, he discovered she had an incestuous relationship with her father that started at four and continued into her teens. As she got older, she used sex to get what she wanted from him. There were also several rapes and sexually abusive relationships before she married you, Mr. Cruz."

"Mr. Cooper, please understand I'm not dropping the charges. She crossed the line; this could have had more serious consequences."

Mr. Cooper was beginning to get emotional because he loved Mary very much. "Mary is pregnant; I know it's my child because of the time frame."

"So, you knew she was having an affair with other men, and still you want her... I don't understand." Cruz was puzzled.

Mr. Cooper smiled, "Cruz, you're a handsome young man, and I know this is hard for you to understand, but as you can see, I am older than Mary... regardless of everything, I love her. She mothers me and pleasures me whenever I want. I do put a lot of demands on her. She makes me laugh, and... frankly, I don't want to be alone."

"Mr. Cooper," Tressa finally spoke. She turned to Cruz, "Baby, let's talk outside… we'll be right back." Cruz followed her down the hall into the library.

"What's on your mind?"

"Baby… I want you to try to understand what I'm going to tell you."

"I can tell by the tone of your voice I'm not going to like it," he replied quickly.

"Please, baby, just hear me out… the most important people to me right now are you and Miranda. I knew from the beginning that something was wrong with Mary… I want to drop the charges in exchange for her allowing me to adopt Miranda. I want to be her mother."

"What are you asking me, woman? You're asking me to forget everything she did to you."

She touched his face tenderly. "I want Miranda to feel totally and completely part of us and the other children we will have. If I adopt her, she'll know that we adore her and that she doesn't have to live in fear that Mary's coming for her… because I'll be her mama. Please, sweetheart, this is what I want."

He took her hand and kissed it lovingly. "I don't deserve you… and I want you to know that it is under great protest," he pulled her into his arms. "I know Miranda would be extremely happy… let's see if he'll go for it."

"Thank you, baby, for letting me do this."

Tressa made her demands and waited for Mr. Cooper's response while he conferred with his lawyer.

"Mr. Cooper," Cruz said, "Mary hadn't met Miranda in three years and had never shown any interest in her except to hurt me. My daughter is terrified of her… now you understand why we want this. These are our demands, please take your time and think about it… but know this… Mary is forbidden to come near her, adopted or not."

"I understand. Now I know why Mary never brought her around… I agree with your demands… they are reasonable for her treatment and freedom. I know she won't get the treatment and care she needs in prison. She will be released from the hospital in two weeks. I will arrange for a live-in doctor to stay with us, and someone will watch her 24/7 when she's in the bathroom. She would have intensive therapy; we are hoping for a good outcome. I'll have my lawyer draw up the necessary papers… I want this done before she comes home. I have power of attorney and can sign on her behalf. I appreciate your consideration; I am indebted to you both."

On their way out, Mr. Cooper ran into Miranda and her grandparents. As they opened the door, he looked sad; Miranda looked so much like Mary. He stared at the beautiful child with wide eyes and innocents. His heart was crushed, knowing she would not be part of his family. Miranda ran past him into Tressa's arms. He turned towards Cruz and nodded, letting him know it was the best thing for the child.

Cruz's parents were delighted to hear that Tressa would adopt Miranda, but all Miranda understood was that she had someone to call mama.

As the family continued to arrive, Amparo was the perfect host. She reveled in the company of the bride's parents, Audrey and Demi, who felt like family immediately. Jesse and his family arrived a day early, along with Tressa's uncle Joaquin and Brydus, who brought along their two sons and a two-year-old daughter who stole everyone's heart with her doll face and cuteness. There was so much excitement the estate was in sweet chaos.

The men had their bachelor party in town, raising hell along the way with Jesse and Cheo. The two played the worst tricks on Cruz. When Cruz was drunk, they put makeup on him, took his shirt off, and had him take pictures with some female impersonators. They dragged each other from bar to bar, and the owners were more than happy to join the party. Tajo threw water to wake Cruz up and torture him some more. The guy stumbled into their rooms at daybreak.

The women had their party at the mansion; music was cranked up, and the drinks were in excess. Jesse's wife Renee bought not one but two exotic male dancers who kept them entertained all night. Yadira purchased different kinds of sex toys and wrapped them up as gifts. When Tressa opened them, she screamed with surprise, wanting to throw them at her. Audrey and Amparo laughed so much their faces hurt.

"To think we have to do this all over again," Audrey said.

Amparo squeezed her hand and replied, "I can't wait… I am so happy."

Audrey hugged her neck; they both had too much of a drink.

"Me too," Audrey agreed.

Tressa was chased around with the sex toys, and the male strippers tried to make a sandwich with her dancing. Ellen had the most fun; she put money in their g- strings and bumped and ground with them. At the end of the night, when Tressa was too drunk to walk, they picked her up and threw her into the pool. Afterward, everyone else jumped in; the pictures would tell funny stories once they regained their senses.

Cruz begged Jesse not to show Tressa his pictures with a cross-dresser, but it was too late. During the wedding rehearsal dinner, they were displayed proudly on the walls. They even put a little fancy women's hat on him.

Tressa was not spared; they had pictures of her being sandwiched between the dancers and a look of dread on her face when they picked her up and tossed her into the pool.

The rehearsal and the dinner went beautifully; they enjoyed each other's company well into the night.

Cruz managed to steal Tressa away for a few minutes. From the upper terrace, they watched as their families interacted with each other as if there had known each other for years. He held her tightly in his arms and kissed her passionately; she laid her face against his chest tears of happiness escaped her. "Why are you crying, my love… getting cold feet?"

"I'm just so happy; tomorrow you will be my husband… and I will be Tressa Quintanilla Montenegro," she kissed him.

"That sounds like music to my ears, my love… destiny has many twists and turns in a person's life. I would have never imagined being married to the world's most beautiful and wonderful woman this time last year."

She cried harder, "Stop it…" she said, "you're making things worst. Thank God our wedding is at night… look at our families; they'll be hung over tomorrow," they laughed, "it's a beautiful sight."

"I won't see you until tomorrow evening, so I want to give you my wedding gift to you." He pulled out a burgundy velvet box. It was a beautiful teardrop ruby necklace encrusted with diamonds.

"Oh my God, Cruz, it's beautiful." He kissed her again, trying to hold back his passion for her. "Wear it for me tomorrow. Let me see it around your sexy neck as you become my… wife," she clung to him as if he was going away forever.

They partied late into the night, carrying the groom up the hill to Tajo's house to let him sleep off his drunkenness. The three powerful men stayed up and discussed plans for the country and their children's future.

Tajo put his brother to bed; he smiled because it would be his turn next. He thought about his soon-to-be wife and knew it was meant to be. Tajo instructed the servants to prepare the house for Cruz and Tressa's honeymoon. They wouldn't be leaving for a few days, and he wanted to give them privacy.

"Good night, brother… I love you, man."

The following morning estate was ablaze with activities-people running back and forth, cleaning, and setting up for the happy couple's celebration. The women took charge; Alex took over the kitchen and garden setup. Renee made sure the musician and stage were set up. The men were in charge of doing what the women needed to get done. Jesse and Cheo woke Cruz with a mimosa and aspirin.

"Do I have makeup on," Cruz asked, afraid they had played a joke on him; they laughed.

"No, son, we just wanted to say good morning and ask you how you're feeling," Jesse replied.

Cruz drank his mimosa and swallowed the aspirin.

"So, are you ready for this big step, son?" His father asked him, knowing he was more than ready.

"Papa, this has been the most remarkable week… just watching our families and friends come together, making Tressa my wife. I'm more than ready. I can't thank everyone enough for making this time in my life special."

Well, I want you to know that the Quintanilla family is thrilled to have our families joined by two special people…

We have big plans for this side of the country. The Quintanilla women are strong and loyal... Tressa is a remarkable woman, and I know she will make you very happy," Jesse said, giving him a strong hug.

Audrey, Amparo, and Yadira attended Tressa as she prepared for her big day.

"Tressa, you need to come out of the bathroom now so that you can slip into your dress," Yadira fussed at Tressa through the bathroom door.

Audrey watched all the activities happening right outside the window. It was a beautiful sight with all the lights and red and white roses adorning the ceremony area. Tressa looked at herself in the mirror. Her hair was expertly done, and her makeup was flawless. When she finally came out of the bathroom, Audrey's eyes were moistened as she held back tears of happiness for her daughter.

"My baby... you look so beautiful," Audrey held her hands, admiring how exquisite Tressa looked.

"Mama, you're going to ruin your makeup," Yadira said, "come, Tressa, let's get you into your wedding dress." Tressa was shaking as they laced up her dress with the red ruby necklace adorning her neck. Her hair was done up in beautiful long curls that hung loosely down her back. She wore a simple a-line umpire dress that was low cut in the front. Tressa was trembling as Yadira handed her the bouquet; she hugged her sister tightly. "I'm so glad you'll live close by."

"I don't think I have a choice; I love that man," they giggled. "Sisters to the end, Cruz is lucky to have you."

"I think I'm the lucky one; to have a man that makes me feel special."

The musicians played a sweet Spanish melody as the wedding party set up. Cruz waited for his beautiful bride to join him at the altar. "Tajo, you still have my ring?" He asked.

Tajo laughed; he could tell Cruz was nervous. "For the fifth time, my brother, I have it right here," he patted his pocket.

Cruz's nieces were the flower girls. They laid out rose peddles along the white carpet leading to the altar. Miranda was the junior bridesmaid dressed in white and red, accompanied by the Jr. Groomsman Tressa's brother Demi Junior. When Tajo saw Yadira in her fitting navy blue dress, it took his breath away. He winked at her; the chemistry between them was electrifying.

The music changed to 'Here Comes the Bride,' and everyone stood up as Demi walked his daughter to the altar.

Demi couldn't content himself and started crying the moment he saw her. However, he wasn't alone; family members on both sides cried tears of joy.

Tressa focused on the extremely handsome man who waited for her at the altar. He would be her husband, and how much she loved him, Tressa thought. She looked faultless in her white dress, dark hair, and red lipstick. When Demi gave her hand to Cruz, he wore a huge grin and wondered if he must have done something right in his life to be the luckiest man in the world. Cruz peeled back the veil and kissed her impulsively for everyone's joy.

Jesse laughed, losing his place as he presided over the marriage ceremony. Tressa went first as she tried to remember the vows she had memorized. They were sweet and from the heart, but Cruz stole the show when he fell to one knee and professed his undying love for her and how she completed his life. There wasn't a dry eye in the place; even Jesse choked up a little before he pronounced them husband and wife. The crowd cheered as the couple took their first kiss as husband and wife; the confetti was everywhere.

The celebration continued as the couple joined their guest in the mansion's grand hall; the entire estate was adorned to accommodate the people who arrived from different parts. Family and friends joined in to wish the couple joy and happiness. Everyone except for Nina, who watched how Tajo and Yadira held on to each other. When she had asked him for a dance, he would only dance a fast number with her. She was heartbroken, needing to do something quickly, or else she would lose Tajo forever.

The next morning both families gathered for breakfast to talk about the happy couple and enjoy each other's company since they would be departing soon; they would have a final dinner as a family before they journey back to their homes.

Tajo stood up to get everyone's attention clicking his glass. "I am so honored to be part of this wonderful family, the union of Montenegro and the Quintanilla families. Tonight, before my family and Yadira, I would like everyone to be a witness as I ask my beloved soulmate to be my wife."

Yadira was surprised as he got on one knee in front of everyone and purpose, "Yadira, would you be my wife and make me as happy as my brother is now... I love you." Yadira had a knot in his throat. Everyone held their breath as they waited for her answer.

"You crazy fool. Yes, I can't wait!"

Everyone cheered as Tajo put the beautiful diamond ring on her finger. The families had another reason to celebrate and plan another glorious wedding.

Tressa and Cruz left on their honeymoon a month on a sunny island the following week. Sandra and Logan announced they had caught the marriage fever and were going to elope. Sandra cried throughout the ceremony. Logan had been her life savior; she was in love and didn't want her family to ruin their special love for each other. Logan thanked Tressa a million times for introducing him to the woman who brightened his life.

Yadira and Tajo started making plans for their union. They decided to get married on her parent's ranch.

The happy couple couldn't wait to start their life together as man and wife. Mary watched from her window. Her mind was fuzzy from all the medication they made her take, "This is not the end. Cruz- my love, soon I will be well, and we can continue where we left off." Her laughter echoed throughout the house.

To be continued – Yadira, Black Beauty